# THE JUGGLER

Also by Sebastian Beaumont:
*Thirteen*

# The Juggler

Sebastian Beaumont

MYRMIDON

Myrmidon Books Ltd
Rotterdam House
116 Quayside
Newcastle upon Tyne
NE1 3DY
www.myrmidonbooks.com

Published by Myrmidon 2008

A catalogue record for this book is available from the British Library.

ISBN 978-1-905802-26-5 Hardback
ISBN 978-1-905802-27-2 Trade Paperback

Set in 11/14.5 Goudy by
Falcon Oast Graphic Arts Limited, East Hoathly, East Sussex

Printed and bound in the UK by CPI Mackays, Chatham ME5 8TD

1 3 5 7 9 10 8 6 4 2

LOTTERY FUNDED

To Peter Burton
and to my parents with love

# CONTENTS

# 1. Going Forth

Later, Mark's wife accused him of running away. His old friends agreed with her. They were the kind of people who didn't understand that a person might need to go away for a while, or forever if necessary, so they would see it – with a predictable inevitability – as running away. But the fact was that he'd fundamentally shifted, although he'd been unaware of it most of the time. And then, one day, it had become unbearable. He hadn't planned it, it had simply happened.

Mark would feel a strange sensation from time to time, a discomfort in his skin. Not an itch, exactly, but a fidgety thrill of disgust that would shiver through him. Vaguely, he knew it was the life he was leading that was causing this unease, paradoxically making him feel trapped; paradoxical because he'd made all his choices willingly and they had led to the desired outcome, which is to say, a good qualification as an engineer, marriage and fatherhood at the age of twenty-nine. So why the discomfort? Because of the inevitable *but*. This was the surprising and scary thing, there always seemed to be a but. Right now he could formulate it as 'I have everything I want, *but. . .*' It was this particular *but* that had caused the tremor of disquiet.

Then he did what people aren't supposed to do. He left his home, his job, his wife, his friends, his seven month old baby. . . everything. He set out, with a flyer advertising a night club in his pocket that had an address written on the back in spidery pencil. And a small, hard bag of the sort that photographers carry their lenses in. But this bag did not contain photographic equipment. This bag contained £40,000 in cash.

Sitting breathless on the train, he knew with a desperate certainty that if he'd missed this departure, the three hour wait for the next train would have proved too much and he'd have given up on his wild, impromptu flight. There was a window of time, a brief moment in which Mark saw, without fully understanding why, that he must give in to this impulse to get away, or give up on himself entirely.

Mark's mood on the journey was a mixture of exhilaration and panic. He was *doing* something. He wasn't sure what it was, but that was far less important than the fact that he was doing it. It came as a shock to realise that he'd never in his life set in motion a course of action without knowing precisely what the outcome was likely to be, and it was this uncertainty that caused both the exhilaration and the panic. It was like doing the high jump. He had cleared the hurdle of escape and was now in the process of landing on the other side of the bar. He was unsure of what it might mean, to do this, except that there was something unequivocal and irrevocable about having jumped.

The train went through a long tunnel shortly after the journey started and, as it plunged through the darkness, Mark's ears depressurised and it was as if his whole life was being sucked out of him and ejected into the air that he was leaving behind. The four-and-a-half hour journey was spent looking out at the fields and towns that he passed – an endless procession of ordered existence – or at the early primroses that were in bloom beside the tracks.

He pulled the flyer from his back pocket and looked at the address scrawled there in smudged pencil: *1 Baker's Yard*.

As the train neared its destination, he could see a jumbled skyline of buildings ahead of him – corporate, private, religious – that made up the town, beyond which he could see the hills. To the west he could see the rearing cliff that dominated the skyline, crowned with its fine eighteenth century lighthouse, beneath which, he knew, were the famous caves. There was a sign by the track here, saying that the station was one mile away and he closed his eyes briefly, trying to still his nerves.

The station was one of those tall, Victorian iron-and-glass structures that made him feel that he was coming to a place of scale and substance. The station forecourt wasn't particularly busy, but those people who were there had an air of intent and purpose that was obscurely inspiring. Outside, across a wide cobbled square, there was an avenue that sloped down to the river, flanked with arty shops, galleries and pubs. The older architecture was ornate, but not overblown, while the newer blocks of flats were made of glass that was tinted blue or green, with stainless steel railings and small but functional balconies. It was more or less what one might expect from a town that had made its money from its small port and fishing fleet a hundred and fifty years earlier and was now beginning to reassert itself in a post-industrial, even post-modern way.

The first thing he needed to do was to acquire a map of the town, in order to find his way to that all-important address, and he crossed the shiny blue-grey cobbles of the square to a small newsagent, outside which stood a series of buckets filled with bunches of tulips, carnations and freesias.

When he went in, he immediately noticed the smell of confectionery. It was one of those shops that sold hand-made chocolates in a glass cabinet by the till. This, and the waft of airy perfume from the freshly cut flowers, mingled to give an impression of indulgence and lethargy. The woman behind the counter was wearing loose pale clothes and dark tights, and looked like a dancer or someone who'd just stepped out of an aerobics class. She was reading a magazine from the extensive rack beside her and she glanced up at Mark when he came in, but didn't stop reading until he went over to speak to her.

'I'm sorry,' she said when he asked, 'we don't have any town maps at the moment. We should have had the new edition in last week at the latest, but–' she shrugged, '–you know what councils are like. And with the start of the tourist season only a week or two away. . .' She shook her head in mock despair, then smiled. 'But tell me, where are you going? I expect I'll know where it is.'

He showed her the address.

'Oh, well!' she laughed. 'You're in luck! It's just round the corner.'

She gave directions and, before he left, he bought a magazine about the area – a county he was not familiar with. He didn't particularly want the magazine; he bought it to give her a little custom, for being so helpful.

'Are you here visiting friends?' she asked as he paid.

'No,' he told her. 'I think I might have come to live here.'

She smiled as he said this, but he could tell that his words had closed her off, quite suddenly, and made her sad. It was as though she heard this all the time, and knew how impossible or vain the hope might actually be.

As he walked the couple of blocks to Baker's Yard, Mark dropped the magazine into a bin. He realised with embarrassment as he did so that he had no idea what he was going to say when he got there. It wasn't as if he knew why he'd come, or who he was hoping to meet. . .

**Last night.**

Live stand-up comedy was not something that Mark would ever have considered going to see on his own, but the babysitter had fallen through at the last moment, and Amy had persuaded him to go without her. She was feeling tired and under slept. They both were, of course, but Amy especially. They'd been given tickets to see Ewan Rees at The Joker cabaret bar. Tom, a work colleague, was supposed to come along too, but he'd called to say he was unwell, and so Mark found himself sharing a table in the bar, a few feet from the stage, with three strangers who talked loudly about the refit that had just been completed at the folk club down the road, and how the acoustics there were now rubbish.

Comedy. There was something unfunny about sitting in a venue bursting with raucous energy when he was feeling so tired and so in need of relaxing conversation with familiar friends. To be sitting here alone, drinking far too fast, was making him feel alienated and sorry for himself. The warm-up comedian had done a routine about free will and had sung the song 'I did it my way' in a sneery way, and had then sworn at the audience for believing it. Though Mark had laughed along with the others, it felt as though his body was doing the laughing of its own accord, while his mind was saying, 'But I have never done anything *my* way. Ever. I don't even know what my way is.'

What had happened to his life? How had he ended up here, with a wife he didn't love, and a baby – Tyler, or Ty as they called him – that he could experience at times as a little miracle, a wonder, but whom he nevertheless resented with a cold, white anger? And how could he be anything but disgusted at himself for feeling such resentment towards another human being, a person who shone when loved, and who deserved something so much better than parents who were locked into mutually annihilating disinterest?

From this distance, though, Mark's feelings for his wife had a tinge of affection to them. Wasn't this how it often happened in relationships? The irritation that comes with disinterest obscures the positive qualities, so that all that's left is something grim and gritty and loveless. In fact, Amy had a great sense of humour and purpose. But these things hadn't been visible to Mark for some time.

Even his job left him with a sense of dissatisfaction. He was employed by Themerex, a small company that specialised in research into aero and fluid dynamics. Mark's specialist area was 'parasitic drag': how much extra energy it took to push an object through air or water if you attached something to it. There were applications in the automobile industry, but mostly in aviation and shipping. Like many research companies, Themerex lurched from grant to grant, from financial uncertainty to the brink of financial disaster. Mark expressed the company's status to himself as 'teetering'. But this word seemed to encapsulate his entire life. His relationship was teetering, his job was teetering, *he* was teetering. . . on the edge of taking up his father's offer of far more lucrative employment. And doing that would, of itself, represent some kind of desperate, humiliating reneging on his dreams.

His father owned a small building firm, and he was pressurising Mark to come and work for him installing central heating systems. Although both his current job and the one that was on offer from his dad might be referred to as 'engineer', the gulf between the two was massive in terms of interest and self-respect. As a youth he'd done decorating and renovation work for his father, and he'd hated it. To agree to work for him again, however glamorous a title his father gave the position, would represent a giant backward step; failure even.

He thought of his teetering relationship. Was it teetering on the brink of collapse, or was it merely yo-yoing up and down in a self-perpetuating cycle that could last a lifetime? He knew that Amy had been unfaithful to him, at least twice, and he'd nearly been unfaithful to her, but he couldn't bring himself to make any judgement about these things, except for a small flicker of hope that Amy might have gained a little pleasure from her clandestine activity.

There was another teetering too, into increasing levels of debt. Amy was a spender, where Mark was a saver, and this added extra stress to their relationship.

Then there was being on medication. Anti-depressants were a kind of teetering, or perhaps a desperate attempt not to teeter out of sanity, and into. . . well, judging how he was feeling right now, they weren't being successful. He had never felt so alone in his life. Although perhaps it was something more than loneliness. His world was becoming a laughter-free zone, so perhaps this was the place to be. A place where, for a couple of hours, laughter was the intention.

Ewan Rees burst onto the stage with a mixture of energy and affected ennui. At the same time, a waitress placed another pint in front of Mark, and he began to drink, without thinking. He slopped a little on to the table as he picked up the glass, and noticed a flyer there, beside a food menu advertising jalapeno burritos and chicken goujons with a blue cheese dip. He picked the flyer up but didn't read it, and put it down again away from the spillage of beer.

Mark didn't really listen to the comedian at first. His patter phased in and out like a poorly tuned radio, drowned out by his own cyclic thoughts. There was an odd, jolting moment, though, when Mark felt the utter ridiculousness of laughing. He stopped so abruptly that he felt engulfed by a strange, black emptiness that caught him unawares and left him a little breathless. There was something in the laughter of others – their will-to-happiness – that, quite suddenly, and irrevocably, made Mark absolutely aware of the absence of happiness within himself.

Quite what happened next, Mark was never clear about, but there was a blurred, drunken moment before he 'came to' and found himself the centre of attention.

'Yes, you,' Ewan Rees was saying to him, 'I suppose you left your wife and baby at home to come out drinking. That's a laugh, isn't it? What did she tell you, that the baby-sitter couldn't make it? Oh, my *God*, and you believed her? He believed her, ladies and gentlemen! Of course, she only told you that because she's having it off with the man in the flat downstairs, the one with the bulge in his wallet, the one with the BMW and the sexy smile. And she wanted you out of the way.

'Now, I know you've thought of being unfaithful yourself, but you haven't got the nerve, have you? It's not that you don't want to, or that you don't fantasise about it. It's because you're too scared to go through with it. You're too scared that you're a crap shag. Well, let me tell you, mate, you *are* a crap shag. Your wife told me when I was fucking her.'

Why were people laughing? This wasn't funny. He felt a quivering in his gut, and wondered if he was going to be sick. The others at his table were laughing, too. Why? What was happening? And how did Rees know these things. . . ?

'Why don't you and your very insignificant little ego fuck off out of town, if you can manage the haulage costs for that chip on your shoulder. You don't even know how to please yourself, let alone anyone else, so go elsewhere, mate, where you can fuck up only one life instead of three. And don't tell me you don't know where to go. The answer to that is staring you in the face.'

At this, Rees turned his attention away and the laughter moved on, but Mark felt so dumbstruck that he was aware of no sound except the buzzing in his ears. He didn't want to move while Rees was on stage, for fear of drawing attention to himself again, and so he stared down at the table. And noticed the flyer again. He picked it up. It was glossy and plain black with white print, and read: *Club Covert. The Key is Classified. Give yourself a treat tonight. Your passport to extensive cocktails on the wrong side of the tracks. If you want a new perspective, turn over a new leaf, look on the other side. Make your Mark. Your custom is confidential. Your intentions are covert.*

Why did it seem to have been written for him? And why was there a flyer for a night club at the other end of the country on the table in front of him? He turned the flyer over. Handwritten on the back, in pencil, was an address, *1 Baker's Yard.*

While Ewan Rees was at the far side of the stage humiliating someone else, Mark got up, furtively in case he should draw attention to himself, and snuck across to the exit, then down past the bar and the box office and out into the car park. It was cold outside, and the air was refreshing, but it did not clear his head. He felt more confused than he could remember, and also a weird anguish that made him breathless.

There was a low wall at the far side of the car park, on the junction between Station Road and West Street, and he crossed to sit on it in the shade of a large road sign. There was no way he could go home while he felt like this. His stomach raged with acidity, and his mind was foggy. He could detect the beginnings of a headache behind his right eye. He leaned forward and was sick against the post of the traffic sign, a brief but copious outpouring, and as he leaned back, coughing slightly, he tried to remember how much he'd had to drink. He thought for a while and could only remember drinking three pints. He took his money from his pocket and checked his change. He'd come out with twenty pounds, and the money added up. He really had only drunk three pints, so he couldn't be drunk to the point of being sick. So what was this nausea? A kind of ghastly reaction to having a twisted truth flung in his face and having people laugh at it?

He looked up at the sky, at a sliver of moon, and took a deep breath, then closed his eyes. He was calming down a little now, but still felt scalded. Facing Ewan Rees's tirade had been like having had his entrails drawn out of him and placed on stage for others' merriment and there was something deeply humiliating in that.

He opened his eyes and looked at the flyer again. What did it mean: *If you want a new perspective, turn over a new leaf, look on the other side*? And as for *Make your Mark.* . . that was something that had been said to him as an unfunny joke for as long as he could remember. 'Make your mark, Mark.' It was the capital M on the flyer that made it seem to be addressed to him, personally.

He didn't see the man straight away, but noticed his dark

leather shoes first, in his peripheral vision. The man was stationary. When Mark looked up, he was sure that the man was staring intently at the flyer in his hand. He was wearing a dark blue suit with a white shirt and a loosened tie. He was tall, very tall. Perhaps six feet five, and slim with it. His face was distinctively chiselled, his high cheek bones accentuated by the fact that his long black hair was pulled back into a pony tail. He smiled at Mark and leaned forward, placing the bag that he was carrying at Mark's feet.

'Make sure Jonathan gets this,' he said, and turned and walked away.

Mark stared after him. The evening was getting stranger. . .

He looked down at the bag, then picked it up. It had several side pockets and one main zip, which he opened, looking around him to see if there was anyone else in the vicinity. No sign of anyone. He opened the bag, and saw the £20 notes at once. They weren't in neat bundles, but loose. He couldn't tell how much money was in there, but it was a lot.

Mark had experienced a range of feelings over the course of the evening, but this was the first time he'd experienced cold fear. He didn't know anyone called Jonathan, let alone know anyone who might do the kinds of things which would require dropping bags of cash off in car parks late at night. He zipped the bag up again and got up. Looking round once more, he started to walk away, his back tense, as though someone might jump him from behind at any moment. He'd been mugged a couple of years before, not far from here, and that was how it had happened – a blow to the head out of nowhere, from behind.

Once out of sight of the car park, he started to run. Wasn't this the most suspicious thing a person could do in these circumstances? But he had to do something with the surfeit of adrenaline that was pumping through him. He almost wanted to laugh. Surely this was the funniest thing that had happened all night? He ran past the station and across the red sandstone bridge over the river by the town hall and into the tree-lined avenue that lead to the park. It felt more private beneath the trees and he stopped to get his breath back, standing under a sturdy lime tree. He could see the moon through the bare branches above him and it looked ludicrous, impossibly far away.

As he glanced around him, he realised there was a Thistle Hotel round the corner where he'd be able to get a room. He stood, glancing down at himself – fairly smart in black jeans, a thick dark blue shirt and grey Craghopper fleece.

'Stay calm,' he told himself and walked back to the main shopping thoroughfare that led up from the town hall to the football ground. There, by the Odeon and the traffic lights, was the Thistle Hotel, which he entered as casually as possible. He went up to the reception desk and took a room on the third floor. Only when he closed the door to the room and clicked the lock did he think to wonder why he hadn't gone home.

He looked around the anonymous room, and dropped the bag on the floor by the bed. What should he have done? Called out to the man who'd given him the bag and told him that it was a case of mistaken identity? Handed the bag back and hoped that it would be left at that? In principle, he could imagine arriving home with a bag of money and saying to Amy, 'You'll never guess what happened to me this evening. . .' but in practice, it wasn't a happening thing. And it wasn't as if the money was the only surreal thing that had happened to him this evening. The man in the flat downstairs *did* have a BMW and Mark wanted to go back and say to Amy, '*Have* you been shagging Richard, then?'

He emptied the cash onto the bed and counted it, slowly and methodically. There was £40,000. Not enough to change a person's life. But enough to. . . he found he couldn't answer the rest of that statement. Enough to what? Make things easier for a while? To stay on in his job and not worry that next month's salary might be his last? To carry some more of Amy's spending for a while? Or perhaps it was enough to enable him to walk away?

He went into the bathroom and took a shower, which helped to calm him down a little, and coming back into the bedroom he suddenly felt overwhelmingly tired. Not sleepy particularly, but exhausted. He dropped his towel to the floor and got into bed, enjoying the thickness of the sheets and the fresh-laundered feeling of the cotton. There was something comforting about the anonymous bed – he always slept well in hotels. The pillow was slightly too bulky for him, but he drifted off to sleep almost immediately.

It was nearly nine when he woke. He lay in bed and wondered what Amy would be thinking. Would she be angry? Worried? Relieved? He looked at his mobile, on the bedside table, and couldn't bring himself to switch it on. Putting yesterday's clothes back on, especially his socks, made him experience a pang of something like self-pity, but that was quickly superseded by a desire to wash and shave. He took £100 out of the bag and put it into his back pocket, then slipped out before breakfast and bought himself a disposable razor, shaving cream, toothpaste and brush, plus deodorant and some underwear.

At 9.40 he came down for breakfast feeling clean and fairly

rested, but still with the residual anxiety of the night before and a sense of deep uncertainty about what he was doing. And that was a valid question: 'What *am* I doing?' He brought his bag down to the dining room with him and kept it under his chair – leaving it in his room while he went shopping had made him nervous.

He discovered that he was ravenously hungry and ate a huge plateful of 'the works' with coffee, fruit juice and toast.

*It's as if I don't know when I'm next going to eat,* he thought, *as though I'm about to leave on some kind of adventure trek across the wilderness.*

Packing in his room was easy, a question of putting his toiletries – including the mini soap and shampoo that came with the room – into one of the side pockets of the main bag. He then split the money into two, putting half of it in the plastic carrier bag that his toiletries had come in, and placing it with the rest of the loose money in the bag. He turned his mobile on and, although it warbled to alert him to the texts that were waiting for him, he ignored them and sent two short texts of his own. The first was to work, which read: *Not coming to work today. Or ever. Cheers. Mark.* It made him smile, although part of this was embarrassment. The second text was to Amy: *I'm not coming home. Sorry.* He switched the phone off and sat on the bed for a while, thinking of Ty, who would be with his grandmother for the day now. He remembered moments with him, when he would look up and gurgle with pleasure, squirming slightly as Mark gave him tickly kisses.

Next, he went to the Post Office and bought a flatpack cardboard Parcelpak into which he placed the bag containing £20,000. He addressed it to 'Tyler Gage and Amy Ferrer' and sent it first class Recorded Delivery. Did it make him feel any better that he was sending this money? Did it make him feel less of a shit for walking away? No. But perhaps it made it more possible to do what he felt he would have done anyway, at some point.

He was lucky to find that a train was leaving in fifteen minutes for the town on the flyer that he'd picked up the night before. He bought a single ticket, then went across the road to the river and threw his phone into the water below the weir.

As Mark sat on the train, he felt another beat of sadness and guilt. He was leaving Ty behind and the sense of betrayal in that was huge. He remembered Ty in his little jumpsuit and tiny yellow trainers. He had such pale blue eyes, and Mark remembered staring into them in wonder sometimes. In fact, it was on one of these occasions that the seed of Mark's eventual departure was sown, when Amy said to him: 'You used to look at me like that, once upon a time.'

But there is never a moment when all the conditions are perfect for instigating radical change. Mark's sense of betrayal of Ty was something that was real and massive, and yet it was still not enough to keep him from leaving.

He wondered to what extent he was an asset as a father. He was empty. On medication. No good to anyone, particularly not to his wife and son.

He didn't find the address at first – even with the simple instructions that he'd been given by the woman in the newsagent – because Baker's Yard looked like the gap between two houses rather than a street. In fact, it was a narrow alleyway that opened up after twenty feet or so into a tiny cobbled courtyard that contained a single small tree and a house that looked to be an old workshop, though presumably it had also once been a bakery. The reason why it was number one Baker's Yard was clear as he approached it. It was the only house there. Its slate-tiled roof was in need of attention, and the dormer windows badly needed a lick of paint, but it had a settled look to it, with hanging baskets on either side of the front door whose trailing greenery had yet to come into bloom. Early herbs grew in window boxes on the ground floor.

He deliberately didn't stop to think what he was doing but rang the bell and waited. There was a high wall round the courtyard and this gave an almost menacing and claustrophobic feel to the place. If it hadn't been for the hanging baskets and the laburnum, it might have looked like a tiny prison yard. The afternoon was beginning to fade. The sun had already set behind the crowding buildings that huddled around the tiny yard.

'Hello?' said a wary voice, from above. Mark looked up and saw that a small, frosted glass window high above had been opened a couple of inches. He could hear a woman's voice but couldn't see her face.

'Hello,' Mark said. 'I've come here to. . .'

And then he stopped, and laughed a brief, involuntary laugh, before shrugging.

'I'm not quite sure why I have come,' he admitted. 'I seem to have been given an invitation.'

'Ah,' said the woman, as if that was an explanation in itself, but her voice remained wary. 'What is the password?'

Mark thought for a moment.

'I'm not sure what you mean.'

'Unless you arrive accompanied by someone from the house, how would I know to let you in? There is an established password and if you don't know it then I can't help you.'

Mark felt a sensation of confusion and was about to say

something when the window above him clacked shut. He stood looking up at the rotting window frame for a few moments before turning away and wandering the short distance back up to the main street.

There was a small café across from Baker's Yard, on the next block up towards the station, and he went in and bought a cup of watery coffee. It hadn't occurred to him what would happen if he wasn't welcomed at Baker's Yard, and when he thought of this, he wondered why he'd made the assumption – on an unconscious level at least – that he would be welcomed. Who in their right mind would turn up unannounced at an address they'd found in a comedy venue and expect to be taken in? But then, he wasn't in his right mind, was he? Walking out of his job and his relationship. Jumping on a train to who knows where with a bag of money belonging to someone else. . . Somehow, though, he knew instinctively that it was the state in which he'd been existing for the last couple of years that wasn't his 'right mind'. Perhaps you have to do something a little mad – become a little mad – to find what your right mind is?

If he wasn't welcome at the house, then what should he do next? Going home was out of the question, so the obvious solution was to find a hotel or guest house and hole up there for a while until he came up with a plan. He had more than enough money to do that. This decision reinvested in him a sense of purpose. He left the café and wandered back towards the railway station, reasoning that there must be some sort of hotel in that part of town. He bought himself a pastry and ate it as he walked. Idly, he drew the flyer for Club Covert from his pocket. Looking at it, he read its enigmatic message again: *The Key is Classified.* Of course! A password is a key. Why hadn't he realised immediately? He turned and quickly made his way back to Baker's Yard, resisting the urge to break into a run, and went up to the door and knocked loudly. The window upstairs opened wider this time and a woman leaned out and looked down.

Before she spoke, he called up to her, 'It's classified! The password is "classified".' He felt disproportionately proud of himself for having worked it out.

Again, the window closed with a bang, and there was a deep silence. Mark began to feel uneasy again. Perhaps he wasn't so clever after all. Maybe that wasn't the password. In fact, it was unlikely to be that simple, he reasoned, and he began to feel foolish. But then he heard the sound of footsteps coming down a staircase and a few moments later the door opened. Mark stared in astonishment at the man standing in the doorway.

'Oh, hello!' said Ewan Rees. 'It's you.'

Mark was filled with incredulity and anger in equal measure. A hot flash of resentment sparked in his chest, suffusing his body with sudden heat. Rees seemed so unsurprised to see him that it was infuriating.

'*Ewan Rees!*' he gasped.

'That's my stage name,' he told Mark. 'My real name is Don. Please, come in.'

Don leaned over and shook Mark's hand, laughing at the over-formal gesture as though it was a joke. It was a simple and uninhibited laugh of pleasure – very different to the artificial stage-laughter of the previous night. Mark, bewildered, hesitated for a moment. Things were happening too fast. Disturbing and coincidental things that shouldn't happen at all were all happening at once. He remembered a ride he'd once had at the funfair as a child, where you stood in a cylindrical room with your back to the wall as the room rotated faster and faster. Eventually, you stuck to the wall and the floor started to drop away. He felt the same vertiginous lurch now, only this time the world of logic had dropped away and was showing no sign of returning. He took a deep breath before following Don into the ground floor sitting room. The ceiling was low, with exposed beams, and the roughly plastered walls were hung with brightly coloured abstract designs. Don looked different here, in his own environment. Last night, on stage, 'Ewan' had been wearing a red flamenco-style shirt, tight black jeans and with his hair gelled slickly back. Now he was wearing baggy, faded chequered trousers, an old white shirt and his hair was uncombed after sleep. Although he must have been somewhere between thirty and forty, there was a boyish quality to his face that, at certain angles, made him look impossibly young. It was disconcerting.

'Coffee?' Don asked.

'Only if I'm welcome here,' said Mark stolidly. But he didn't really know what he meant by that. Actually, he now felt inclined to leave and continue his search for a hotel in town. Surely he couldn't stay here. Not with Ewan Rees, who'd publicly humiliated him the previous night. He shifted his weight from foot to foot, indecision gnawing at his belly.

'Sit down,' Don said with a friendly smile, gesturing generally round the room at no chair in particular. 'I'll be back in a moment. Ailsa!' he called up the stairs, 'It's someone from my gig last night. Come down and say hello.'

Left alone in the sitting room, Mark sat down and rested his hand on the bag beside him and then looked up as Ailsa came down the stairs. He saw that she was a tall woman with shoulder length wavy hair, glossy with hair product. She had a rather thin face with delicately upward-slanting eyes. She wore intensely red lipstick, accentuating the cast of a mouth that gave Mark the impression that she was perpetually amused. She gave Mark a pleasant, welcoming smile.

'Hello,' she said.

'Hello,' Mark answered. The woman seemed vaguely reassuring and this had a normalising effect on him, which was most welcome.

'So you worked it out after all!' she said.

'Yes,' said Mark.

'I hope I didn't sound too suspicious earlier,' she continued, 'but you have to be careful these days.'

'Hence the password,' said Mark.

Ailsa nodded.

'So,' she said, 'you've already met Don?'

'He was outrageously rude to me last night,' Mark told her. 'If I'd known that he was going to be here. . .'

'Yes?' Ailsa looked at Mark. 'Then you wouldn't have come? Is that what you were going to say?'

Mark shrugged.

'Don't worry about Don,' Ailsa went on. 'He says the unsayable when he's on stage. His observations can be painful if they strike a nerve, and we all have those!'

She brushed back a stray ringlet, tucking it behind a small, neat ear. She looked at him brightly.

'Have you come to stay?'

Mark cleared his throat. 'I've come looking for somewhere to stay here in the town. I wonder if you know anywhere. A good hotel perhaps?'

Ailsa regarded him for a moment.

'Or you could stay here,' she said carefully. 'Isn't that what you were hoping for when you came here? To find refuge?'

'I don't know what I was hoping for,' Mark told her.

Ailsa looked at him steadily and said, 'Not allowing yourself to think about why you are doing something is a kind of deceit. Part of you knows what you're looking for, but you can't bring yourself to acknowledge it. You'd probably say you were acting by instinct, coming here and knocking on the door and not thinking beyond the moment.'

'Yes, that's *exactly* what I was doing,' Mark replied.

'But unless you can be honest about what you're doing and what you want, you'll inevitably get it wrong.'

Mark frowned. He'd liked Ailsa at first, but now she was becoming as antagonistic as Don. And she seemed to be talking in riddles.

'What if there was no one here, or if we were unfriendly?' she asked him gently.

'Like I said, I would go and find a hotel,' Mark told her. 'I almost did that before I came to you, anyway.'

'You see,' said Ailsa, 'you're still resisting what you already know.'

She looked down at the sofa that he was sitting on, and then at the flyer that he'd placed on the arm beside him. His eyes followed hers.

'A flyer,' she said. 'Don't you see? *You* are a "flyer".'

'A flyer?' said Mark, and laughed. 'You mean as in, "I have taken flight from my home". Do you think that's bad?'

Ailsa laughed.

'The question I would ask is, "What does flight mean to you?" But you would say, "I don't know". And then you're back to not knowing. As to whether *that's* bad – it might be fantastic – but then again. . .' She trailed off and looked out of the window for a moment. 'I used to inhabit one kind of not knowing. About why I was so self-destructive, mostly, and I nearly died as a result of it. And now I inhabit another kind of not knowing that seems to be saving me. It's a conundrum.'

Don came in with a tray of coffee for the three of them.

'You *are* planning to stay?' he asked Mark as he sat down.

Mark nodded slowly.

'I don't know why I was so surprised to see you here,' Mark told him. 'It didn't click that you'd put the flyer on my table in the club last night.' He tapped his temple with his index finger. 'I wasn't thinking that coherently. But now. . .'

'As it happens, I *didn't* put it on your table,' Don said, laughing happily, 'but that's not important. I *did* know that you needed a push, and so I did a little pushing.'

'Pushing is an interesting word for it,' said Mark. 'It felt more like dismemberment.'

Don laughed.

'Good word, dismemberment. Because it's a gutsy thing to do to jump on a train and get away. It's a bowel thing – a gut feeling – that allows you to do something like that. And as for what I said last night, I'm not going to try to explain why I said what I said to you, because I did it on instinct. All I can say is that you can judge me as you like, but judge me as Don and not as Ewan Rees.'

Don sipped his coffee and Mark noticed that his eyes sparkled with an easily kindled delight. Mark looked out of the window, at the high, broken cloud over the rooftops, and at the sunshine dappling through the branches of the laburnum tree that shaded the window. He reminded himself that 'Ewan' and Don were not the same person.

Suddenly his resentment died away, and the air seemed to buzz with fresh possibilities.

'So,' Mark said at last, 'Ailsa was saying something about the possibility of me staying here. . .'

'Right. If you've come to live in this town,' Don said, 'then

I'd better explain the situation here before we go on, and then you'll have a better idea of where you stand.'

He leaned back in the sofa and looked at Mark.

'Firstly, Andy is away at the moment, so you can have his room for a week or so – he's cool about that kind of thing. We all are.'

'I'd like that,' Mark said. 'As a stop-gap, I mean.'

Don smiled. 'As for finding somewhere more permanent to live down here, it can be quite hard, but the summer season hasn't started yet, and the annual influx of students has settled, so you'll probably find it as easy as it ever gets – which is to say fantastically difficult. Anything cheap gets snapped up straight away. There's a weekly paper that comes out the day after tomorrow which has a lot of flats and rooms to rent, but you have to get it practically as it comes off the press if you're going to have any chance of getting something. I have to warn you, though, most of them will want references and a deposit.'

'I have money and good credit,' Mark said. 'And I don't mind staying in a hotel for a while. But what about work? Are there many jobs around here?'

'There are a couple of agencies that might be worth signing up with,' Don said, 'and there'll be plenty of seasonal work in a week or two, to tide you over while you look for something more permanent – if that's what you want. What is your profession?'

'I'm a qualified engineer,' said Mark, 'I work in aerodynamics. But in a more practical sense, I have also done quite a lot of renovation – doing up houses before they're sold on. I don't enjoy that kind of work, but I can always fall back on it.'

'I should imagine you'll do well anywhere with skills like that,' said Don. 'There are one or two jobs that need to be done here.'

He raised his hand, gesturing generally, and laughed.

'It's a joke! I'm an architect myself, by training, but I cut my teeth on making sure buildings function effectively. I usually do such jobs myself, it's good for my psyche, so please, leave that side of things alone here.'

Mark nodded.

'Now, I'm going to start on the dinner,' Don said. 'You can come and help if you like, and then you can go and get some wine so that we can toast your arrival.'

Ailsa smiled at them both in a vague sort of way, then got up and wandered off upstairs. Mark followed Don through to the kitchen.

'Unfortunately,' Don told him, 'we don't have room for another tenant in the cottage at the moment, or I'd offer you a more permanent room.'

Mark shook his head as if to shake water from his hair. 'You're very kind. But somehow this is all a bit. . . I don't know. Sudden. Vertiginous. *Unplanned.* My life to date has been ruled by planning. My work demands it.'

Don smiled. 'Vertiginous is good, if you mean you feel as if you've fallen over the edge of a cliff. That's how most of us come to live here – sudden chance meetings, or word of mouth.'

'Then I'd better stay. Keep the tradition,' Mark smiled.

The kitchen was a low-ceilinged, functional room that had a large oak table in the middle, with some bread and a bowl of fresh vegetables on it. Don delegated some simple tasks and Mark stood there doing things he'd done innumerable times before; peeling vegetables, frying onions, stirring a sauce, but this afternoon it all seemed as though he was doing it for the first time – or for the first time in this way. He wondered how that could be: that he could do an action so many times that he forgot he was doing it, and then there was a change of environment, and suddenly it seemed new and fresh? His interaction with Don was like that. By accepting Don's offer of a room he'd already placed himself in a relationship that invited a kind of closeness – being a guest elicits a certain friendliness – but Don was, at the same time, a stranger. Mark found that these two things created an unusual dynamic of both connection and detachment.

It seemed natural to ask Don about his life and where he'd come from – his accent was vaguely Cornish, Mark thought, though he couldn't be sure.

'Look,' Don said in response to Mark's question, 'it's one of the rules of the house that we never ask questions like that. I'm not trying to be dismissive – or even evasive. It's just that some of us here have had, well. . . difficult pasts. It's not that you can't talk about that sort of thing, but it should be at the invitation of the person you are talking to. Both parties have to be ready and able to accept the obligations that conversations of this kind might raise.'

'Yes, of course,' Mark said. 'That's fine. I'm sorry.'

'Please don't apologise.'

Mark felt himself blush, and realised how little his old social skills seemed to fit here.

'What would you have said, for example,' Don added, 'if I'd asked you to tell me about yourself? Would you have told me that you were so unhappy that you were making yourself ill?'

Mark stared at Don.

'Ill?'

'When I saw you yesterday, you were completely washed out – a husk. Don't you agree?'

Mark closed his eyes and felt an odd sensation, something like hunger, in the pit of his stomach.

'Yes,' he said after a pause. 'I was ill. I must have been ill for a long time but I hadn't realised it.'

Don grinned, and swept some carefully chopped vegetables into a pan.

'You had realised it, in here.' He touched his solar plexus with his palm. 'But you had to deny it in order to carry on.'

Mark turned to chop some tomatoes for a salad and felt a constriction in his chest.

'Today,' he said, 'is the first time in nearly two years that I haven't taken my anti-depressant medication. I forgot to bring it with me. I don't know what effect it will have on my body if I stop suddenly. . . it seems so strange to think that I'd been taking it for so long and never saw it as a sign of illness. My mother is on anti-depressants. One of my cousins is on anti-depressants. One of my work colleagues is on anti-depressants. This kind of illness seems to be something that a person might endure, rather than seek to recover from. It's so odd, and now I've realised that I haven't had my pills today, I feel nervous and a little overwrought. I don't know if that's psychological or a symptom of withdrawal.'

'You see where this conversation has gone?' Don said. 'If you are in an honest space, even though you ask serious questions in a light and artificial way, they will still lead you into deep water. Now,' he added, 'why don't you go out to the offlicence? There's one back up towards the station. Get a couple of bottles of wine – red preferably, unless you're particularly keen on white, in which case get one of each – and we'll open one straight away.'

As he left, Mark looked at his watch. It was nearly six o'clock.

*

26

He crossed the quiet street at the end of Baker's Yard and went out onto the main avenue leading up to the station. Looking above the shop fronts, he noticed that the buildings were of red brick inset with decorated golden sandstone window surrounds, topped with broad lintels. They made him remember family day trips to Chester when he was a child. These buildings weren't as old, or as ornate, as those in Chester but they did exude that same air of gentle living from a bygone age, and a sense of placidity and friendliness. Even the ultra-modern glass-fronted office blocks by the station, and the boxy residential flats behind them, didn't diminish this sense of elegance.

Mark's home town was modern and vaguely institutional in feel, even though the old school and council buildings were Victorian; they had been somehow subsumed to the characterless offices that surrounded them. It wasn't that the buildings of his home town were modern, it was that they were conceived as low-cost structures, and not as places in which people might feel at home – unlike this town, which embodied a kind of cultured homeliness, even on first sight. Perhaps that was why the woman in the newsagent had sounded so unsurprised when he'd said what he had about maybe living there. Perhaps on arrival, everyone had the impulse to stay.

The off-licence was small and empty except for a young woman behind the counter who had ragged-looking hair and one of those spikes through her lower lip. She smiled at Mark as he came in.

'So you're a friend of Don's?' she said.

Mark was surprised by her question.

'How do you know that I know Don?' he asked.

'We all know Don round here,' the woman laughed. 'I used

to stay in the cottage with him and the others. It was a kind of staging post for me. And not just me. Don has a terrific paternal compulsion and a fantastic instinct about people who need to be. . . helped.'

'Yes, but how did you know–'

'Look,' she said, and pointed out from where she was standing by the till.

From here, framed by the entrance of the street opposite, it was possible to see the entrance to Baker's Yard and, beyond that, the door to the cottage.

'I saw you arrive. I also saw you go away and then come back again. It took you quite a long time to work out what the password was. . . but don't worry, some people never get it, so you've done well.'

She smiled a secretive smile, Mark thought, as though there was something important that she wasn't telling him.

'This may not seem to be a particularly small town,' she went on, 'but everyone still manages to know everyone else's business. I'm Holly, by the way. Welcome. If you're going to be staying with Don and the others for a while, I expect we'll be meeting socially anyway, so we might as well get acquainted now.'

'I'm Mark,' he said, then asked her opinion on which wine he should buy.

'They always drink this organic mersault,' she said, indicating a tall, darkly green bottle, 'when they can afford it, which isn't often. It's biodynamic.'

He bought two bottles, said goodbye, and wandered back to Baker's Yard. *The others.* He wondered what Holly meant by that? He didn't know whether it sounded comforting or ominous. When he got to the cottage, the front door was slightly ajar and he could hear voices inside. He felt a wash of shyness that halted him as he raised his hand to push the door open. He didn't feel quite ready to meet anyone else yet. He wanted to talk some more to Don first. Still, he couldn't stand on the doorstep forever, and so he took a long breath and went in.

Don was talking to a man who was considerably younger than himself and who looked up as Mark came in. He was tall and wiry with short dark hair and had a kind of poise about him as though he'd been praying. He looked at Mark with a certain curiosity but gave no indication as to whether he would be welcoming or not.

'Here,' Mark said to Don, handing him the wine.

'This is Gareth,' Don said, taking the bag.

Gareth shook hands with Mark, again a gesture that seemed oddly out of place here. Gareth smirked, and tried to put on a deliberately over-serious expression.

'Organic mersault,' Don laughed, then looked up. 'Thank you. It must be Holly on duty this evening.'

'Yes.'

'She always knows how to talk people into spending twice as much as they were expecting to.'

'I don't mind. I liked her.'

Gareth turned abruptly as Mark said this and went off upstairs. Mark watched him go.

'Don't worry,' Don told Mark after Gareth had gone. 'He's always wary of new arrivals. Everything will be fine so long as you let yourself be natural.'

Mark laughed and thought: *I don't really know what that means.* As far as he could see, his life had been one long process of not being natural. In his relationship with Amy, he had drifted into a cordiality that covered a yearning gap; a gap that made every aspect of his waking life one big unnatural cover-up of his real self. And it all went back as far as he could remember. The question of whether he could be natural was simply not a question that he would have thought to ask at first, and then, in time, it was one that he forgot how to ask. Because he knew he couldn't answer it.

'I don't know how to be natural,' he said, quietly.

He didn't expect Don to laugh at this, but he did – and in such a hearty and unrestrained way that it caused a flash of irritation.

'Don't think about it,' Don said as he busied himself with opening the wine. 'That's the thing. Do and say what you feel without trying to work out whether you *should* say it or not.'

He opened a battered old oak corner-cupboard and took out three glasses.

'There must have been a time when you were natural,' he said and handed Mark a glass before filling it with wine.

'What if my natural reaction is that I dislike Gareth?' Mark said. 'What if I feel that he resents me being here?'

'Then say so. Indeed, you just have.'

'But I'm a guest in your house,' he said. 'And besides, I'm not sure if I do think that.'

'Look,' said Don, 'I'll take Gareth his wine and then make sure everything's on track in the kitchen. I won't be long.'

On his own, and in the wake of Gareth's apparent hostility, Mark confronted the possibility that he'd made a mistake big time in idly assuming that he could simply jump on a train, accept the first offer of a place to stay, and find himself a new life.

The meal was a surprising anti-climax. He'd already met Gareth, of course, and Ailsa, who came downstairs as the food was served. The fourth and fifth members of the household were a Dutch couple called Ingrid and Wim who were ordinary, pleasant, ran a small clothes shop near the seafront, and seemed light and superficial. Just like the people Mark had left behind, in fact. But then what had he expected? Did he think that he was being invited into a world of bohemian emotional extravagance and pithy conversation? Had he expected everyone to gather at the table and talk intensely about their lives, and other significant things?

He thought perhaps he should try to encourage the conversation beyond the daily chit-chat of people who were familiar with each other, but remembered Don's instruction from earlier not to enquire about anyone's past, and he felt this as an inhibiting restriction. Still, no one seemed to mind his silence – if anything they seemed to expect it. Gareth also sat quietly through most of the meal, eyeing Mark suspiciously, which made him feel even more uncomfortable. He gathered, at one point, that Gareth was a potter, and that figured, somehow. Cord-like veins protruded from the backs of his strong, flexible hands, and his silence was the silence of someone who was thinking in three dimensions. Mark wanted to ask him about his work, but didn't know whether this would also transgress house rules and so he kept quiet.

Later, when Ingrid said goodnight and went off up to bed with Wim, she said, 'Drop by at the shop tomorrow if you go out wandering. We're just off the harbour as you go into the Old Town.'

Gareth followed them up and, when Don and Mark were alone, Don said, 'You look disappointed.'

Mark said, 'I'm sorry, I expected–'

'–your new life to begin with something more. . . sparkling? More psychologically dramatic?'

Mark smiled and nodded.

'There is a process going on here,' Don told him. 'It's not to do with conversation. It's to do with being aware of yourself. Everything that you do needs to facilitate that.'

As Mark pondered this, Don leaned towards him and whispered with a sense of urgency that made the hair on Mark's scalp prickle.

'You will either make a success of this or you will fail, but, either way, the only way you can achieve something worthwhile is to give up having any expectations and let what is happening to you *happen*.'

When Mark went upstairs to bed, he wasn't even vaguely sleepy. He thought of Ty and Amy, and felt a whisper of self-pity, or perhaps self-recrimination. But this was quickly subsumed to a powerful sense of determination that had no object. He felt a sense of responsibility to do something constructive and dynamic. If he was going to walk out on his job, his wife and his son, then he needed to honour this with a sense of urgency not to waste time and opportunity – even if he had no concrete sense of what this might entail.

He realised he had a flyer for a club in his jacket pocket, and so he went and got it out. **Club Covert**. He smiled to himself. *Covert*. How apt, he thought, seeing as everyone else had gone to bed and he was considering slipping out to have a look at the place.

He took some money from under the bed, and wandered up to the taxi rank at the station where he jumped into a cab and said, 'Club Covert please.'

The taxi driver mumbled a sound that could have meant almost anything and set off down towards the river. There weren't many people around, and the riverside was deserted. They went over an arched stone bridge and turned right towards what appeared to be an industrial estate on the far side of the harbour. It looked as if it had seen better days. Several of the warehouses had been demolished to be replaced by makeshift car parks in which second hand cars were parked up, their prices prominently displayed on their windscreens. There were another couple of industrial units, and then a boatyard in which a dozen or so yachts were standing dry for maintenance and repair. On the far side of this, by the harbour wall, was another warehouse, in good repair this time. It had no windows, but several vents, one of which was letting out delicate plumes of what looked like steam. There were two bouncers standing by large double black doors, each of which had a small round window, with nautical-looking bolted steel surrounds. No name was apparent.

The taxi stopped and Mark got out and paid the driver, then went up to the entrance. One of the bouncers nodded to him without speaking and opened the door. Inside there was a small lobby with a red carpet. There was a dimly lit, polished black desk with a cash register behind which sat a woman of about forty in a plain black evening dress. She smiled at Mark and asked him for his entrance fee, which seemed quite reasonable and which – according to the small printed ticket that she issued to him – would have entitled him to a free 'dance' if he'd arrived before nine o'clock.

A waitress asked him if he was on his own and then took him into the club itself, which Mark instantly recognised as a lap-dancing club. Nevertheless, and in spite of a thrill of embarrassment, he followed her, resisting an urge to flee. He was directed to a small table near the bar and the – also small and currently empty – stage. He ordered a whisky with ice, and when the waitress left, he looked around. To the left there was a long bar, out of which sprang metal poles at regular intervals, bolted to the ceiling. He was relieved to see that none of them had anyone dancing at them. There were tables throughout the main area, with either lounge chairs or red sofas at them. It wasn't particularly busy, but there were a few groups of men, mostly between twenty-five and thirty-five he guessed, drinking and laughing and flirting with the half dozen or so girls. He noticed a 'menu', which he picked up and glanced at, and which explained the pricing system here. Drinks could either be ordered from the bar or 'one of our friendly waitresses', and were not overpriced. For the cost of three or four drinks you could get one of the girls to 'dance' for you for the duration of a song. It was around half that price if you wanted them to chat. The music itself seemed to be a half way house between non-descript dance music and bland soft rock.

Mark felt a prickling sensation of increasing embarrassment. As he glanced across the club, a woman two or three tables away started taking her clothes off in front of a strangely indifferent young man, who sat with his smartly suited legs apart and his hands placed on his thighs, neat and immobile. Mark was surprised that the 'dance' went all the way to full nudity and felt uncomfortably voyeuristic witnessing it. The man appeared to be watching television rather than a real person. The woman, Mark thought, looked quite ordinary, though attractive enough in a homely way, and he was surprised that the man wasn't showing more pleasure at her performance, seeing as he'd agreed to pay money to witness it. There was something about the way the woman ground her pelvis and pouted at the man that seemed not only false but curiously unerotic. Pornographic, yes, but – in the flesh – also somehow toe-curlingly uncomfortable. When the song ended, the woman smiled, accepted the note that the man handed to her, and turned from him to slip her panties back on. The man glanced to his friends and said something that they all laughed at, while the dancer walked away.

Mark had no time to think more about this before a woman wearing what he at first thought was an absurdly skimpy nurse's uniform, but which he then realised was supposed to be nautical, came up to him and said, 'Hi, are you on your own this evening?'

She was slim, with a cool languor to her movements that made him think 'feline'. She had long dark brown hair that was slightly wavy and a face that was rounded, but with noticeable (and accentuated) cheekbones. She was pale, with a slightly haunted look to her that made her seem vulnerable in a way that was particularly attractive to Mark – it was a trait that tended to bring out the rescuer in him. Her breasts looked augmented but not to absurd proportions. His immediate response was to blush deeply.

'Yes, I'm on my own,' Mark told her, astonished by her beauty, but made extremely uncomfortable by it, too.

'You could ask me to dance for you if you like,' she said, and then noticing Mark's flush, said, 'or you could always buy me a drink.'

Mark stammered slightly as he said, 'I'd love to, but I think that buying you a drink might cost me more money than I can afford. What do you drink? Champagne, I expect.'

She laughed back.

'If I can get a man to buy me champagne, then that is what I drink.'

Mark had seen the price of champagne, so there was no chance of that, and the idea of purchasing a stranger's time felt curiously unpleasant anyway, almost abusive.

'Never mind,' she said, and wandered off to talk to some

men at a table by the stage who were beckoning her over. They were all wearing suits, with ties loosened, and looked, Mark thought, as though they were competing with one another, as if they'd placed a bet on who could pull the best dancer.

As the woman who had spoken to him 'danced' for one of the men, he wondered if there was, perhaps, an etiquette here? No leering, or touching by the men, but a studied and apparently insouciant semi-boredom, followed by rather childish glee once the woman had wandered off. There was something vaguely disturbing, too, about the fact that he was now seeing the woman who had spoken to him, completely naked. He found he couldn't watch outright, but looked down at the table and glanced across furtively, which seemed worse somehow than blatant staring. What made it particularly strange was the knowledge that if he'd seen a photograph of this scene, he would have found it arousing. But in the flesh it was far too obviously voyeuristic. A sexual fantasy can be many things, but the reality of the transactions he was witnessing reminded him of the taxi journey he'd taken down here. There was a 'meter' ticking, although the journey was rather different.

He took another sip of his whisky and, as another of the women caught his eye, he quickly looked down.

The first woman came back over to him again.

'Look,' she said in a friendly voice, 'you might as well come clean and tell me why you've come here. Anyone can see that you're getting about as much fun out of all this as I am.'

Mark took the flyer out of his pocket and showed it to her.

'I saw this,' he said.

She picked it up.

'I've never seen one like this before,' she said. 'Are

you sure it's for *this* Club Covert? Where did you find it?'

He mentioned his home town.

'That's half way across the country,' she said, laughing even louder.

Confused, he looked at the flyer again. She was right. *There was no mention of location at all.* Why had he imagined that it was here, in this town, rather than somewhere else? Why had he bought a train ticket to somewhere that he knew nothing about when the flyer hadn't actually mentioned the name of the town? He rubbed his forehead, upon which he could feel a light patina of cold sweat. Surely the name had been on the flyer before? But now it had gone. It was ridiculous. . .

'You're in the wrong place.' She read the flyer. '"*Turn over a new leaf, look on the other side. Make your Mark.*". Well, you're not going to turn over a new leaf here, are you, unless you want to turn over the wrong kind of leaf. But then, maybe that's the point, I guess? And what *are* your intentions?'

Mark looked her in the eyes.

'My intentions are to start my life again, and to learn to be with people without taking them for granted, and to not carry on being with someone when there's no love left in the relationship.'

'Great. And a club like this is the place to do that?' she said. 'Wow, you have a fine set of aspirations, but a majorly weird idea of where to start looking to fulfil them. Good luck to you.'

She turned to go and Mark said, 'Hey, please stay and have a chat. I can't buy you champagne, but maybe I can pay for your time for a while.'

She looked around the club. He could see her doing a mental calculation as to what chances there were of getting better business elsewhere. Then, she looked back at him.

'Okay,' she said. 'But, it's not easy with someone like you. I don't have any patter for you. I can start by saying my name is Ruby, but you're not going to follow that by asking about the size of my breasts, are you?'

'Umm,' he said, 'it's not that easy for me to strike up a casual conversation with you, either. . .'

'And don't think I listen to any old thing that people say, just because you're paying for my attention. I can walk off any time. I could have you thrown out if I wanted to.'

'Do you want to?'

'Actually, I'm curious about you. What's your name?'

'Mark.'

'Well, I'm curious about you, Mark, but only because you've found your way in here for the most ridiculous reason I have ever heard.'

'How did you find your way here?' he asked.

'Ha, ha,' she laughed mirthlessly. 'I'm happy to talk about you but let's leave me out of this. And if you pressed me, I would lie, so don't bother with any of that. . .'

'Okay,' he said. 'So, why were you so sure I wasn't here for the same reason as everyone else?'

'Show me the man here who's looking down at the table with embarrassment. Embarrassment, yes, that happens quite a lot here, but if you're going to be embarrassed you might as well have a look while you're at it.'

Mark found himself shrugging, and blushing again.

'You're quite cute when you blush,' she said. 'I would have been more happy to dance for you than most. But don't ask me now, it's too late. I only dance for strangers.'

'I'm still a stranger.'

'Let's put it another way. You may be a stranger, but I quite like you, and I'm afraid I *can't* dance for someone I like. I have to imagine that the blokes I dance for are brainless arseholes. I'd need more money than you could afford before I danced for you now.'

'How do you know how much I can afford?'

'It's obvious,' she said. 'Look at the suits in here. Then look at your get up. No offence – I mean it's one of the things I like about you – but, given what you're wearing, you clearly live a life in which you have to be careful with money.'

'What nights do you work here?' he asked.

'Why?'

'Just wondered.'

'Don't come back here, Mark. I won't dance for you. The other girls will, of course, but given what you want to do with your life, you'd be a fool to spend your money on it.'

Mark took a deep breath and said, 'You're right, Ruby. Thank you. It's not something I'd enjoy.'

'Enjoyment is a relative word,' she told him. 'For example, in what way are you enjoying yourself right now? I have enough experience to know when a man is sitting in such a way that he's pretending not to have a hard on. . . But maybe you're not enjoying *that*, either. Maybe you're embarrassed by it? Or ashamed?'

'I'd rather not think about it,' said Mark. 'Perhaps I'll go home now.'

In the taxi on the way home, Mark reflected on whether he was pleased to have gone to Club Covert or not. Part of him wanted to go back to Baker's Yard and get some more of his money, then go back to the club and buy a bottle of champagne to drink with Ruby. But what was that about? A desire to impress her? He might have idle money this week, and for a few weeks to come, but it was finite. It was not in any way comparable to an executive salary. On reflection, the idea seemed puerile, and a little sordid, too.

He felt even more sordid when he masturbated in bed, later, unable to sleep and over-stimulated in many ways. When he'd finished, he lay and looked at the dark red and brown Rothko print that hung on the wall of his room. He felt confused and ashamed, but the shame felt like something old, and not particularly to do with this evening. Gradually, his thoughts began to slow down. Interestingly, his last thoughts were of how distant his home now seemed, even though it was only a few hours away. Amy would have gone to bed alone. . .

The great surprise was that Mark didn't feel guilty about this, although the thought of Ty caused a small, intense pain in his chest.

# 2. Sense Desire

Over the next few days, Mark began to explore the town. Every morning he took some cash from the photographer's bag, which he kept under his bed, and wandered wherever his feet would take him. These days were sharp and clean, with a keen breeze. Thin spring sunshine broke suddenly from behind banks of turbulent clouds that raced away towards the northwest. There were short, sudden showers that seemed to come out of a blue sky, and which always caught him by surprise. The wind was cool on his face, slightly numbing his nose and the tips of his ears. The waves skipped in the sea breeze, topped with crenulations of foam. He was constantly surprised at the bitter, salty sting of the air. Somehow he'd imagined that spring in a seaside town would be warm, even balmy. Now he realised that he needed a better coat.

On the fourth day of his wanderings, he was out early and the breeze seemed keener than ever. Mark found himself narrowing his shoulders and lowering his head in an attempt to keep warm, offering as few angles to the wind as possible. He was barely taking in his surroundings. Now was the time to get some suitable clothes, he thought, remembering that Ingrid and Wim had a little shop nearby. He decided to go and see what they had to offer. It was shortly after 9.00am, so the shop would be open.

As he walked along the seafront, he stopped to watch a fire-eater who was performing, wearing a blue, yellow and red harlequin costume. It was something he would never have seen at home, but here in a tourist town it seemed to be absolutely ordinary. Unremarkable. He huddled inside his light jacket and shivered as the man juggled his burning torches with nonchalant aplomb, finishing off by blowing a plume of flame into the air. He was of indeterminate age, tanned, with weathered skin and callused hands – a circus man, or a traveller. It was fascinating and absorbing to watch him. His assured movements made such deft skill look effort-less. Mark stopped to lean against the railings, where a handful of other people stood, but, sadly, the man had finished. He doused his torches, to a scatter of applause from the few people who were up and about so early, then began to pack his things away. Mark went over and dropped a pound into the man's hat.

'Cold, isn't it?' he said as he did so.

The man didn't reply. Instead, he leaned down, carefully picked Mark's coin out of the hat, and handed it back to him.

Mark didn't know what to say. He looked down at the coin in his palm for several seconds before looking back at the fire-eater.

'What's wrong with my money?' he asked.

'I don't want it,' the man said. 'We don't want your sort here. Locals and tourists are welcome, but we don't want runaways, renegades or *parasites*. . .'

Mark laughed. Who was this guy?

'How do you know I'm not a tourist?' he asked.

'Look at you,' the man said. 'You're wearing ridiculous clothes. You wouldn't know *how* to be a tourist. And you have such a. . . *hungry* expression.' The man stared belligerently into Mark's face. 'I've seen it before, hundreds of times. If you're not careful you'll end up sleeping in the gutter, and then you'll be in trouble.'

He put his doused torches into a sports bag which he zipped up. Then he picked up his hat and emptied the handful of coins from it.

'Go home,' he told Mark, pointing a finger towards Mark's chest for emphasis. His hand was blackened from handling the extinguished torches. 'I suggest you get on a train and go back to your woman and your son and give up this ridiculous fantasy that you might actually be able to change your life in any meaningful way.'

Mark was shocked by the challenge in the man's voice, the subdued violence, the unexpected hostility, and most of all the accuracy of his words. How did the juggler know that he had a wife and son? The other people who had been watching the fire-eating smirked at him as they began to wander off. Mark dropped the coin back into his pocket.

'I don't know how you know what you know,' he said to the man, 'but I've got just as much right to be here as you.'

The man shrugged but didn't respond.

Mark laughed again. 'This is ridiculous,' he said, 'you're just trying to intimidate me, and it's not going to work.'

He walked away and was about to cross the road at the beginning of the Old Town, when the man called to him again, from behind.

'Go home! We don't want your sort here.'

There was something about this town, Mark thought.

Everyone seemed to be challenging him. And yet, in other ways, people had been extremely welcoming. But not to begin with, he reminded himself. Don and Ailsa had been challenging too, at first. Mark remembered the woman in the newspaper shop on the day of his arrival, and thought he was beginning to understand why she'd looked so sad when he'd said that he was hoping to stay – she'd known that he would encounter this sort of hostility.

The Old Town was built on the slope leading up from the harbour to the headland. Above this he could see the fine lighthouse, which had looked resplendent from the train when he arrived. Now that he was closer he could see that it was disused – the lower entrance boarded up and sprayed with the pointless graffiti of the dispossessed. To the west, the harbour had been turned into a marina with pontoons that bristled with sailing boats. On the eastern side, the last few commercial fishing vessels were docked. From there, a group of steep streets or stairways meandered up the slopes towards the lighthouse, characterised by the jumble of architectural styles from Tudor to Edwardian; pubs, antique shops, boutiques and private residences. One of the first shops on that narrow, cobbled first street was Ingrid and Wim's, in a low-slung, beamed cottage, with their sign – a suit of clothes, dancing by itself – swinging lightly on two thin chains. It squeaked mournfully as it swung to and fro. Mark had to stoop a little as he pushed the door open and went in.

The shop was far larger inside than he would have imagined from the tiny frontage. The rear of the building had been extended, and the premises widened out naturally as they went back, so that the rear of the shop was two or three times as broad as the front. There was no one else there except for Ingrid and Wim, and Ingrid smiled as he came in. She looked smart and business-like this morning, calm in a way that Mark hadn't noticed at Baker's Yard. Wim had a slow, casual manner that made Mark begin to relax simply by virtue of being in the same room as him. He had that languor of move-ment that suggests a complete lack of stress bordering on the soporific. Mark wondered why he'd thought of them as being even remotely ordinary or dull before.

'Hello,' Ingrid said, then paused, noticing his expression. 'You look a little. . . disturbed?'

He was surprised that she could tell, and laughed.

'Oh,' he said, 'I just had an encounter on the seafront. It was odd more than disturbing,' and he explained what had happened.

'I'll get you a coffee,' she said, 'there's some brewing in the back. Shoppers don't really come out before ten thirty, so we might as well put our feet up for a while.'

Wim pulled a chair from behind the counter and placed it beside the leaded window, then gestured for Mark to sit. He did so and noticed that the window ledge was of silvery dry wood, cracked here and there in long thread-like lines. It was prob-ably hundreds of years old and made Mark wonder how many other people had casually laid their arms along it in the past.

'You have to understand,' said Wim when Ingrid had left, 'that this place is very parochial in some of its attitudes. I should know, I'm a foreigner and I've encountered my share of intolerance because of that. But if you stay here and work hard and make a contribution to the town, then they will come to accept and even respect you. So many people come down here to doss for a while in the summer, to make a noise, explore the caves and leave their rubbish and beer cans behind. As soon as the townspeople realise you're not going to be doing that, they'll leave you alone.'

Ingrid returned with a pot of coffee and some mugs. The fresh aroma made Mark feel briefly homesick. Not for the home that he'd left behind, but for a routine in which he had the comfort of certainty.

'I have to tell you,' said Ingrid, as she passed him a cup, 'and this is simply an observation – but I know exactly why that fire-eater assumed you were one of our unwelcome visitors.'

Mark laughed, surprised.

'Why?' he asked.

'Because in a way the man was right, you *do* have a look about you. Smart, but. . . as if you're wearing an off-duty uniform; as though your clothes have been bought for you by your mother.' She held up her hands as if in apology. 'Not that I'm condoning the haranguing,' she added quickly. She stopped and looked at Mark with gentle eyes. 'There's something else, too, but it's difficult to put it into words.'

Wim smiled and touched Mark's arm by way of reassurance.

'You must forgive Ingrid,' he said. 'She says things as she finds them. Sometimes it is not so very. . . tactful.'

'Well,' she shrugged, 'I'd rather that than sit here saying polite things like, "I can't think *why* that awful man might have said such a thing to you."'

She looked at Mark again, then turned to glance out of the window, as though trying to work out what to say next.

'You see,' she said, 'when a town has a certain reputation, then it sometimes comes to be that way by attracting the sort of people that will make it true. Ever since the sixteenth and seventeenth centuries, when the caves were used for smuggling, and later when William Garston wrote his gothic novel about the ghostly goings on in the Old Town, it has attracted odd characters of every kind imaginable. Of course, it has also exerted a pull on more sensible people, like myself and Wim, and you,' she smiled, 'but you have to forgive the townspeople for being wary.'

Mark looked down at himself and then across the shop to his reflection in a full-length mirror on the far wall. He saw a man in his late twenties, with a perfectly ordinary hairstyle, wearing perfectly ordinary high-street clothes. He was nonplussed. Surely it was a look that should make him invisible rather than a figure of persecution?

'All right,' he said to her, 'I don't exactly understand what you mean, but if I'm going to make a go of it here, perhaps you could kit me out with some clothes that would make me fit in. You should know. After all, you run a clothes shop.'

'Well, it's true that we could,' said Ingrid, 'but I don't want you to feel that I said what I did just to get some custom out of you.'

'No, no,' he said, 'I know you wouldn't do that.'

'Okay!' she laughed. 'Let's have a look, then.'

The next twenty minutes were rather hilarious. While Wim saw to an American couple who had come in, Ingrid brought item after item from the racks for him to look at.

'Some of these are rather brightly coloured,' she said, 'but there's nothing wrong with that, is there?'

Mark bought a couple of pairs of trousers, a pair of shorts, three shirts, several tee-shirts, a sweater, a fleece-style jacket, two pairs of shoes and a hat. They were all in either primary or pastel colours that he would never have dared to wear back home. And the cut of the cloth was fuller, but somehow more sculpted, too. He was pleased by the quality, and the fact that he hadn't been offered clothing that seemed to be "fashionable" as he hated the idea of trading one kind of uniform for another.

Everything was going extremely well, in fact, until he came

to pay. Rather than pay in cash (he felt it might look odd if he was seen to be carrying as much cash as he actually had on him), he gave Ingrid his credit card. But as she took it over to the till to swipe it, she stopped.

'Oh, I'm so sorry, Mark,' she said, 'this expired yesterday. I'm afraid I can't take it.'

He took the card from her and examined it. She was right. He pulled his wallet out and removed his debit card. It had also expired the day before. He wondered why he hadn't been sent new ones, before he'd left home. But then, not getting things that had been sent to him was par for the course these days. Amy quite often put his post carelessly to one side, only for him to find it weeks later, unopened. . .

'No problem,' he said. 'I'll pay in cash. I've got plenty.'

He counted the notes out on the counter and found that he had enough, with some left over. As he was about to leave Ingrid said, 'Hang on,' and began to rummage among some leaflets by the till. 'There's something else that might be useful to you. Here we are,' she said, finding and handing him a card, 'this is a good hairdresser. It may seem like interference on my part, but if you've bought some new clothes, you might as well. . . *consolidate* things. And it's not far from here, actually. You usually need an appointment, but I wouldn't have thought Thursday morning would be particularly busy. Say you're a friend of Don's and they might manage something.'

Mark left, still wearing his old clothes, but laden with carrier bags, and set off to his bank at the far edge of the Old Town. On the way, he passed the hairdresser that Ingrid had recommended, Ray's Place. It was one of those smart establishments with chrome trimmings and acres of pale polished wood – highly intimidating to someone used to going to the same barber once a month and unthinkingly asking for 'the usual'. There were four stylists; two male and two female – so clean cut and good-looking that he suddenly felt, for the first time, that Ingrid might genuinely be right about his appearance. Normally able to walk into a new place or situation and be affable with strangers, he felt that if he walked into Ray's Place, they would all look at him and wonder what someone as dowdy as himself was doing in a place like that. He lost his nerve and hurried on.

*I'll leave it for the moment,* he thought.

At the bank, there was no queue and he went straight to the till. The cashier looked at his credit card briefly and said, 'I'm sorry sir, I'm afraid I can't help you right now. We have a problem with our server this morning and we have no access to the network – it's down at the moment, so we can't verify your details. It should only be another hour or two before we're up and running again. Perhaps you could come back later today?'

There was nothing he could do, so, accepting the cashier's apologies, he left and made his way back to Baker's Yard. Now that he'd walked right across it, he realised that the Old Town was only a very small area of the town; a quaint corner attached to the mostly Victorian streets that led up to the station. As he walked along the flagstoned alley back to the seafront, he felt the old, beamed buildings towering over him; more than that, he could feel the oppressive weight of history itself bearing down on him from above, while the rest of the town, although decorative, hid nothing. It had no sense of a past.

As soon as Mark got back to the cottage, he went straight upstairs and tried on some of his new clothes. As he stood in that low-ceilinged room, in front of the mirror, he felt a dull thump of disappointment and thought: *This isn't me. I am not this person.* The clothes were of that tailored kind that accentuate the body, make a feature of it rather than conceal it. It wasn't that they were sexual, but more that they were assured; confident, almost flaunting. Now, here, in this new town, he wanted to arrive unnoticed and quietly find a place for himself in which he would have to make no grand statements of confidence and not have to resort to bravado of any kind. Admittedly, given the reaction to his old clothes, he acknowledged that they were unsuitable too, but surely these new ones were also inappropriate. What a fool he'd made of himself in buying them!

*I can't wear them,* he thought, and began to take them off.

When he was dressed in his old clothes again, he went out to buy himself some lunch and to do some more exploring of the town. He ended up sitting in a café between the station and the sea that looked out over the cliff and the old harbour. There was a breakwater that provided a modest anchorage with a beautiful stone quay, crumbling now in places, but still largely intact, with perhaps half a dozen small trawlers. Mark knew nothing about the fishing industry but was surprised to find that any fishing took place here at all. He'd somehow imagined that fish no longer inhabited the seas around the UK.

There was a little harbour like this down at Lyme Regis in Dorset, within walking distance of the cottage where he and his parents had stayed with his aunt, uncle and his cousin Rod, seven years in a row between the ages of nine and sixteen. Rod, eighteen months older, and such a strange mixture of sureness and shyness; of wisdom and craziness. They had been so close, like siblings, or even closer Mark used to think when he sometimes anticipated things that Rod was going to say, or want to do. This weird, semi-telepathic communication at odd moments had lasted throughout their childhood, but had gradually waned, on Mark's part at least, though Rod had never stopped being frighteningly insightful. Wasn't that why they'd drifted apart? Mark's academic success and aspirations had become more and more of a preoccupation, but Rod had dropped out of school after GCSEs. It began to seem that the seamlessly parallel course of their lives was diverging at an ever-increasing rate. Rod took a job as a gardener – was still a gardener, as far as Mark knew, twelve years later.

At the front of the café there was a counter selling sticks of rock, decorative boxes of fudge, and postcards of the town. On impulse, Mark bought himself a postcard and a book of four first class stamps. The postcard was an aerial view of the Old Town, with the harbour visible at one side, and the lighthouse and cliff top at the other. He wrote:

*Dear Rod,*
*I bet you're surprised to get a card from me after all this time. I'm staying here now. I don't know for how long. The old harbour here reminds me of the harbour at Lyme Regis. Do you remember? The cliff here is said to be riddled with caves and tunnels. We'd have loved it, back then.*
*All the best.*
*Mark.*
*p.s. I can't give you my address as I haven't got one yet.*

It was six years – no, now he thought about it, it must be more than seven – since he'd last seen Rod and he was surprised that he could remember the address. Of course, it was quite likely that Rod had moved on by now and wouldn't get the card, but somehow that didn't matter. The writing of it was as important as the receiving.

When he left the café, he posted the card and wondered what to do next. Although he knew that at some point he ought to start registering with as many of the employment agencies as he could, he ended up in the art gallery and museum instead, pondering the exhibits: fossils found in the cliff; a display showing the town's history of smuggling and of its importance as a port in the time of Henry VIII, a rather dreadful portrait of whom hung in the main hallway (a poor copy of a Holbein). There was a model of the Old Town in a great glass case showing how it would have looked in 1799, before the rest of the town had been built – a tumble of buildings, jostling together on the hillside as if desperate to keep their balance.

Although it could hardly be described as warm, the wind died down somewhat over the course of the afternoon and Mark wandered off to the harbour to walk on the breakwater. Most of the boats had been brought out and propped up on the shingle. To Mark's untrained eye they seemed decorative rather than functional: part of the tourist rather than the fishing industry. From the quay itself, he could see down into the water of the harbour. The tide was more or less high and there were fronds of seaweed gently swaying in the clear water, their air bladders like dull beads sewn into cloth. The barnacled stones of the bottom were so clear that, when Mark sat down to stare into the water, he could see, after a time, the small dark fish that swam there and an occasional scavenging crab. In fact, it so reminded him of his childhood holidays in Lyme Regis, that he couldn't resist the temptation to paddle and took his shoes and socks off. When he dipped one of his feet into the water, it was searingly, bone-numbingly cold. He pulled it out, and sat patting his foot on the sandstone of the quay, making dark, wet footprints on the cold surface. He'd never been to the seaside outside of the summer season and it had never occurred to him how cold the water could be at the end of April.

It is strange how, with places that he only visited in summer, he somehow imagined that they were eternally like that; always bright, always busy, always warm – always friendly. On his way back, Mark noticed that the fire-eater was setting up again at the entrance to the Old Town, so he stopped to watch. As the man soused the ends of his fire sticks with kerosene, he looked up and saw Mark.

'Still here, are you?' he said, aggressively and somewhat pointlessly.

'There's nothing to stop me from watching,' said Mark. 'You might not want to accept my money, but you can't stop me from watching.'

The fire-eater glared, took three large strides over to Mark and held one of his unlit juggling sticks under Mark's chin.

'Can't I?' he said.

The kerosene fumes made Mark feel giddy and he glanced round at the people who were gathering to watch, expecting someone to help. But they simply stared at him, as interested by this altercation as they would be by the fire-eating. The man pulled at his harlequin sleeves as though to smarten himself up, then gave Mark a shove. Mark didn't flinch. The man went back to his bag and stood there.

'The show will commence,' he said loudly, 'once this *gentleman* has left.'

Mark shrugged to those around him and smiled, but didn't move. As the static quality of the moment settled around them, he realised that there was no reason to hang around.

What point would it make? Instead, he caught the fire-eater's gaze directly and stared at him defiantly, refusing the man's insolent gaze and not being cowed by it, then turned to make his way back to Baker's Yard.

'The sea is freezing for another few weeks,' Don told Mark. 'But don't worry, there's a current that arrives at the end of May. You can tell because a thin scum of algae appears on the surface. After that the water's still cold for a while, but it's bracing rather than freezing. You'll be on the beach on the next properly sunny day and then you'll be surprised at how hot it can be – even if you can't go in for a swim.'

Ingrid and Wim turned up as Don was saying this.

'Your clothes,' Ingrid said. 'You haven't changed into them.'

Mark laughed. 'I'm not quite up to it yet,' he told her.

'Don't worry,' said Wim, 'you look fine as you are.'

'Incidentally,' Don said to Mark, 'did I tell you that it's our monthly "house night out" soon?'

'No,' said Mark, 'what does that mean?'

Wim grinned. 'Don't look so nervous at the prospect, Mark,' he said, flicking his dark fringe back before sitting on the sofa.

'The last Wednesday of the month is live music night at the Harbour Tavern,' Don said. 'It's become a bit of an institution at the house to go along. There's invariably a bit of a buzz down there and we always enjoy ourselves. It would be great if you wanted to come along.'

'Of course. It sounds fantastic.'

Don went upstairs to have a bath and Ingrid and Wim went through to the kitchen to prepare the dinner. Mark followed them in.

'Do you always eat together?' he asked.

'We try to eat together, when we're all around,' Ingrid told him. 'Gareth often comes in too late, but otherwise it's another one of the house institutions. Of course, we take it in turns to cook.'

'It works very well,' Wim said. 'You can cook tomorrow, maybe. What do you think?'

'Of course,' Mark said. 'I'd be glad to.'

'Good.'

He offered to help, but was refused, so he leaned against the wall in the kitchen and watched the simple domesticity. How relaxing, he thought, how pleasant, to be in a household with no atmospheres, no unspoken irritation.

'I'm not sure if this is an admissible question,' he said, 'but it seems strange that Don has this dual existence as a comedian on the circuit as well as. . . well, he told me he was an architect. But he actually seems to be some kind of a landlord.'

Ingrid wiped a lock of hair from her forehead with the back of her hand. 'Yes, it does seem strange but he really is an architect as well as a cabaret performer. As an architect he has something to do with the reclamation of derelict sites. You should ask him about it sometime, when you're having *that* kind of conversation. It's interesting work. He does a project every now and again, and then he has a few months of travelling around, performing. He always takes most of the summer off, too, which is the opposite of us, in a way. As shopkeepers here we're quiet all winter and then busy in the summer season. Don works in the winter and takes the summer off.'

'Don said that I shouldn't ask people in the house direct questions about their lives,' said Mark, 'and I assumed he included himself. I'm just trying to be. . . circumspect.'

'Mmm,' Ingrid said, 'I suppose Don might seem to be a secretive person. But I expect he'll tell you more of his own accord, in time.'

'It's a good rule, in principle,' said Wim. 'It was a relief to me and Ingrid. We were so pleased that we never had to *explain* why we'd come here. It's such a relief not to have to talk about your past if you don't want to.'

'Yes,' said Mark, unconvinced, 'I suppose so.'

But how did you get to know people? That was the thing. It ruled out all his usual tactics.

*But then,* he thought, *have I ever REALLY got to know anyone?*

There was Rod, of course, but it wasn't Mark who had put the effort into that. He heard Don's voice in his head saying, 'Be natural'. Even if he didn't know what that meant, exactly, he supposed that it was a reference to not trying too hard. Not thinking of tactics but letting things happen. But that was difficult. What was a person but the sum of his past? Could you communicate that without talking about it? In a way, yes, he supposed. Wim was utterly relaxed, for example, and that must have come from somewhere. He didn't have to explain it for Mark to be able to identify it as a trait. But maybe it was an intrinsic part of his personality and not a product of his past?

Seeing as he couldn't ask relevant questions, the conjecture seemed pointless.

*At least,* he thought, *I don't have to tell anyone how DULL my life has been.* That was a relief. It might, he thought, have been fun to try and invent a more interesting past. But would it be plausible? And would it be sustainable?

'How,' he said aloud without really meaning to, 'did Don manage to invite me down here in the first place?' It seemed that he was in a household of such different people to himself. He would never fit in, no matter how much he might want to or how much he might try.

'Don,' said Ingrid, 'is the most instinctive person I have ever met.'

'You must believe that he was right to invite you,' said Wim. 'That's the way we feel about it.'

What did that mean? That Ingrid, Wim and Gareth might think him an inappropriate guest but would put up with him because they "believed" Don was instinctively right?

'Look,' he said, 'I'll go and get a bottle of wine for the meal.'

'Okay,' said Ingrid, 'but get a bottle of cheap stuff. There's no need to be cajoled by Holly into spending a fortune.'

'Let me give you some money,' said Wim, 'so you can get two bottles.'

'No, no,' said Mark, 'I can get two bottles.'

The meal that evening was livelier than on previous evenings. Mark had bought two bottles of champagne, which had been smiled at. Ingrid looked almost embarrassed when she admitted to not liking champagne and slipped off to get a bottle of wine that she did like. Mark ended up feeling self-conscious, as though the others thought he'd bought the champagne in order to show off, when in fact he'd done so as a celebration of his fledgling new life. But what constituted celebration here was a question in itself. The fact that he'd spent money on champagne meant nothing.

Gareth did not appear at dinner, which made Mark feel less inhibited, and he was able to talk about his exploration of the town. This meant that he had something to contribute to the conversation that wasn't self-referential. It was rather difficult, but he supposed it would get easier in time, as he came to have more experiences that he'd shared with these people. If he continued to see them, of course, once he'd found somewhere else to stay. Perhaps the town would be like university? The first friends he'd made there were not the people he ended up remaining friendly with.

'Do rooms often become free in this house?' he asked at one point.

'From time to time,' said Don. 'Why, would you be interested?'

'Yes, absolutely.'

'There's a possibility that Andy might be moving out in the future. He has to go away more and more these days, so I expect he'll be moving on soon. But not for a while. Two or three months, I should say.'

'All right,' said Mark, 'I'll get that paper you told me about and see what's around. But if a room does become free here. . .'

'Of course,' said Don. 'Of course, we'll let you know.'

The next few days passed in a blur of exploration and laziness. He remembered Ty often, and felt terrible moments of guilt and loss. But there also came with this feeling a growing sense of relief at not being trapped in a life that was gradually suffocating him. He had fantasies that he might have brought Ty down with him, and in his fantasy there was no conflict or discord, and Amy was happy about it, and he could somehow create a life and an environment that would be suitable and sustaining for Ty. As soon as he pushed this fantasy, though, it collapsed or evaporated and left him feeling even more alone than before. Somehow the word 'sacrifice' seemed appropriate in here somewhere, too, but Mark wasn't clear about exactly how it applied to him.

He kept on thinking that he would get the paper and look out for somewhere else to live, and perhaps try to find some work. But there was no rush. Andy contacted Don to say he wouldn't be back for another week or two, and so Mark stayed on in the house. In any case, he could move into a bed-and-breakfast or get a holiday flat for a few weeks if he had to move out. . . he didn't need to make decisions about what kind of place he wanted to live in just yet. Maybe he could look for another house-share. . .

He went to a different café next time he stopped off for a coffee. It was on the edge of the Old Town and had a small terrace with wonderful views. From this elevated position, he could see out over the harbour to the sea, and to one side there was the hill and the lighthouse on its promontory. The chairs on the terrace looked almost too fragile to bear a person's weight, seeming to be made of thick, white-painted wire. But they were obviously well up to their task, and Mark admired them. The impression of frailty, but the fact of strength, seemed inspiring and rather helpful right now.

As he sipped his coffee, Mark saw Ruby from Club Covert, walking down from the station with two other women. They were going to be coming past the café so he leaned forward and waved.

'Hey, Ruby!'

She noticed him and smiled, then hesitated briefly.

'Let me buy you a coffee,' he called to her.

She said something to her companions, one of whom he recognised as another dancer from Club Covert, and then came up onto the terrace. She was wearing jeans and a light cream-coloured sweater. She looked incredibly ordinary, as though the last thing she could possibly be was a table dancer.

'Hello,' he said, 'what can I get you?'

'A double latte, please,' she said. 'And thank you. I was having an argument just now, and I'm afraid I used you in a rather mercenary way to extricate myself.'

'Glad to be of help,' he said, then grinned as he gave the waitress his order.

'And, please, don't call me Ruby,' she told him. 'That's my stage name. My real name is Natalie.'

'Natalie,' said Mark, nodding. 'How are you? Have you been somewhere?'

Natalie looked slightly cagey at this question, and Mark laughed.

'It's all right,' he told her, 'I'm staying in a house where we're not allowed to ask questions about each other. Perhaps it's true of everyone in this town. I think I'm getting the hang of it.'

'No, it's okay,' she said, 'I had a meeting, that's all. I have to get back soon to get ready for work, but I don't have to rush. In fact, it's quite helpful not to have to get back straight away. I share a place with those girls I was arguing with. We all work at the club and one of them is having a bit of a hard time. It's best to stay out of the way if I can.'

Mark nodded. He noticed again how pale she was, and how frail – although this seemed to be a psychological rather than a physical quality.

'You look great,' he said. 'I mean, you look. . . real. In the club all the girls looked *themed*.'

'It's true,' said Natalie, looking at him briefly and then out towards the distant, bright horizon.

'You have to be an actress to work somewhere like Club Covert,' she told him. 'We're all supposed to be "types." It's not a role you'd ever get an Oscar for, but I'm an actress by profession and it's certainly the hardest role I've ever had to play. All that semi-audience participation, for a start. . . I did a term on physical theatre at drama school, but even that didn't prepare me for this.'

She shrugged. 'At least it's only for a while.'

She looked out over the town. In profile she looked serious, and perhaps a little unhappy. Mark thought she looked more attractive like this, but less sexual – a strange realisation, as he had never thought of sexuality and attraction as being separate before.

'So,' she asked him, 'what do you do?'

'I'm on the lookout for a job,' he told her. 'Sort of. I'm an engineer by profession, and so there are probably quite a few things I could try my hand at, but I'm not really in any hurry at the moment.'

'Lucky you,' she said. 'Enjoy it. I hope to take some time off, to travel for six months or so, perhaps, once I'm back in the black again.'

He smiled.

'You're talking about leisure,' he said. 'I suppose I have leisure now, in a way, but it seems more like a kind of limbo to me. I think maybe I'm incapable of taking time off for leisure.'

'It's hard to use leisure time well,' she said. 'I had a gap year before going to drama school and I did nothing that I can look back on and think, "That was a good use of my time."'

'I know what you mean,' he agreed. 'I had a gap year, too, and just worked for my dad. I hated it. What did you do with yours?'

'I got a part-time job in a bakery,' she told him. 'I lived at home and spent the money going out partying with friends every weekend. But the partying appealed to such a small part of myself that I became smaller and smaller, until that's all that was left. These days I think that time is far more precious than almost anything else.'

'I went out partying when I was at university,' said Mark. 'I loved every minute of it.'

'I don't mean it wasn't fun,' said Natalie emphatically. 'It was. But fun has to be balanced with other things, doesn't it? You can't eat cake all the time. Also, I found that I got a bit mixed up around the difference between pleasure and happiness. I discovered that you can experience pleasure even when you're unhappy. That was something that I didn't even notice at first. I mean, we all got drunk and took drugs and had sex, and every individual *part* of that gave me pleasure, but the pleasure masked the fact that *underneath* it all I was actually unhappy. What a strange shock it was to discover that!'

'What did you do when you discovered it?'

'I went to drama school and learned to channel my unhappiness into the characters I played. That way I could pretend it wasn't me that was feeling unhappy. I could feel my own unhappiness, but pretend to myself that I was acting. Delusion is a funny thing, isn't it? How did your unhappiness present itself?'

'How do you mean?'

Natalie looked at him as if the answer was obvious. 'No one uproots themselves unless they're trying to escape unhappiness,' she told him.

Mark laughed. 'You're right,' he said. 'But it's not something I thought I might be asked about in a café on a sunny morning like this. . .'

'You don't have to talk about it,' she said. 'There are definitely some things we need to keep to ourselves.'

Mark shook his head. 'I. . . well, I was on antidepressants for nearly two years and they made it possible for me to continue to live a meaningless life. Now that I haven't taken them for a while I feel more. . . real.'

'You look real. What made you take antidepressants in the first place?'

'It might sound a bit mad,' said Mark, 'but I don't know. Even at the time, I wasn't sure. I found it harder and harder to get up in the morning to go to work, and my doctor asked me this question: "Have you lost interest in the things that used to make you happy?" When I said yes, he told me I was depressed and prescribed me medication.'

'Medication!' said Natalie, with a bitterness that surprised him.

'I took my medication because it seemed to help,' Mark told her. 'But the word "help" is a bit of a misnomer. I felt at the time that I was being helped because I was able to go to work again and was more or less able to function – we conceived our son in that period – and it all seemed better. But underneath my coping, I was as unhappy as ever, even though I wasn't so aware of it. It's odd, being unhappy and not even knowing it.'

'I suppose a lot of us have experienced that,' said Natalie. 'I certainly did. I had no idea what genuine happiness might feel like, and so I mistook what I was experiencing for the real thing.'

'That's exactly it!' Mark exclaimed. 'And then when I was on medication, I didn't really know what I was feeling. I was a walking, talking puppet being powered by the medication that I was taking. And I worried that this was bad, but at the same time I felt that if I stopped taking the pills I would cease to function again. . . And yet, here I am, off my medication and feeling like myself again, and I'm not unhappy. It's a kind of miracle.'

Natalie looked at him, casually, but with a certain interest.

'You have a son?' Natalie said.

'Yes,' he said, and looked away.

They sat in silence in the sunshine and Mark closed his eyes briefly to still the beat of his heart, and to savour the feeling of sunshine on his face, and to try and somehow forget – or ignore – the fact that he'd left Ty behind.

'I asked you about your aspirations when you were in Covert,' Natalie said after a while, 'but I can't remember what you said?'

He smiled. 'To become happy. I seemed to have stopped being unhappy, which is amazing. But I don't really know how to become happy.'

'Happiness is a fruit,' said Natalie. 'That's what my mother always used to say. You can't get fruit unless you sow and nurture a seed.'

He thought about this for a while. 'How wise,' he said, then added: 'And what about your aspirations?'

'To get away from Club Covert,' she said. 'To not have to waggle my fanny in the face of over-confident upstarts who think that because they pay to look at me they can talk about me as though I wasn't there.' She laughed sadly. 'But I'll stop as soon as I've paid off the money that I owe.'

'How much do you owe?'

'Four thousand,' she said. 'You'd have thought I could pay it off quickly with what I earn, but it's more difficult than I thought.'

'Won't a bank lend you that kind of money?'

'No,' she said, 'I have a zero credit rating, I'm afraid, and the money is a personal debt, which is much more. . . *problematic*. That's why I'm at Club Covert, of course. You don't think we do that kind of thing because we enjoy it, do you?'

Again she looked out across the town to the sea, and this time Mark could see her sadness more clearly. He could see her lower lip begin to tremble and the tears begin to well up in her eyes.

'I came down here to try and make my fortune. To have an adventure and to find myself. And look at me,' she murmured, 'I've come to this. . . '

She started crying in earnest at this point and Mark, embarrassed, patted her lightly on the arm, not saying anything but leaning in towards her with concern.

'I'm sorry,' she sniffed. She tried to laugh but failed, making a guttural croaking sound instead, 'I didn't mean to start crying. I can usually get by without crying. I thought I'd got past doing that. It's probably quite a good sign, really. I've felt numb recently, so feeling like this is probably an improvement.'

Mark watched her for a few moments. There was something poignant about witnessing the distress of someone that he didn't know. Of course, the honesty of the last few minutes gave him a sense of connection with her that was deeply stirring, and her mention of coming down here to make her fortune and to find herself put him in mind, quite suddenly, of what he was trying to do, and how easily it might go wrong. Hadn't the fire juggler told him he had a 'hungry' expression? That was exactly what Natalie had now – he could see it clearly – a great hunger, that he now recognised in himself. The juggler had predicted that Mark might end up sleeping on the street. Although Natalie wasn't sleeping on the street, working at Club Covert seemed a psychological 'rock bottom' equivalent, and the quality of her crying underlined the truth of this. In an eerie way, it was like looking at himself. There was a part of him that would cry in exactly this way, if only it could find a voice.

Quite suddenly, he decided. . .

'Look,' he said, 'I can let you have the money. I've got some cash at home that I don't really need. You can have four thousand pounds of it.'

She looked at him, completely confused.

'What do you mean, you can let me have the money?'

'What I say,' he said. 'I feel a bit uncomfortable about the money, to be honest. It doesn't feel as if it's mine, and it would give me pleasure to help you out. Genuine pleasure, I mean.'

'But what strings are attached?'

'None.'

She laughed at this, a little maliciously, he thought, and said, 'There are *always* strings attached, believe me.'

'No,' he said, 'really. Come with me and I'll get it for you. I'm not going to make any demands on you. I'm going to give you the money. What you do after that is up to you.'

He stood up and dropped a tip on the table, and Natalie followed him down to the street. They walked back to Baker's Yard in silence. He asked her to wait in the sitting room, and went upstairs and carefully counted out four thousand pounds, which he brought downstairs. He went into the kitchen to get a carrier bag and stuffed the notes into it, then came back and handed her the money.

'It should be in a brown envelope really, shouldn't it?' he smiled, 'but a carrier bag will have to do.'

Natalie looked into the bag and then up at Mark.

'You're really giving this to me? No strings?'

'Yes, I'm really giving it to you. No strings.'

She took a deep breath. He could see the exhilaration in her body, in the way that her breath seemed to stick a little as she breathed in, so that she made a sound that was half way between a gasp and a sigh.

'Thank you,' she said in wonder. 'I'm sorry. That seems *so* inadequate for what you've just done. You've saved my life.'

'You know where I live, now,' he told her. 'It would be lovely if you wanted to meet for coffee sometime, but it's *not* a condition. I'll leave it up to you.'

'You're an amazing person,' she said. 'I have never met

anyone, *anyone*, who would do this for another person – a stranger. I would never be able to do it.'

Mark felt embarrassed, and mumbled something. She threw her arms round him and kissed him on the cheek.

'If I go now,' she said, 'I can get the debt paid off this afternoon. . .'

'Go,' he said. 'Go and do it.'

After she'd gone, he felt a little deflated. He wasn't quite sure what he'd done. Had it been an act of generosity? The money didn't seem to be his, well it *wasn't* his, was it? So giving it away like that wasn't at all the same as if it had been his own life savings. But he had still given it away, and that was intrinsically generous, wasn't it? Yet if that was the case, why didn't he feel pleased with himself? Why did he feel this sense that he'd done something foolish? And was he kidding himself in saying that there were no strings attached? Of course he was. He hoped that she would be grateful to him and would make that gratitude obvious in some way. He couldn't bring himself to be explicit about what form that gratitude might take, but it certainly included them both spending time together.

# 3. Ill Will

When they went out for the house night out the following evening at the Harbour Tavern, Ingrid tried to persuade Mark to wear some of his new clothes, but Wim shushed her. Mark had actually been shopping again since his visit to their boutique, and had bought a pair of safe blue jeans and an equally safe pale blue shirt, which he wore with the old jacket that he had arrived in. No one at the pub seemed to have any opinion on how he looked and once he'd had a drink or two, he forgot all about it.

Don was right, there was a buzz to the atmosphere and he was pleased to see that Holly was there. He ended up sitting beside her. The bar was bustling and noisy with conversation and music. The band had yet to come on but their instruments, set up on the small and slightly tatty stage, glinted enticingly under the lights – especially a trumpet that had a small black electronic box taped to its underside.

At one point, Wim leaned forward from the other side of their small table and chatted to Mark and Holly about their taste in music. They laughed together about the song that was currently blasting through the sound system. It was a track from twenty years back that had been vilified by trendy people at the time, but now it had been nostalgically embraced as a classic anthem by the current generation.

'Of which Mark and I are two!' Holly laughed, jigging in her seat and raising her arms above her head as though about to perform an impromptu belly dance.

'I'm not really young,' said Mark, 'not if you go by being up to date with the music scene. As a matter of fact it's going to be my thirtieth birthday on Friday.'

Holly tilted her head back and laughed and the light glinted on the steel labret that spiked her lower lip. 'We'll have to have a party,' she said.

Several other people turned up, and as they did so Mark began to see why he might have been considered to be conservatively dressed. What had seemed to him to be routinely ordinary, was in fact worryingly bland. Most of the people here wore baggy clothing in natural materials, with the sort of informal footwear that made Mark think of travellers, or music festivals – the sort of people that his old friends back home would smirk at.

The strangers were introduced, but Mark didn't catch their names. They were all former members of the household in Baker's Yard. This monthly Wednesday evening was clearly a "past and present" house party, and Mark liked the idea of this. He enjoyed the way in which almost everyone came up to him at some point and gave him a few encouraging words of welcome. He hoped that, before long, he would be properly acquainted with most, if not all, of them.

Gareth turned up as the band came on, and Mark offered to buy him a drink, which earned him his first brief, but genuine, smile from the potter. He asked what kind of day Gareth had had.

'Oh, you know,' he said, 'a bit hum-drum. And you?'

'Good,' he said. 'I'm beginning to get a feel of the place.'

Gareth patted his shoulder when Mark gave him the drink. The music was easy to listen to, and the sound of laughter and conversation made Mark feel happy. He was pleased to be included in the conversation around him; it made him feel a part of things, rather than a greenhorn newcomer. Much later, at around closing time, when the band had finished their last number, Mark said to Gareth, 'Are you sure you don't mind me staying in the house?'

'Of course I don't mind.'

'You seemed wary, that's all.'

'It doesn't always work, you know,' he said with an apologetic shrug. 'And I hate to invest energy in people who are going to creep back to where they came from once they've realised they're not going to fit in here. It's not easy, you see. That's all I can say to you that I know to be true. It seems so easy at first, but it's not. And when people find out how difficult it is, they often give up.'

'And I look like someone who would do that?' Mark asked.

'Yes, actually, you do,' said Gareth before smiling at Mark's surprise. 'But I suppose you can't help that.'

Mark went to the toilet before they left the pub and splashed his face with cold water. He looked at himself in the mirror. It was extraordinary! He did look dowdy; impossibly staid. How could he have preferred to look like this when he had the clothes that Ingrid and Wim had sold him? It was absurd.

After the pub, they all went on to a house about a third of the way up the hill, along a flagstoned alleyway and up a flight of worn sandstone steps. They'd bought some beers at the bar and there was a real party atmosphere amongst the group as they arrived, although Mark noticed that none of them were drunk, or even close to it. How refreshing. His evenings out back home invariably degenerated into slow-motion mumbling rather than actual conversation.

The house they came to was quite narrow, but the first floor sitting room had floor to ceiling windows that looked out over the lights of the Old Town and the harbour beyond, where the waves could dimly be seen splashing against the breakwater. Beyond that there was an utter blackness. The room they were in was sparsely furnished. Some of the tables and picture frames seemed to be made from driftwood. The owner of the house, a wild-haired designer called Leon who looked to be around forty, lit a dozen candles in two candelabras to provide the only light, and put on some music that seemed to have church bells in it, and some kind of string arrangement, and breathy sounds that made Mark think of waves, or of wind in the trees. He was handed a beer, and Ingrid came to stand beside him at the window. Mark put his arm over her shoulder and looked at the dark reflection of the two of them in the glass of the window, and felt insanely grateful.

'I'm so glad I came,' he said. 'I feel so welcome and *accepted*.'

'That's how it is here,' she said. 'But only if you allow yourself to be a part of it.'

The laughter and conversation continued around him, and after a while, when Wim came over to talk to him, Mark said, 'Are there really caves in the hillside here?'

'Yes, of course,' said Wim. 'There's one right at the end of the alleyway outside. It's got some railings to stop people getting in, but like so many things here, they were put in so long ago that they're coming apart and it's easy to clamber in around the side.'

He turned to the rest of the people in the room.

'Hey,' he said, 'Mark has never seen the caves. Why don't we show him?'

There was general assent at this and a certain buzz of excitement, as though someone had suggested taking part in an arcane ritual.

'Let's take the candelabra with us,' Ingrid said. 'There's nothing more atmospheric than candlelight!'

Outside, there was a crisp coolness to the still air. They made a curious procession as they went along the narrow walkway to what appeared to be a dead end about fifty metres ahead. Leon had brought a torch and lighted the way as one after the other the dozen or so people clambered round the loose end railing and into the darkness. Don went first holding one of the candelabras, then Holly and the others and, finally, Leon, who took the second candelabra. A thoughtful hush had descended on the group and Mark realised that this place had a particular significance for them.

Once inside, they moved along what might have been a miner's tunnel for about twenty metres, then the floor of the tunnel sloped steeply downwards so that it was necessary to scramble down the pathway. Mark found this difficult as the light was so poor and he was unfamiliar with the path. The way led to a cave which in turn opened out into a huge cavern with a high roof that couldn't be seen in the darkness. Mark stood in the dim flickering light and looked around him.

Holly touched his elbow as she came to stand beside him and she pointed to a small recess in the wall as the tunnel entered the cave. She put her hand in and pulled out a candle and a lighter.

'I keep them in here,' she said, 'in case I want to visit the cave on my own.'

She lit the candle and handed it to him. It was a few inches long and quite thick and Mark found it helpful to be able to have this extra light for himself. He could see that there were three exits to the cavern; dark openings of irregular sizes, one of which they had entered by. The walls here were rough and looked natural rather than hewn. The rock itself was ragged pale, like fine grey sandstone, pitted here and there and studded with quartz-like stone. It looked dry, though the air had the smell of ferns or moss and reminded Mark of green-houses.

He was taken by surprise by the sound of humming, a mysterious all-encompassing sound that seemed to come from all directions at once.

'The acoustics are amazing here,' Wim whispered to him as Mark looked around to see where the noise was coming from. It took him a few moments to realise that it was Ingrid. Her eyes were closed and she continued to hum for a while before gently singing a short, wordless chant with a simple melody that several other people in the group joined in with, harmonising with it so that, with the echoes around them, the effect was choral. Mark felt his neck prickle and his scalp tighten as the haunting sound encompassed him, and, after a minute or so of listening, he joined in. His voice, a lean baritone, gave a depth to the chant that pleased him and helped to give a unity to the sound. To one side of him was Don, who had a light tenor, and on the other side was Ingrid, a pleasing soprano. It was difficult to tell how the others sounded because they all melded together so completely. Wim and Gareth weren't singing at all, but were listening, eyes closed, enthralled. The effect on Mark was electrifying, and he allowed himself to inhabit the sound as fully as possible as it segued into variations of melody and volume. This was an act of communal behaviour that he simply couldn't imagine experiencing back home. After a while, the chant came to a muted end by communal assent, and he felt breathlessly alive in the vivid silence that followed.

'Well done,' said Holly when they'd finished. 'What a resonant voice you have. It really added something; rounded us all out. I wondered if you'd join in.'

'Do you do that often?' Mark asked. 'It was amazing!'

'Not often,' she said. 'Sometimes it feels right for us to come down here.'

'The tune,' he said, 'where does it come from? It was lovely.'

'Oh,' she said, 'one of us generally sings the first thing that comes into our head.'

People started to file back up the short scramble to the way out. Mark blew his candle out and put it back in the recess with the small red lighter. There was a gentle silence and Mark could see that those around him were either pensive or smiling gently. When he came to clamber up, though, he lost his footing and with a cry that boomed back and forth, he fell, landed on his back and slithered the few feet back to the floor, nearly knocking Holly over as he did so. She laughed a loud, reverberating bark of laughter as she grabbed the person next to her to keep her balance.

'Are you alright?' Gareth asked, concerned, as Mark lay looking up, disorientated.

'Mmm,' he said, then sat up and smiled. 'Not the serene ending you'd want after that lovely singing.'

Gareth laughed and helped him up, and then there was laughter all round; a wonderful bright noise that made Mark yelp with such uninhibited amusement that he felt light-headed and clean. Outside, there was more laughter, and Leon invited everyone in for a hot drink. It was only when they were upstairs and Mark had been handed a cup of tea, that he noticed that he'd torn the elbow of his jacket, and ripped his trousers at the knee.

As they walked back to Baker's Yard, Mark tried to remember the tune they'd been singing, but, although it had been so simple, he found he couldn't remember it. For a moment he would think he had caught a thread of it, and then it would slide away, like water through his fingers. Ungraspable.

When they returned to Baker's Yard he was pleased to see that Holly came with them. When she wordlessly followed him up to his room, he was even more pleased, and their lovemaking sealed the evening perfectly.

The following morning, Mark made love to Holly again. He was fascinated that the spike in her lip did not seem sharp or in the way, but tickled him slightly as they kissed. There was something strange about her that he couldn't quite fathom. She seemed secretive, somehow, even though everything about her suggested openness. It was an apparent contradiction that Mark wasn't bothered about right now, but he noticed it.

When he got up, he put on his bright clothes. Pale yellow linen trousers, close-fitting at the waist but otherwise baggy, a blue tee-shirt and a red, green and white top. Then he looked at himself in the mirror. Why had he previously thought they were impossible? Today he was pleased with them. Holly smiled appreciatively. He put his torn clothes into the bin, along with the other clothes he'd arrived in, and then they went down to have breakfast with the others. Ingrid, when she saw him, smiled but didn't mention what he was wearing.

After he'd walked Holly to the off-licence, he went to Ray's Place to see if he could have his hair cut. Ray, the proprietor, was there and when Mark mentioned that he was a friend of Don's, he said, 'All right, I'll do you myself. How about eleven thirty?'

Walking back to the cottage along the harbour quay, Mark looked down once more into the clear water, the still air scintillating with dazzling light, the day warming up delightfully. He felt a sense of peace more profound than he could remember. The previous night had been a revelation. The pub, the music, the genuine friendliness and, later, the extraordinary singing in the cave, followed by making love to Holly – it all made him feel that he was fitting in. Even the fact that his singing voice had filled a space in the chanting made him feel a sense of destiny, somehow, and purpose in being here.

He noticed that there was a builder's merchant at the point in the harbour where the trendy cafés stopped and the more functional building began – the proof that it was indeed a small working port. In a moment of happy desire to give a gift, he bought a tape measure and went back to the cottage to measure the rotting frame of the upstairs bathroom window. He noticed a cracked pane in the kitchen, too, and by the time he went to have his hair cut, he'd bought a new window frame and wood for the surround for the bathroom, cement to repair the window ledge, and a replacement pane for the kitchen.

When Ray asked him what he wanted, Mark was at a loss. 'I have no idea,' he laughed. 'I thought you might tell me.'

'Ah, you're one of *those* friends of Don's,' Ray said and smiled. 'Welcome to our town. You look like you're settling in already.'

Ray cut the hair right up off Mark's ears, and short up the back, but left a good length on top which he brushed forward. It suited the shape of Mark's head. He had never thought of that – to accentuate his good features; his ears and the line of his neck. When he left, he caught his reflection in the big mirror by the door and was surprised – almost shocked – at the difference. He looked confident, colourful, handsome even. Next, he went to the small supermarket up towards the station and bought some food for dinner and then he popped in at the off-licence to buy a bottle of wine that the others would like. Holly laughed when he came in.

'My,' she said, 'now *that's* what I call a transformation! You look so much better. I knew you were going to fit in from the moment I saw you – or from the moment you bought that organic mersault with such enthusiasm. You should grow a beard, you know, and then you'd look great.'

'Shall I see you later?' he asked. 'Why not come for a meal this evening?'

'I'd love to.'

He looked at her and laughed. 'This is the point at which I would usually give you my phone number, but I'm afraid I don't have one at the moment. I'll go out and buy one this afternoon.'

'Don't bother,' she said, 'there's no signal here. It's one of the more charming quirks of this place. No one uses mobiles.'

When Mark arrived back at the cottage Don was there, looking strange, Mark thought, and purposeful.

'What's all that stuff upstairs?' he asked.

'The wood and the frame?' Mark said. 'I thought I'd replace the window upstairs for you. It's seen better days, and you mentioned that there are some jobs that need to be done around the house. It's a small way in which I can show my appreciation at being allowed to stay here.'

'No,' said Don.

Mark wasn't quite sure what he meant.

'I'm sorry?' he said.

'No,' he said again. 'I said it was *my* responsibility to do this sort of thing, Mark. This is *my* house and if there's anything to be done to it, I'll do it, not you.'

'Look,' said Mark. 'The frame I've bought is in the same style as the one upstairs. I'm not going to ruin the period feel of the place. I know what I'm doing.'

'What you really need to ask yourself,' said Don, 'is who you are doing this *for*.'

'I'm doing it for you,' Mark told him.

Don looked at him so directly that Mark flinched and began to feel uncomfortable. It was strange. When Don looked at you, you knew you were being looked at, that you were really being taken in. There was no escape from that look.

'Really,' Mark said.

Don thought for a moment before speaking.

'Even though I told you quite clearly that it was my responsibility to do these things? In fact, I asked you explicitly to leave them alone.'

'Okay, okay,' said Mark, raising his hands as if to ward off the accusation. 'But don't you want the rotting window frame to be replaced?'

'Actually, no,' said Don.

'Well, let me replace the broken pane in the kitchen.'

'No,' said Don. 'These things are exactly how I want them. When I said that there were things to do in the house, this wasn't the kind of thing that I meant.'

'I thought it would give you pleasure, that's all,' said Mark.

'You thought it would give *you* pleasure,' Don told him. 'You didn't ask me. In fact, you knew I didn't want you to do it. But you assumed.'

'I'm sorry if I've offended you,' said Mark.

'You haven't offended me,' said Don, who looked even more intense for a moment before smiling slightly. 'I just need to be clear with you about what I want and what I don't want. I hope that you would do the same.'

'Okay.'

As Mark went up to his room, he wondered about this. When had he ever been clear to others about how he felt? Sometimes... but only in anger. And, when he thought about it, only when he was drunk. That's what it took – alcohol – before he could say what he felt. But being angry and drunk always stopped people from listening to him. He couldn't imagine being clear and calm at the same time, as Don had been. He thought of arguments with Amy and realised that they had simply been the angry outpourings of two people who weren't listening to each other.

He went back to the off licence to buy another bottle of wine for the meal, though really it was so he could say hello to Holly again. But she wasn't there, so he wondered about buying some spirits and mixers, but was unsure whether this would be acceptable, and so he didn't and bought a couple of litres of fruit juice instead.

As he turned to leave, he noticed the man who had come into the shop behind him. It was the tall, slim man with the pony tail who had given him the bag with £40,000 in it. His heart thumped as he got eye contact, and this turned into sheer panic when he noticed the man noticing him. The man opened his mouth to speak, but Mark slipped past him and grabbed the door, then ran out onto the street. He sprinted down the road, away from the station and Baker's Yard, and jumped into an alleyway that led down to the river. He stood for a moment and tried to get his breath back. It was ragged from shock rather than exercise. When he peered round the corner and up the street, there was no sign of the man. He still hadn't come out of the off licence. Mark waited for a while, and then the man came out. He didn't look down towards where Mark was hiding, but walked off up towards the station.

Mark made himself wait for five minutes before setting off back to Baker's Yard. What did this mean, randomly bumping into someone he'd last seen under such bizarre circumstances, hundreds of miles away?

Mark leant back against the wall and felt a horrible lurching in the pit of his stomach. Was it a coincidence? He quite suddenly felt unsafe. In the moment that he became scared, he wondered why he'd ever felt safe at all. He'd absconded with £40,000 of illicit money, which was something that people could get *angry* about. But then, he'd come across it anonymously. There was no reason why anyone would have known who he was, or where he'd gone. Most double-crossing is done by people who are well known to those who are being double-crossed. . .

This didn't make him feel any better. The fact was that the man with the pony tail was here, had seen him and recognised him.

The meal at Baker's Yard went well, in spite of Mark's recurring feeling of unease at having seen the man with the pony tail. He mentioned the incident to Holly when he saw her, without explaining fully about the money, and she laughed.

'All sorts of people come and spend time here,' she told him. 'If the man had been looking for you, personally, he would have come out of the shop and chased you, surely, or shouted out for you to stop.'

This was a comforting thought, but the man had definitely recognised him and it was difficult to interpret what this might mean – for him to have noticed Mark, but not to have given chase. It was impossible to imagine a scenario in which the man was indifferent. Mark realised after a while that these thoughts were circling round and round in his mind without getting anywhere, and so he tried to put them to one side.

Holly was very relaxed in the cottage – it had been her home, after all. She knew Ailsa, Gareth, Wim, Ingrid and Don well, and chatted to them easily. It helped to give Mark a sense of legitimacy, if not actually of belonging. He had a right to be here and to invite a guest to their meal. Although he was accepted here and had, strangely, been invited, he realised that he didn't in fact belong here yet. He still didn't know what was expected of him, or what was allowed. He was still smarting from Don's assertion that he was only thinking of himself when he'd decided to replace the bathroom window and the pane of glass in the kitchen. It confused him to think about this. Didn't people help each other in the world? The idea of 'doing someone a favour' was deeply ingrained in him, and was so much a part of what made someone a 'nice bloke' that Mark felt bemused at Don's reaction. He had been so dismissive of Mark's willingness to help. It was mysterious, and rather irritating.

This, coupled with the rule that he should not ask anyone about their past, made Mark feel deskilled and he found it difficult to function casually. Holly seemed to sense this and smiled at him reassuringly from time to time. He smiled back and felt a stirring of desire that confused him, too. Back home, he had resisted a number of blatant attempts at seduction, on the grounds that it would constitute infidelity to Amy – someone he no longer loved, and with whom he only rarely had sex. But here, he'd slept with Holly without a moment's thought, or even a flutter of conscience.

*Is this the new me?* he wondered, and smiled because he didn't know what this meant.

Later, when he made love to Holly he was shocked by how uncomplicated it was. His previous experience with sexual partners had been characterised by a feeling of yearning so intrinsic to the physical sensation that he'd thought it was the same thing, was a part of how human beings experienced sex: that sex was, in fact, an act of yearning. But for what? And what was it with Holly that made him *not* yearn? He thought of what Don had said about 'being natural', and again had a sense that he did not know what this meant.

The following day Holly left early, and Mark slept in until late morning. When he got up, the house was empty, and he sat in the sitting room drinking tea and wondering what he should do. He still had plenty of cash upstairs, and so there was no hurry to make a decision. The sun was shining again and so he decided, once more, to go out and enjoy it. This time he went down to the eastern end of the harbour, to look at the working vessels there and to see if, perhaps, there was somewhere to buy their fresh produce. He was impressed by the working feel of the far quay. There was no public access down onto the wooden pontoons, but from where he stood, looking down from the public thoroughfare, he could see the nets and the lobster creels by the boats.

There was a small, slightly run down café here, with a couple of Formica tables on a small terrace set back from the quay. It was warm enough to sit outside and so he ordered himself a coffee and sat on a rickety metal chair in the pale sunshine, looking out towards the upmarket cafés and bars on the other side of the harbour. There were a couple of minia-ture fir trees in large pots beside him that sheltered him from the light breeze, and some steps leading down from the terrace to the waterside. Two fishermen came along the quayside, wearing old blue boiler suits, and stopped at the next table to drink a glass of beer and to talk.

Mark was feeling almost sleepy, which seemed peculiar after the long night's rest he'd just had, but he realised it was a contented, soporific feeling of relaxation rather than sleep. He closed his eyes and enjoyed the sounds of the harbour. The lapping of water, the cry of the gulls, the clanking sound of wires against masts, the distant sound of boat engines further out towards the harbour mouth. When he opened his eyes again and looked up the quayside, he saw Don walking along the water's edge towards the town, accompanied by a tall man. As they came closer, Mark realised with a chill of fear that it was the man with the pony tail.

The fir trees beside Mark screened him quite well, and by leaning back in his chair, he could observe them without being seen himself. They were turned away from him, and were conversing in a friendly way. As they talked, the man took out a couple of large mortise keys. They were on a key ring with a yellow tag that was attached to a short length of pale string. Don put the keys in his pocket, and the man patted him heartily on the back and started to walk away up the harbour side. A familiar beat of fear caught Mark as he watched the transaction, followed by an anxious puzzlement about the connection between Don and the man with the pony tail.

Don turned and walked towards Mark down the cobbles of the waterside. As he drew level with the café, he looked up and smiled at Mark, and came up the steps to the café with a cheerful bounce to his step.

'Hello Mark,' he said. 'I didn't see you there. How are you? Fancy another coffee?'

Mark nodded and Don went into the café to order. He was gone for a few moments and then he came out and sat next to Mark. He looked out at the water in front of them, towards the masts of the yachts on the other side of the harbour. The slatted pontoons were dappled by reflections from the sunshine on the water.

'Lovely morning,' he said, and sighed.

Mark didn't reply immediately. He nodded and shaded the sun from his eyes with his hand as he looked out to sea.

'Don,' said Mark eventually, 'who was that man you were talking to?'

'What man?' asked Don.

'The tall man with the pony tail. He gave you some keys.'

Don looked, for a moment, as though he'd been caught out, but the surprise only lasted for a second. Long enough, however, to cause a tiny flicker of paranoia to arise in Mark's chest.

'I can't tell you, I'm afraid,' Don said.

'Why?'

Don glanced down at his coffee for a moment before looking up at Mark.

'I can't tell you why.'

'Because you were talking about me?'

'Look,' said Don, 'this is not what it seems. . .'

Mark ignored this.

'Why were you talking about me?'

'I'm not going to lie to you,' Don told him.

Mark found that his voice was getting louder.

'You don't have to lie to me, just tell me what you were saying about me?'

'I. . .' Don hesitated. 'In spite of the fact that you are drawing your own conclusions about why I was talking to Sean—'

'His name's Sean, is it?' Mark asked. 'What did he have to say about me?'

Don laughed, which only made Mark more angry.

'Mark,' he said, 'cool down. When people mention each other it isn't always to say bad things.'

'Yes, but Sean probably wants to find out where I am. He may be looking for me.'

'Why?'

Mark looked at Don. It was a touché moment. He had been manoeuvred into a corner from which he was unable to challenge Don further.

'I. . .'

'Yes, well,' said Don. 'Sometimes you can't say, can you? But you're angry, Mark. That's a bad starting point for a conversation.'

'Well, if I see people I trust talking to people I don't trust, it makes me feel nervous, that's all.'

'I'll take that as a compliment,' said Don. 'Why don't you trust Sean?'

'I think he might know something about me that I would rather he didn't know, that's all.'

'Something that I should know?'

'It's not something that I would choose to tell you,' said Mark. 'You said when I first met you that we shouldn't ask each other about our pasts.'

Don laughed, loudly and happily. 'That's right, I did,' he said.

'But you still can't tell me what you were saying?'

'No.'

Mark sighed, then stood up. 'I thought I might make a go of this town if I tried hard enough to fit in,' he said, 'but I get a sinking feeling that I'm not going to be given the chance.'

'I'm afraid you can't blame your burgeoning paranoia on the town or its residents,' said Don. 'You brought this particular problem with you from *outside*, and I guess you're going to have to take responsibility for that.'

'But you're not helping me,' said Mark. 'You more or less told me off yesterday because I wanted to give you some help around the house. And now I discover you've been talking to someone who might wish me harm.'

Don laughed again – why was that so infuriating? 'It must seem strange and perhaps a little threatening,' he said.

'Yes,' Mark told him. 'Yes, it does.'

Don shrugged, and Mark turned and walked away. He couldn't read Don at all. He seemed to be goading Mark into anger, while speaking with such apparent kindness and good humour. Mark didn't want to feel anger about this, but it seemed to spurt suddenly from somewhere, and so he shook his head to clear his thoughts. What was going on? Was Don playing with him? Anger was such a strange emotion to be feeling, here, now. . . it was an unwelcome sensation. He hadn't felt anger for a long time. Just a sort of numb emptiness. He remembered singing in the cave a couple of evenings ago, of how his voice had fitted so well and how he himself had felt that he was in harmony with those around him. Don had seemed to be the link between himself and these people, but now he was being secretive and obstructive, in a way that seemed unhelpful and perhaps even sinister.

When he returned to the cottage at the end of the afternoon, only Ailsa was there. It was Friday evening and Wim and Ingrid were away for the night. Gareth was out with friends, and there was no sign of Don.

'It's like this sometimes,' she said. 'People are so spontaneous, you can't assume that there will be people here to talk to. I'm going out in a minute myself. Will you be okay on your own?'

'Yes,' he said. 'Of course.'

'Good.'

She smiled kindly and went upstairs.

Left on his own, Mark decided to go out and get something to eat. He went to his room and got some money and then walked over to the off licence. Again, Holly wasn't there and so he went down the main street towards the river. He realised that he had no idea where Holly lived, had simply assumed that she was accessible via the off licence, which seemed overly simplistic. Now that he was out in public, he found that he was unable to relax because he was constantly on the lookout for Sean. Still, Sean was distinctively tall, and so would be easily visible if he was out in the streets.

He found himself in the trendy part of the harbour, where the river met the sea and where there were little man-made islands in the shallow water near the bridge that ducks had colonised for their nests. There was a restaurant there serving Japanese cuisine and so, having never tried it before, he went in. He sat by himself and watched a couple of flamboyant chefs performing their culinary acts in an open plan kitchen. The food was excellent, and, as Mark listened to the general chatter and laughter around him, he suddenly felt more lonely than he could remember ever having been before. There was no one in this town that he could call in on or casually ask to meet up with. He didn't know where Holly was, and there was no one who knew him well and who might keep him company. And as for Natalie, he'd very deliberately not asked her where she lived.

When he left the restaurant, he sauntered along the river, not yet ready to go back to Baker's Yard. There were lights strung along the water's edge for some way, with shops and a couple of bars. Then it became residential, with a long terrace of Victorian sandstone houses. There was a road here that led up the hill to the station so he took it. It was cobbled and completely deserted. There was something desolate about the quietness. It reminded him of standing on station platforms on Sunday evenings as he waited to return to boarding school after a weekend at home. How deeply depressing that had been, and how vividly he could remember it now!

The road curved up and round, and as it approached the station, he began to see people again. He passed a hotel, a bar and a Thai restaurant and before long he was in the Friday night bustle of bright lights and lively people again. This made him feel even more alone, and strangely uncertain. It was an odd uncertainty because he still didn't feel – even for a moment – that he had done the wrong thing in coming to this town. He simply didn't know how to feel safe and at home here.

He remembered a friend who had emigrated to Australia and who had become deeply homesick there for a considerable time before beginning to feel at home. There seemed to be a moment in a new place, after the excitement of arriving had worn off and before comfortable familiarity had set in, when everything seemed a little melancholy. He remembered getting emails from his friend that would say, 'I'm making new friends, but they still don't *know* me yet.'

He wondered briefly if he suffered from a dependent personality. Perhaps he only really existed as a person if there was someone with him to validate his reality? The people at Baker's Yard had all been friendly and inclusive (although there was now this odd question mark regarding Don). Holly had been acceptant, too. But this didn't seem to have translated into comfort for Mark yet. And then there was his medication. Wasn't that something that he'd used to help him cope with the feeling of loneliness that had permeated his being three or four years ago? Now that he hadn't taken it for some time, perhaps he was returning to his 'normal' mood. Perhaps this strange emptiness was what his pills had been covering up. Or perhaps it was withdrawal.

When he got back to the cottage there was no one there. It was only ten, but he felt enervated and tired so he went to bed, falling asleep immediately.

*

In the morning he awoke feeling empty, still, but there was a different quality to the feeling now. Today, the emptiness resembled hunger, as though he hadn't eaten for a long time. He was reminded of the way he'd felt when recovering from a nasty bout of flu. He hadn't had an appetite for over a week, but woke up one morning feeling well again and ravenous. His body had felt empty and light, as if it might start to levitate if he let himself go.

He was wondering whether he should get up when the door to the bedroom opened and Holly came in. She crossed over to the bed, and kissed him.

'Happy birthday, Mark,' she said, and lay on the bed beside him.

Mark smiled at her. 'Thank you,' he said.

She smiled back and laughed.

'I looked for you last night,' he told her, 'but I don't know where you live.'

'There's no point in giving you my address,' she said. 'I'll be moving house in the next week or two. I'm not sure where I'll be going, I've had several offers. It partly depends on whether I get a job I'm going for or not.'

'What job?'

'Mental health support worker at a refuge. I was filling in some time at the off-licence, before moving on to something more useful. It's funny, though. I enjoyed the off-licence far more than I thought I would. I never thought I would ever be a purveyor of intoxication. . .'

She laughed and kissed him again.

Over breakfast, she said, 'I've made plans for the day. You don't have to do anything at all except come along. I'm glad it's sunny. Have you been to the lake yet?'

'No,' said Mark.

'I've arranged a picnic, and I've managed to get hold of a boat. There'll be quite a few of us around today, so you'll have a chance to meet up with some of the people from the house-night again.'

There was something in Holly's light tone of voice, and the sensation of being lifted by it, that reminded Mark of his feeling of emptiness from the night before.

'I hadn't realised that time is the key to these things,' he told her. 'No matter how much you like a person or a place, it takes time to get to know them, doesn't it? That's so obvious, I suppose. But it's eleven years since I last experienced going to a new place and being surrounded by strangers – when I started at university. Familiarity is such an important part of my life, and that was only really highlighted when I lost it.'

'But,' Holly said, 'it's amazing how fast you can regain it. Don't forget, we've all done this, Mark. Everyone you're going to be seeing today has done it. And it's the *kind* of familiarity that you establish that is going to be vital. Remember that bad things become familiar too, if we do them often enough.'

'I think,' he said, 'that I'd like to become more familiar with you.'

She smiled and looked him in the eyes, and there was a sparkle there, of happiness and promise.

They left together on bicycles at about ten-thirty. Mark was riding the bike that belonged to Andy, the man whose room he was sleeping in. Both cycles had rear panniers that Holly had filled with food and drink, and they rather hilariously rode down the cobbled street to the river, Mark singing long notes near the top of his range that wobbled with vibrato as their bikes crashed down over the slate grey cobbles. Holly was laughing too much to sing and they arrived at the foot of the hill breathless.

The river at that point was tidal, and the pale green water was flowing inland. Mark had never seen this before, and it looked back-to-front to him that the water was flowing *away* from the sea. It made him smile. They turned and cycled along with the water. After a short while the buildings stopped and they left the road and went onto a path along the top of the raised river bank. It was built up to stop tidal flooding of the pasture beyond, which must have been salt marsh before the land was protected from the sea.

A couple of miles later, they came to a weir where the tidal water stopped. After that, the river was reedy and meandering, with hawthorn and elder on the far side. They got off their bikes and walked the last few minutes to where a lake opened up and stretched for a mile or so, wooded on one side, and with open pasture and some boat houses along the other.

As they made their way around the waterside, they came to a narrow lane that wound away from the lake and on behind some large houses that sat in grounds. After passing a couple of these opulent residences, which resembled small hotels, they took a path that went back down to the lakeside. Mark followed until they came to a large wall with an iron gate in it. Holly said 'Hang onto my bike for a moment, would you?' and he took the handlebar and held it for her. He looked down at the panniers, and wondered what goodies they might contain.

He heard the jingle of keys as Holly opened the gate, and looked up. Beyond the gate there was a stretch of lawn that led down to the edge of the lake. They wheeled their bikes through and onto the grass. Mark looked around. There were rhododendrons up towards the house and above these he could see some chimneys, but that was all that was visible of the residence.

Ingrid and Wim arrived almost immediately and in moments had a couple of blankets laid out by a chestnut tree that stretched out over the boathouse and the edge of the lake. One or two of its far branches grew down until they almost touched the water. The leaves were large but looked pale and newly grown, soft and fresh. As Holly began to open their panniers, Mark heard a bicycle bell behind him and he turned to see Gareth arriving on an old bone shaker, laughing and waving. He skidded to a halt by the gate.

'Great day,' he called, 'it's so warm. I thought you were mad to suggest a picnic so early in the year, Holly, but this is fantastic.'

Holly smiled and continued to unpack what she'd brought. Gareth wore a rucksack in which he had some cherry flavoured root beer, and soon there was an array of food and drink in the sunshine. Leon, the wild-haired designer, arrived with Ailsa and a couple of other people that Mark had met only briefly at the Harbour Tavern. Once they were all sitting, or lying back on the blankets, they were each given a plastic cup full of Gareth's dark, intensely flavoured drink, and they toasted the spring sunshine, and Mark's birthday.

'Who does this house belong to?' asked Mark, as he drank.

'A friend of a friend,' said Leon. 'He has an open-lawn policy for certain people.' He raised his beer towards the hidden house and murmured, 'Bless him.'

A small cloud went across the sun and the brief drop in temperature accentuated the fresh quality of the air.

'Thirty, eh?' said Leon to Mark. 'An important age. Young enough for new beginnings, old enough to know your mind.'

'I wish I *did* know my mind,' laughed Mark.

'Don't worry, Mark,' said Ailsa, 'Leon is joking. He's fully aware that your mind doesn't know *anything*. It simply exists.'

She play-punched Leon and lay back to look up to the sky.

'Actually,' she said, 'I've found that the concept of knowing or not knowing can be unhelpful.'

'But you said to me when we first met that not knowing is a good thing,' said Mark.

'Hmm,' said Ailsa, sitting up and looking out over the water. 'But if you remember, I did also say it was a conundrum.'

She drank a little of her beer and savoured it before speaking again.

'I can talk so easily about knowing and not knowing. But perhaps in many situations a part of me knows and a part of me doesn't, so that the statements "I know" and "I don't know" might both be true at once. I might say, "Yes, I know that I love this person", but a part of me might not know at all. I might say, "Yes, I want to go and live abroad," but another part of me might be painfully unsure about it.'

She shrugged.

'Anyway, Mark here is thirty years old and he doesn't know his mind. I'll certainly drink to that.'

She drank and handed her glass to Gareth for a top up.

'Where's Don?' Gareth asked.

'Off somewhere. There's a deal he needs to get sorted, I think. He didn't tell me what it was.'

The thought of Don going off somewhere to get a deal 'sorted' made Mark suddenly uncomfortable and he wondered if he'd been 'sorting a deal' yesterday with Sean. This made him realise that he was relieved that Don wasn't at the picnic.

'What kind of deal would that be?' Mark asked.

Ailsa didn't answer. She sipped her beer and looked away from Mark and out across the lake.

'Something to do with his work as a comedian?' Mark asked.

Again, Ailsa remained silent. No one said anything. Holly busied herself with getting some olives out of a jar. Gareth was rummaging in his rucksack. Wim and Ingrid were whispering something to each other. Leon was looking down at his hands.

'All right,' said Mark. 'I'll get these rules eventually. The problem is that it's difficult for me to be clear about what constitutes a prying question.'

Ailsa smiled, and looked at him briefly with friendly compassion. She handed him a plate and, taking one herself, began to help herself to food. Mark followed suit and soon had a plate piled high. He lay propped up on his elbow and ate with his fingers as conversation began to flow around him. At one point Holly made him take his shoes and socks off and come down to the lakeside to paddle. The water was icy, but not numbingly cold, and he stood ankle deep on the fine shingle there. The refreshing coolness made his skin tingle. Holly shrieked loudly when she stepped into the water and jumped out again immediately, and when Mark followed her out, he found that the cold had made him feel wide awake and alert.

Holly sat and leaned against him as she ate, and poured them both some juice. The sun was warm on Mark's face, but the side of him that was out of the sun felt chilly and he was pleased when Holly said, 'I think it's time to go out in the boat and do some rowing.'

She leaned forward and pulled her jacket towards her, reaching into the pocket and pulling out a couple of keys with a hefty iron clasp – large mortise keys with a yellow tag that Mark recognised immediately.

'Where did you get those?' he asked Holly.

'Don got them for me,' she said.

Mark felt the world drop away for a moment.

'Wait,' he said, 'the keys don't belong to someone called Sean, do they? A tall guy with a pony tail?'

'You know him?' asked Leon. 'That's weird! This is the house where he lives.'

Mark closed his eyes, his mind racing.

'So, Sean knows that I'm going to be here today? That I'm going to be having a picnic and then going out boating on the lake?'

'I don't know what Don will have told him,' said Holly. 'What's wrong Mark? You've gone pale.'

'Sean was the guy in the off licence I told you about. The man from back home who's after me.'

'After you?' asked Gareth, trying not to smile.

Ingrid leaned over to Wim and whispered something to him. He laughed and looked down at the blanket. Mark had a sudden sense of certainty that they knew about the money.

'Something's going on!' Mark said. 'You all know, don't you? You're all in on this.'

'All in on what, Mark?' asked Ailsa.

'I didn't steal the money,' Mark said. 'I was *handed* it.'

'What money?' asked Holly.

Mark suddenly had a sick feeling, as he looked around them, that the people here were neither benign nor friendly.

'Sean knows that I'm here! He wants to punish me for running off with the money. Don't you see? He knows I'm going to go out boating, on the lake. . . Has he organised a boating accident, or something?'

It all seemed sickeningly clear.

'Come on, Mark,' said Holly, 'it's us, the Baker's Yard

brigade. We don't wish you harm. And I have no idea what money you're referring to.'

'No,' he said. 'I have a bad feeling about this. This can't be a coincidence. . .'

He stood up, feeling precarious and threatened. No one moved, either to reassure him or to stop him.

'Look,' he said, 'I'm sorry, I can't stay here. I need to go and think about this. I don't feel safe at all.'

'Safe!' Ailsa laughed. 'I should hope not. The last thing we would want is for you to feel *safe*.'

'So you *do* know about this,' said Mark.

'Mark,' said Holly. 'This Sean thing has nothing to do with us. Ailsa was teasing you. She has a rather inappropriate sense of humour, sometimes.'

Mark backed away and grabbed his bicycle, then jumped onto it and set off through the gate and onto the undulating path back up to the lane. No one shouted after him, which seemed particularly incriminating. It was comforting to know that none of them had phones, otherwise he would have felt even less safe.

The lane bent round for a couple of hundred metres before it met the main road, which he turned onto and headed back into town. He pedalled as hard as he could, but still he seemed to be moving almost in slow motion. Only his ragged breath showed how much effort he was putting into this flight back to town. As he drew level with the first of the houses of the conurbation, his breath suddenly gave out and he let the bike freewheel for a while, slowing down on the slight upward incline. As he came to a stop, he began to think more clearly. He realised that if Sean knew Don, then he was likely to know where Mark was staying. He was surprised that he hadn't made the connection before, when he'd first seen them talking together on the quayside. He was amazed at how effectively he had been able to hide this knowledge from himself, in order to prevent himself from having to act on it. But he had to face it now. Sticking his head in the sand would be disastrous at this point. The thought made him feel a massively increased sense of threat. Someone really was out to get him! There was a pub ahead, on the far side of the road, and he cycled across to it, leaned his bike against the wall and went in to buy himself a whisky. He calculated that the safest place, right now, was amongst a crowd of people. Nothing could happen to him there, and it would give him time to think of what to do next.

The bar had clearly been a country pub at one point, but in recent years the town sprawl had eaten up the surrounding countryside and it now perched uncomfortably on the outskirts, neither fish nor fowl – its bucolic décor strangely incongruous in its new urban setting. Mark ordered himself an Islay malt, and took it outside into the beer garden at the back where he could keep an eye on the bicycle. It was just after half-past two and still warm in the sun. He desperately needed a few minutes to calm down, gather his thoughts and come up with a plan.

The beer garden had about a dozen tables, three or four of which were occupied. As he sat down at the table nearest to the car park, a silver Mercedes pulled up and stopped on the gravel on the far side of his table. Mark looked across as the driver got out and, with a thump of recognition, he saw that it was Sean. He smiled affably at Mark, in the most friendly manner, and came over to him. The smile was not at all reassuring; it reminded Mark of his childhood fear of clowns. He had always hated them. Those eternally smiling faces – what was *behind* the smiles, he had always wondered. When Sean arrived at the table, he smiled again and said, 'Hello Mark.'

'How do you know my name?' Mark asked, his voice husky with fear.

Sean ignored this and sat down beside him, looking completely calm and perhaps rather pleased with himself. He looked around the beer garden and smiled at the patrons. Continuing to sound friendly, he leant in close to Mark and said, *sotto voce*, 'I don't want to do this, Mark, but sadly you've left me no choice. I'm sure you realise that there's a protocol in circumstances like these. You ran off with the money, and I'm afraid this is the consequence.'

He took a flick knife out of his pocket and pressed a catch to make the blade snap straight. Mark leapt to his feet, but Sean was even more swift and in a moment had Mark in an agonising arm lock. He kicked Mark's legs from under him so that he fell heavily to the ground, face down. Sean then knelt on the small of his back and, releasing Mark's arm for a moment, and with an incredibly swift and adept movement, he took Mark's right earlobe between his fingers and sliced it off.

'You won't be surprised to hear that Jonathan wants his £40,000 back,' he said, grunting with exertion. 'I trust it won't be a problem for you to raise it by, say. . . tomorrow at midday?'

He didn't wait for an answer, but got up without haste and turned to walk back to his car, waving in a friendly way to the shocked patrons at the other tables. Once in his car, he drove back out of the car park and turned right onto the main road, away from town, towards his lakeside home. Mark sat, stunned, looking at his untouched whisky, paralysed by the searing sensation of his wound, which – after a few brief moments of feeling almost nothing at all – burst upon him with overwhelming intensity and almost blinding pain. He grabbed at the main part of his ear, which was slippery with blood, as was his neck. He wanted to pinch the wound closed, but there was nothing to get hold of. His first thought was to look for the earlobe that had been cut off, but he realised that Sean had kept it. His second thought was to run away. His third was that he needed to get to a hospital, fast. He remembered that there was one on the hill, between the station and the promontory.

At that moment the barmaid came out and saw him, and screamed.

Before anyone had time to call an ambulance, or offer him a lift to the hospital, Mark leaped up, grabbed his bike, jumped on it and set off back towards the town. Blood streamed from his ear in alarming quantities as he did so, spattering his shoulder and his leg as he pedalled furiously.

*

Fortunately A&E wasn't busy. Early afternoon on a Saturday was clearly a good time – if it's possible to think of it in that way – to have an earlobe sliced off by a pissed off gangster. The duty doctor, who had roused himself from some kind of stupor when Mark arrived, seemed overjoyed to have something more complicated than a sprain or a bump to work on, although he was a little disappointed that Mark didn't have the piece of his ear that had been removed. When he'd cleaned up the wound a little, he told Mark that, in that case, there wasn't much for the stitches to get a purchase on. There would be quite a scar.

Mark had been both surprised and relieved, after the first searing pain, to find that his ear had settled down to a dull throbbing that he could cope with without too much difficulty. Even as he'd cycled to the hospital it had been bearable. Here in the hospital, of course, the local anaesthetic meant he felt no pain at all, but there was a sense of tenderness all the same, as if he'd been bruised rather than cut.

Another thing that surprised Mark was that the police were not mentioned. He'd imagined that someone would ask him how he'd managed to sustain his injury. But no one had done so. He certainly didn't feel inclined to raise the subject himself, or go to the police once he'd been discharged, and he hoped that the pub hadn't contacted the authorities, either. His hasty exit may have been enough. He wanted as few people as possible involved in this private drama, and he wanted to avoid having to answer any difficult – or incriminating – questions about the episode.

When he found himself on the pavement outside the hospital at last, he looked at his watch. It was less than two hours since he'd left the party. It seemed an incredibly short time, but then he had been seen immediately on arrival at the hospital. He touched the dressing on his ear gingerly. It was rather spongy, and had been attached using dressing strips affixed to his cheek and neck, with a small built-up pad of gauze behind his ear. He'd looked at himself in the mirror in the toilet before leaving, and was amazed at how bulky it was for such a small wound. The whole of the shoulder and neck of his tee-shirt had been drenched with blood, which was drying to a dark red.

He wondered if the others had returned to the house, which was only ten minutes away, and realised that if this was the case then it was not safe to go back there. What would he do then? Warily, he freewheeled down past the station, to the entrance to Baker's Yard. He waited there for a short while, feeling nervous to say the least. After carefully studying the house for a few minutes, he edged his way down towards it. As far as he could judge, there was no sign of life, and when he peered through the sitting room window there was no one there. He left the bike on the far side of the front door and let himself in, then ran upstairs to his room and looked under the bed. The bag and the money were gone.

# 4. Restlessness and Anxiety

Mark slumped to the floor, and stared blankly at the wall. There was something inexorable about all this – and hadn't he expected it, really? Of course it was all going disastrously, horribly wrong. How could anything go right for someone who had abandoned his partner and baby to 'leave it all behind' and start again? It might have been better, he thought, if he'd had some idea of what he was moving towards. Leaving is one thing, but having a destination is surely a prerequisite to a successful journey?

But his current situation was no good at all. Here he was: injured; someone had stolen his money; his credit and debit cards had expired; he had nowhere to go; he knew no one he could trust, and worst of all, he needed to raise £40,000 in the next twenty four hours, or something very bad might to happen to him. And yet. . . and yet, the idea of going home still seemed impossible. What could he go home to? His job, which had seemed so potentially useful when he'd first started in it, had become an exercise in winning grant funding rather than actually doing the useful work that the grant aid was supposed to facilitate. Amy? He realised that he'd hardly thought of her the whole time he'd been here, and that said everything. There was a dull, residual relief at not having to face her on a daily basis, but that was all. Ty: a small pain stabbed at his heart once more as he thought of Ty. Perhaps he was already forgetting Mark. He was so young. Even in this short time he would have grown, and discovered new things about the world, new things that Mark had not witnessed. The underlying sense of regret that he felt at leaving Ty behind remained undiminished it seemed, though perhaps he'd more effectively learned the skill of ignoring it.

He went down to the kitchen and grabbed some carrier bags, then took them up to his room to pack. He quickly emptied the contents of the couple of drawers that he'd been using onto the bed. They were all he'd needed while he'd been staying in Andy's room, because he had so few possessions here. His spare clothing and toiletries fitted into four carrier bags. There was his jacket downstairs, but that was it. He could walk out of the house now, if he needed to, and never come back. But it all seemed suddenly too surreal to deal with and he sat on the bed for a moment and looked out at the sky, which was growing cloudy.

After a while he began to be aware of the unpleasant feeling of his tee-shirt against his shoulder as the drying blood made the cloth more and more stiff. He went to the bathroom and removed it, draping it over the side of the bath where he hoped it might remain as a mystery for the rest of the residents of the house. Then he cleaned himself up and went back to Andy's bedroom to sort himself out. It seemed absurd to be putting on one of his brightly coloured shirts, but all he had was up-beat, optimistic clothing and, for a moment, he couldn't help smiling at the thought. The smile lasted only a moment, though.

Everything was moving too quickly for him. Only a few hours earlier he'd had a growing feeling of stability and contentment. Now there was complete confusion and an oppressive threat of danger that gave him a sense of urgency and haste, but which also, oddly, was almost completely paralysing.

It was only when he heard the door opening downstairs that he was stirred into action. But what could he do? There was someone moving about downstairs and so there was nothing for it but to wait and see if they might go out again, or go into another room so that he could creep out unnoticed. Then he heard them coming upstairs. He quietly closed the door to his room and waited. After a moment there came a knock at the door and, without waiting for a response, Don came in.

'Hello,' he said, 'I wondered if you would be here.'

'Why?' asked Mark, suspiciously. 'Why would I be here at this time of day – when we're all supposed to be out having a picnic to celebrate my birthday?'

'It was a hunch,' he said. 'Why *are* you here, if everyone else is having a picnic to celebrate your birthday? And what's happened to the side of your head?'

Mark ignored this.

'Where's my money?' he demanded.

'What money?'

'Don't tell me Sean didn't tell you about the money?'

Don looked at Mark with a soft expression that Mark took as pity.

'Mark,' he said, 'perhaps you have to lose everything, to lose it willingly, I mean, before something else can really start to take its place.'

'That must be the worst excuse for stealing money that I've ever heard,' he said. He pushed past, crossed the upper hallway and went into Don's room. It was sparsely furnished with only a bed and a small chest of drawers. There were a couple of hooks on the back of the door, with a jacket and coat on them respectively, but that was it. Mark pulled open each drawer in turn, riffling through the clothing. Don stood in the doorway, watching. Then Mark got down on his knees to look under the bed.

'I didn't take your money,' Don said. 'Of course, you have no predisposition to trust me, so I don't expect you will.'

Don looked back to the open door of Mark's room and the bags that were visible there.

'Where are you off to?' he asked.

'Why would you care?' Mark said. 'In any case, there's no way I'd tell you where. You'd probably tell Sean.'

'Wherever you go, I wish you well,' said Don. 'As a matter of fact, I'm going on a short tour soon, so I wouldn't have seen you for a while, anyway.'

Mark walked past Don to pick up his bags, then went down the stairs. Don didn't follow him. Mark left the house and walked out of Baker's Yard and onto the main street. He had no idea where to go. None at all. He needed to get away from Baker's Yard, that was all. First he went to the station to check his bags into the luggage lock-ups there. It was so expensive, per item, that he wasn't quite sure what to do until the attendant directed him to a cheap luggage shop on the next block. Here, he bought a bright red holdall of incredibly poor quality with an inadequate-looking blue plastic zip, but which was large enough to take all four of his carrier bags. When he returned to the station and checked it in, he was pleased to note that he had saved considerably more than the purchase price of the bag. He then walked down towards the western esplanade, away from the Old Town and all the places where he felt he might bump into someone who knew him.

Westwards along the seafront there were a number of swanky new blocks of flats with large balconies and curved, nautical-looking windows in the stairwells. There was a large hotel here too, with a tall glass frontage in marine blue and with a huge atrium, the height of the whole hotel, at the front. He walked on past it and found that he was seething with anger. Towards Don for not being helpful – and for giving him the impetus to get into this mess in the first place; towards Sean, for being here in this town, when Mark had assumed he would never see him again; towards Holly for somehow being 'in it' with Don; to all the residents and ex-residents of Baker's Yard, in fact. All that singing in the caves on his first night out with them. What had that meant? It had seemed so open and friendly, and yet they were all party to an undercurrent of deceit. They'd taken him to the house in which Sean lived. Holly had the keys that Don had taken from Sean, and that meant that there was a collusion somewhere along the line. He couldn't work out what it might be, but it had led with a dark inevitability to Sean's demand for the return of the £40,000. It all made horrible sense. They'd never wanted to include him at all. . . Trap him, yes, but not include him.

On the far side of the hotel, Mark saw a newsagent up a side street and remembered that today was the day that the local paper ran its property section. Even though he knew it was several hours since the paper had come out, he went in and bought a copy. There was a café on the other side of the road, and he went in and ordered himself a coffee. When he sat down he counted out the money he had in his pocket and found that he had just over £50 left.

What he really needed to do was sort out a new credit card. His dad had always been good about lending him money, too, so he'd be all right until he found some work. . .

He glanced through the paper, aghast at the prices that were being asked for rented accommodation. There were plenty of places on offer, but you certainly paid a premium for living in a trendy coastal port! He was used to prices in a depressed north Midlands town. He glanced down the private 'Rooms To Let' column, but most of them were for students to share with families. There was an ad for a small studio flat, and one for a bed-sit with 'integral kitchenette' and shared bathroom. These were possibilities. And then, right at the bottom of the page, separated by a thick black line and in slightly smaller type, as though it had been added as a 'late news' item, was another. "Single room to let in large house in Old Town. Basic facilities. Suit *newcomer*. Rent negotiable."

Mark assumed that "basic facilities" meant that it would be cheap, so he went to a phone box on the seafront and dialled the number. He supposed that the room had been snapped up hours ago, but it was still worth a try. The phone rang for a long time, and Mark grew despondent. The room *had* been let, and now the landlord wasn't answering the phone. It had probably been ringing all day. He was about to hang up when it was answered by a woman with a soft Irish accent.

'Hello?' she said.

'Oh, hello,' said Mark, caught off guard, 'I'm phoning about the room that you have advertised in today's paper.'

'Oh,' she said. 'That was quick! Is the paper out already?'

'Mmm,' he said. 'Is the room still available?'

'Yes, of course. Would you like to come and see it?'

'Yes please,' Mark said quickly.

'When would be convenient, do you think?' the woman asked.

'Um. . . How about now?' Mark suggested. 'I'm down on the seafront by the big new hotel.'

'Oh, well,' said the woman, 'you're quite close, then. We're in the Old Town. Perhaps you could call round in, say, a couple of hours?'

She gave him brief directions which he scribbled in the margin of the paper. Then he phoned the numbers for the other two properties. The lines were both engaged and he spent nearly forty minutes redialling before he got through to the one that had the bedsit on offer.

'I'm afraid you're far too late,' a harassed woman told him curtly. 'The phone's been ringing non-stop. I've already got a number of people coming to look the place over this evening, so I don't expect there's any point you coming too. Maybe you could phone tomorrow to see if it's gone?'

He dialled the number for the studio flat a few more times, but reckoned it would be even more in demand than the bedsit, so he gave up and set off into the Old Town, past Ingrid and Wim's shop, up the stairs past Leon's house, and onto the road which wound steeply up towards the lighthouse. Here, near the top, the houses were all Victorian, on four floors, with large bay windows that looked out across the town. Number 11 was double-fronted and, like the cottage in Baker's Yard, looked in need of some major attention. But the elevated position was spectacular. It was still more than an hour before he was due to see the room, so he wandered on past the house and onto the hill top, where the lighthouse stood by the cliff edge. Here the wind was stronger. The Old Town was sheltered from the prevailing wind – a fact that he only now registered. When he turned his attention to it, he noticed that the lighthouse itself was in a state. The boarded up lower part was covered in layer upon layer of graffiti, and the upper part was crumbling and lined with pale brown streaks which fanned out from the rusting metal frames of its tiny windows. Up here it was relatively flat, and grassy. From where he stood, Mark could see a ridge of hills disappearing off into the distance to the northwest and, at the edge of visibility, a white horse cut into the hillside. Idyllic rural England, he thought, as he sat down on the grass in the lee of the lighthouse, with his back against one of the boards. He looked out across the pasture and saw distant fields of late-season rape, fading back to green from their respondent yellow. To his right the sea was dark and choppy. White horses glinted in sporadic patches of brightness where the sun broke through the low clouds.

He wondered what he should say to the landlady about the dressing on his ear. He guessed it might put her off and so a benign explanation would be important. In the end he decided that a non-committal reference to a bump – whilst cycling perhaps – would be best. He knew that elaborate explanations always sounded the most suspicious

Mark rang the bell of number 11 and had to wait for a while before the door was opened by a smart middle-aged woman who looked vaguely aristocratic, in a faded sort of way. When she saw Mark, she studied him for some moments without saying anything, which Mark found disconcerting, then she muttered 'Oh good,' quietly, as though to herself.

'Pardon?' he said.

'I said, "Oh good",' she told him. 'I mean, you look quite fit. It's just that there's no point showing people around if they're not going to enjoy climbing up and down the hill. It's very steep, as I expect you have discovered, and it can be daunting to some.'

'Good exercise, though,' he said.

'That's what I always say,' she smiled. 'Come on in.'

The hallway was painted white. In the past it might have looked splendid but now it seemed dusty and aged. The carpet, though of good quality, was wearing thin. Although the hall was large and spacious, with a wide stairway, the place had the look of a cheap lodging house and this gave Mark a contradictory sense of both pleasure and disappointment. There were no pictures on the walls, which made it look a little stark, an impression exacerbated by the fact that the hall contained only one item of furniture: a small square telephone table with a phone on it. Hanging from a nail hammered roughly into the wall above the phone was a red biro, presumably for the taking of messages. Beneath the table was a shelf, on which there was a plain note pad, a telephone directory and a Yellow Pages.

'Now,' said the woman, 'come through and have a look at the room first, and then we'll have a cup of tea.' She spoke with a pleasing lilt which favoured vowels over consonants. 'I'm Tara Keane, by the way, *Miss* Tara Keane.'

Mark introduced himself and they shook hands. He liked her immediately. She had a mass of slightly greying dark red hair tied back in a loose pony tail, and wore very little make-up. Her pale face looked calm, her manner straightforward and sensible. She was the sort of person he could trust, he decided, which he found reassuring up to a point. He'd been disappointed in his trust of the residents of Baker's Yard, and so was currently more wary than usual of his instincts as far as that went.

Miss Keane was wearing a voluminous emerald green dress. It reminded him of pictures of his grandmother wearing kaftans in the seventies, and it evoked a nostalgia in him for something obscure and comforting.

She smiled warmly at him and he returned the smile unselfconsciously.

'Is it the dress you're looking at?' she said.

Mark nodded. 'Sorry.'

'Oh, don't be sorry,' she told him. 'It's one of my favourites. I favour the colour of green, you know. Nothing to do with being Irish,' she added quickly, 'I simply find it the most. . . evocative of colours. It's the colour of nature, the colour of life.'

Was he responding to something maternal in her? He couldn't be sure, but he felt at ease with her in an extraordinary way.

'Now, let's see if the room is to your liking,' she said, and led him upstairs. The room was on the first floor at the back of the house and looked out over a narrow, steep sliver of garden. The hill was so steep here that the house immediately behind had a garden wall that was level with the window. The room itself was quite large, with a built-in cupboard on one side of the chimney breast and a wardrobe on the other. On the floor was a large maroon and dark blue patterned rug, slightly smaller than the room itself, which revealed a border of dark-stained floorboards. The bed was of dark wood, and looked old. Mark smiled to himself. The room was perfect.

The rest of the house was pleasant, too. There was a functional bathroom across the hall from his room, and the communal kitchen on the ground floor was large, bright and airy, with a dining table, four chairs and a sofa against the rear wall. It all looked homely and comfortable.

'How many people live here?' he asked.

'I have the front room on the first floor,' she said, 'I'm one of the residents here, by the way, not the landlord. The landlord is Mr Hammond, up in the attic suite. He's an elderly man. He has his own amenities, and leads a separate existence from the rest of us. I expect you'll meet him, in due course. I'm in charge of the running of the house on his behalf, which includes the choosing of *all* of the residents, and in return I get the best room, which seems fair enough to me. We all rub along together quite happily, I find. So don't worry, there's never any fighting over the use of the cooker or bathroom, if that's what you're worried about.'

She hadn't actually answered his question, but he didn't pursue it. There was no sign of excessive clutter or mess, so he didn't suppose it mattered.

'How much do you want for the room?' he asked.

She named a figure that was considerably lower than the prices listed in the paper, but still considerably more than he would ever have paid back home.

'All bills are included, but the telephone only receives incoming calls. As you know, mobiles don't work here, so there's no point in having one. There is a phone box at the top of the road if you want a view while talking to people, or there's one at the bottom of the left-hand staircase as you go down the hill, which is a little closer.'

Mark didn't have to think any further.

'I'll take the room,' he said. 'If that's okay.'

She smiled. 'Good! I thought you might. You look like the kind of person we're after. I have an instinct about these things.'

'About payment,' said Mark. 'It'll take a few days for me to get the money together. And references, if you want them.'

'References will not be necessary,' she said. 'I follow my nose in these matters. You can pay me when you move in.'

'Thank you,' said Mark. 'Paying when I move in would be very helpful.'

'We'll leave it like that, then,' said Miss Keane. 'Now, why don't you come up to my room and let me make you a cup of tea?'

They went upstairs. A couple of the banisters were broken on the staircase, and the landing was shabby, but there was no hint of dilapidation in her room. On the contrary, it had an air of quiet gentility, with smart old furniture and a bookcase that took up the whole of one wall. The branches of a large tree pressed close up to the window, its verdant leaves filtering the room with gentle watery light, which Mark found soothing. Miss Keane went out to get the tea and Mark browsed the books while he waited. The ones that he looked at were academic, traveller's tales or literary biographies. He hadn't got very far when Miss Keane came back in.

'The books belong to Mr Hammond,' she said. 'He has so many that they tend to overspill everywhere. I'm sure he'd lend you any that you were interested in. There's some marvellous stuff in there.'

She laughed and waved him to a chair opposite her.

'Listen to me,' she said with a smile, 'I'm making it sound as if I'm an expert. The truth is, I never managed to *conquer* literature, if you know what I mean. In the early days of my adulthood I always seemed to be too busy with *other* things.'

She laughed then, a deep throaty laugh that surprised Mark. It instantly made her seem more human and less business-like.

'Once you've neglected something as difficult as literature for too long it becomes even harder to make a start on it. Don't you agree?'

'More difficult, perhaps, Miss Keane,' Mark said, 'but surely not impossible?'

'Ah, you're an optimist,' she smiled. 'I like that. And, please, call me Tara.'

It was the first time anyone had ever called Mark an optimist.

'I must tell you,' she went on as they drank their tea, 'that this is a permissive household.'

Mark was shocked and it obviously showed because Tara laughed at his expression.

'Oh, there's no need to look like that,' she said. 'Perhaps you would prefer the term *alternative*? It's interesting that whenever I use the word "permissive", people always think I'm talking about sex, but that's a very limited interpretation of the word, wouldn't you say? Nowadays people are so *inhibited*, about all sorts of things. Everything is so pragmatic and logical. It's all work, work, work and buy, buy, buy, and anything else is regarded with suspicion, as positively *perverse*. I'm sorry, but I hardly feel that that's progress. There was a time when all sorts of possibilities were entertained here. And there was such *joy* then,' she added wistfully.

Mark was surprised that Tara was talking so frankly to him so soon after meeting, but decided to take it as a good sign.

'Of course,' she said, 'I'm not trying to be directive regarding what you do with yourself here. I'm saying that more or less anything is permitted. My only definite rule is – no loud music. The walls are reasonably thick because it's an old house, but there's something so. . . *infuriating* about that thump, thump, thump coming through your bedroom walls at all hours, regardless of how marvellous the music might be to the person who's listening to it.'

Mark left feeling slightly breathless. What had Tara been trying to tell him; that the house was full of weirdoes? It was difficult to tell. Maybe it was Tara who was the weirdo and everyone else was ordinary? And she hadn't mentioned his ear once.

He'd asked to move in as soon as he'd sorted his finances, but that was not possible.

'I'll be away until next Saturday,' said Tara, 'so Saturday 28th would be absolutely the earliest you could move in. Is that okay?'

'Yes, of course,' Mark told her.

It would be fine to stay in a hotel for the next ten days. He just needed to get down to the bank to sort out some money for that. Even given the absence of his credit and debit cards, he was still solvent, so that wouldn't be a problem.

He wondered about Sean and the £40,000. On one hand, the pragmatic course of action might be to leave town for somewhere else. But on the other hand, Mark had travelled to another part of the country only to find Sean here when he arrived, so there was no point in assuming that if he went elsewhere, he would be safe. He felt a sort of bristling anger as he thought of this. There was no way he could pay the money back, and that was that. Would Sean eventually find him and make him pay in some other way? The discomfort of this and the feeling of lack of safety was an unwelcome undercurrent to his already precarious state of mind. Still, he could buy a handful of novels and hole up in a hotel until he moved into his new accommodation.

As he walked, he wondered about Tara; about her outward appearance of formality and her – what was the word? – *permissive* attitudes. It looked as though he was going to be something of a disappointment to her as far as that went. There wasn't much about him that was interesting on that score. But then, being pursued by a gangster had a certain *unconventional* feel to it and might be looked upon in a rather different way by Tara than by most landlords' agents, which could be useful. . . And it was pleasant to know that there wasn't a huge list of restrictive rules to abide by.

He looked over to the cliffs and saw gulls circling there; tiny dots against the sky. Standing at the wide sandstone-flagged walkway above the main shopping street of the Old Town, he saw the fire-eater performing below, wearing his red, yellow and blue harlequin suit. He watched him blow an impressive plume of flame into the air, causing the small crowd to gasp. Mark descended the last stone staircase and, yet again, arrived in front of the fire-eater as he was finishing his act. He walked straight up to him and dropped a couple of pounds into the hat, catching the man's gaze and holding eye contact for a second or two. The fire-eater returned the look for a moment, and then leaned forward to take the coins out of the hat. He didn't look at Mark again, but with a nonchalant flick of his wrist, flung them across the street where they chinked against the kerb and fell down the drain there. Well, Mark thought, that was resoundingly unequivocal. . .

He went into his bank and explained the situation regarding his credit and debit cards to the cashier. The woman pressed a buzzer to summon another member of staff to deal with the query, and asked him to wait. Sitting in a bank like this was a rather surreal experience. It felt like something that he might have done in his past life, but which didn't fit in with this life at all. It was too mundane. After a while, someone came out and took him into an impersonal booth for an interview.

The next few minutes were astounding. And not in a good way. His current account had accrued a small overdraft, and his credit card had exceeded its limit.

'But that's impossible,' he said. 'Last time I checked, I had a couple of thousand in my account, and I'd cleared my credit card completely.'

His first thought was of fraud – that someone had got hold of his new cards and spent his money. Then he thought of Amy. Amy! She knew his PIN, so would be able to withdraw cash using his debit card, and she'd be able go internet shopping with his credit card to her heart's content.

'What's been put on my credit card?' he asked heavily.

The man looked on screen.

'£432 to British Airways on the 2nd of May,' he read. '£278 to Fashion Direct on the 4th. £163 to Perfumes of the World Dot Com on the 4th. £314 to Avis America fly-drive car rental on the 5th. . .'

'Oh god, it's Amy,' said Mark. 'My wife. Can I have my cards stopped?'

The man looked at him and smiled sympathetically.

'If someone has been using your card without your permission, sir, that constitutes fraud, even if that person is your partner.'

'Ex-partner,' Mark corrected him.

'Ah,' he said. 'I see. . .'

Mark took several breaths. He wondered why he wasn't getting angry. Instead, there was a jittery feeling in his chest as though he'd had one too many cups of coffee.

'So what can I do?' he asked the adviser. 'I need some cash. Maybe I can take out a small loan?'

'Certainly, sir,' the man said. 'We would be able to do that for you, based on your current salary.'

'I don't have a salary at the moment,' Mark told him. 'I'm between jobs.'

'That may not be a problem,' the man said. 'Let's have a look at the options.'

But there was nothing that could be done. Mark didn't have any definitive ID with him – neither a passport nor a driver's licence – and he was unable to say when he'd be able to get hold of them. He was clear that he was not prepared to travel home for this purpose; a fact that began to seem more and more suspicious as he was questioned about it. Eventually, the man shrugged, a subtle yet eloquent gesture that was as definitive as anything he subsequently said. He was polite, but in that shrug his body had said, quite clearly: 'You've been shafted, mate, and there's nothing you or I can do about it.'

When he left the bank, Mark stood on the pavement and wondered what to do. He had no rent to give Tara, and no immediate prospect of getting it. . . And paying Sean back was now even more impossible than before.

Mark smiled grimly. Hadn't Don said something about losing everything willingly? When it came to the cash that had been stolen from Baker's Yard, that was one thing. It hadn't been his money. But to find himself with no access to cash and credit, that was different. That was *his* money. *His* credit. As he thought this, and of Amy spending it on perfume and travel, he touched into the anger that was constricting his chest and felt a searing flood of rage that lasted for a moment and then subsided as quickly as it had arisen.

Mark used most of his remaining cash to take the cheapest room in the Old Oak Hotel, which was reasonably priced, if dowdy. It was at the foot of the hill where he'd viewed the room earlier in the day. The little room that he'd taken was at the rear and looked out over the back of a pizza house, where seagulls strutted and shrieked loudly. A noisy extractor fan was positioned only feet away from his little window, which obscured his view and pumped the sweet smell of pizza into his room. It didn't take long before he was sick of it.

There was a phone in his room and so he took this opportunity to call his father. He was surprised when Amy answered.

'I'm staying here,' she said when he asked her why she'd

answered. 'As you know, your father and I get on very well, and if I stay here I have free access to a child minder whenever I need one. Your mother can't get enough of Ty, so it works very well.'

'But why didn't you stay where you were?' Mark asked. 'Didn't you get the money I sent you?'

'Yes, I did,' she replied, 'but your dad made the offer and I took him up on it. It's only going to be temporary. I may be moving in with Richard soon, if all goes well.'

Mark laughed. 'The man with the BMW in the flat below ours?'

'How did you know?'

'Let's say I'm not surprised,' he told her.

'What am I expected to do? You walked out on me.'

'Okay, okay,' said Mark. 'Actually, I needed to talk to you, anyway. About the cash you've taken from my account, and about my credit card.'

'Mark,' she said, 'I don't care about your credit card. I didn't spend that much, anyway. I was amazed that your credit limit was so rubbish. And I thought it was reasonable to take Ty away on holiday after what I've been through.'

'Yes, fly-drive to America,' said Mark.

'Yes,' she said, 'but I didn't go 5 star or anything. You couldn't afford it.'

'But what about the £20,000 that I sent you?' he asked.

'The £20,000 has been helpful in that it has just about sorted out my debts, and it has meant that I'm not out of pocket because of any of this, but don't feel you were being generous. And don't think you can come back, Mark. I don't want you back.'

Mark laughed. 'Don't worry,' he said, 'I'm not coming back. Can I speak to Dad, now, please?'

Amy made a bad tempered grunting noise and the line went quiet. Mark waited for some time before his father came on the line.

'Mark,' he said, 'where the hell are you? What's going on?'

'I'm fine, Dad. Really. But I need to borrow some money, if that's all right.'

'What for?'

'To pay some rent for a while. Amy's been spending on my credit card so I'm a bit stuck. Don't worry, I can pay it back once I've got a job.'

'Mark,' his father told him. 'I want you to come back here and behave responsibly. I've had your boss on the phone asking why you chucked in your job. We've got Amy staying here, and Ty, and it's about time you came back and looked after things.'

'Dad, Amy can look after herself, as you well know. Ty. . . well, I'm sorry about Ty, but I can't come back, Dad. I can't.'

'Look, Mark,' his father said in a wheedling voice, 'this is the time for you to come back and join the business. I can make you a partner. . . it won't just be fitting central heating systems. You'll be able to move on from all that in a few years. You could get a further qualification in accountancy or book-keeping or something and come in on that side of the business.'

'Dad, I'm *not coming back*.'

His father sighed, a sign that he was getting angry. 'Right,' he said argumentatively, 'let's get this clear. I'm not going to give you money so that you can wander about doing God knows what. If I gave you money, you'd only stay away for longer. If you want to come back, I'll pay your fare. I'll even send someone to get you. I'll even come *myself* if you tell me where you are.'

'There's no chance of that,' Mark retorted.

'The sooner you come home the better, or things will go to all hell and back!' his father yelled. 'It's a good thing your flat is in my name or you'd be right up the –'

'Forget it, Dad, forget it,' said Mark and put the phone down.

He went into the small hotel bar and put a whisky with ice on his bill.

The barman looked to be in his forties and seemed friendly enough. They chatted together idly, though the man became more interested when Mark talked of the room he'd been to see that day and explained how it looked as if he might not be able to take it.

'Where is it?' the barman asked.

'In one of those big Victorian houses up towards the top of the Old Town,' Mark told him.

'Oh,' he said, surprised. 'Was it in the paper? I haven't heard anything.'

'Yes it was,' said Mark. 'Today.'

'There's a copy of the paper right here, can you show me the ad?'

Mark thought it was odd that the barman should want to see the advertisement, but he didn't say anything. Everything was odd in this town. Why should the barmen be any different? He still felt bruised, dismissed even, after his conversations with Amy and his father and so he didn't question the man, just picked the paper up listlessly and flicked through to the property section. He scanned the columns carefully, but couldn't see the advertisement.

'Damn it,' he said, 'I can't find it. It was right down at the bottom.'

The barman nodded to himself as Mark flicked back and

forth through the property pages, getting more and more confused.

The advertisement had gone.

'This is *today's* paper?' Mark said, looking at the front and seeing that it was.

'Never mind about the ad,' the man said. 'Is it a double-fronted house, with a dark red door that needs a good lick of paint?'

Mark's mind reeled again. Did everyone know everyone else in this place? Or did they just all know about *him*? Was it impossible to be an anonymous resident here? The barman probably knew Don, Holly and Sean too! He almost felt inclined to ask, then felt a cold thrill of fear run through him. He looked at the barman with hooded eyes.

'Yes, it is,' said Mark warily. 'Why, do you know something about it?'

'I know there's this guy who lives there and rents out rooms. I've never met him but I've seen his housekeeper a few times. They've got a bit of a reputation for being. . . odd. He lives up in the attic and never comes out. My wife thinks he must be mad, or deformed or something. You know, like the elephant man. I've noticed her because she's very distinctive, with all that red hair, and she always looks at you as you go past. Not just looking, either, but *watching*, if you know what I mean.'

He laughed with self-deprecating shrug.

'My wife refers to her as The Busybody, but I think she's harmless. You should go and talk to her and explain the money situation. They're so offbeat they might keep the room free for you while you sort yourself out.'

The advice sounded sensible, although Mark reckoned they'd easily be able to find someone else who *could* pay. Thinking about this made him feel suddenly exhausted. The jitters of earlier had run themselves down and now he felt only an overwhelming tiredness, so he said goodnight to the barman and went to bed, where even the sickly smell of food and the noise of the seagulls failed to keep him awake.

The following morning he checked out of the hotel. When he settled the bill, he found that he only had a few pence left. He had no money for a further night and was now anxious about what he might do next. It was the barman from the night before who was on the desk when he paid up, and, seeing Mark's expression, he said, 'Are you going to be okay?'

Mark shrugged. The only thing that he could grab onto at this stage was the prospect of going to talk to Tara next Saturday, to see if she would take him in, even though he had no money. He might be penniless, but he did at least have prospects. Tara had seemed so clear that he was right for the place, surely that must count for something? Perhaps she might take pity on him. He said something of this to the barman, who smiled helpfully and said, 'Look, mate, if you want to leave any bags here, please do. I can keep them in the store room for you.'

Mark gratefully accepted this offer and went up to the station to reclaim his red bag, which he took down to the Old Oak and gave to the man for safekeeping. He felt nervous and irritated as he left the hotel, at how things seemed to be going wrong, yet again. Yesterday, he'd nonchalantly dropped two pounds into the fire-eater's hat. Now, he was forced to understand how precarious his presence in this town was. Those two pounds might end up being the difference between eating and not eating.

Down on the seafront, everything felt alien. It was bizarre. Now, he wasn't there to simply idle along the esplanade and enjoy the view and the sensation of the cool, salty breeze on his skin. Quite suddenly he had entered survival mode. The environment, the elements, were now things to be negotiated rather than enjoyed. The only thing he could think to himself was, 'What am I going to do? Where am I going to sleep? What am I going to eat?' He was separated from the beauty of the seafront. In fact, he had no point of connection with anything that he saw because he was in a daze of shock that only allowed space for his cyclic thoughts. How could this have happened? How? How had he arrived in a place and in a circumstance where he had no one to turn to? It was inconceivable. The people who walked past might as well have been in another world that he was watching on a screen.

He sat on a bench and stared out to sea. What was he going to do? He had all this time to pass, and he owed £40,000 to someone who might be out looking for him at this very moment. He felt the bandage at his ear and wondered how much further Sean might be prepared to go than slicing off an earlobe. It was a question that didn't bear asking.

Time passed slowly, very, very slowly and he gradually began to feel cold from sitting still for so long. It was lunch time but he didn't feel hungry and so he continued to sit where he was. A slight drizzle began to fall in the early afternoon, and he got up and walked about briskly to try and warm up. He found a small park, on the far side of the river near the bridge at the entrance to the harbour. Here there was a bench under an oak tree that gave him shelter from both the breeze and the moisture in the air.

One thing he found interesting was that he didn't feel miserable. He was far too anxious to feel miserable. There was something in his head that felt like a distant wailing, something elemental, perhaps infant, and desperately needy. He tried to tune into it, but it was too indistinct to get a grip on.

The mere opening to the experience of it seemed to sober him up for a moment, so that he felt a little more calm, in spite of his knowledge that the deadline for giving Sean the £40,000 had now passed. There were things he could do, he told himself. Besides, it wasn't winter and he only had to wait a few days before he could ask Tara if she would take him in.

How odd, he thought, that he'd spent his whole adult life with something to do. With so many options to keep himself busy. There had never been a moment, however brief, when he'd been stuck for a period of time without access to the comfort of shelter, of company, of television, or of the distractions afforded by what money could buy. Food, drink, various kinds of shopping, the cinema, the pub. . .

But here he was, with nothing to do. Nothing to buy. And ten days to spend waiting until he could ask Tara if she would take him in. And what was this quality of waiting anyway? In some ways it seemed like he was waiting for something so ridiculous that he could hardly believe that he was even giving it his consideration. The idea that a prospective land-lord might look kindly on a would-be tenant turning up with no money after ten days on the street. Well, it really did seem ridiculous and quite impossible. But then, Tara had said that she followed her nose in these things and she'd thought he was 'right' for the room.

Focus. It was a question of focus. This was what he needed to get him through the next few days. The fact that Tara had thought of him as a suitable tenant.

By six o'clock a terrible boredom had set in. Mark couldn't believe it was only eight hours since he'd checked out of his hotel. He was still sitting on the bench beneath the oak tree in the small park, and he was beginning to feel cold again.

The weather had cleared after the brief drizzle of earlier, but it could hardly be called warm. He still didn't feel hungry, which was a blessing. He left the park and walked briskly down by the quay to warm up.

He realised, as he did so, that the way he was experiencing time passing was quite new to him. Like the ticking of a clock, he could witness it. He could see the seagulls flying here and there. He could see the waves breaking on the shore, he could see boats as they came into the harbour. All this he could experience as a material indication of time passing, and yet, as the hours ticked by, the following Saturday morning did not seem to be coming appreciably closer. This paradox only really occurred to him now, for the first time.

He'd moved into a new flat with Amy a couple of years ago, and it had still seemed – and looked – new when he'd left to come down here. But in twenty years, thirty years, it would no longer be new. If they hadn't already been changed, the fixtures and fittings would seem old and shabby and unfashionable. Then there was the obvious fact that he would grow old and die. The people who lived in the town would grow old and die. The river, which flowed seemingly endlessly into the harbour, had worn a course for itself that had changed and would continuously change over time. The cliffs on which the lighthouse stood were gradually crumbling. The caves behind the old town would collapse. . . the earth would be swallowed by the sun. Time was irrevocable. And yet. . . and yet, it felt like an eternity between right now and next Saturday morning when he would walk up the hill to talk to Tara.

He managed a wry smile at this thought. The time would come and go whether he wanted it to or not, but wanting the time to pass more quickly between now and then wasn't going to help at all.

By dusk, Mark still didn't feel hungry although he was aware of an emptiness in his stomach. He began to worry about where he might sleep and realised how few obvious places there were to go. He decided to sleep in the park but when he went there he found that it was now locked. The gate into it was too high for him to climb, and it had off-putting spikes on the top. It occurred to him to go and sleep in the cave that he'd visited on the occasion of the Baker's Yard night out, but he wanted to have as little to do with them as possible and so it seemed pragmatic to steer clear of it. If they wanted to find him, that would certainly be one of the first places they would look, and they may well have Sean with them.

He knew there were other caves, but wasn't clear as to their location and so he ended up on the hill, at the lighthouse. Here, there was a doorway on the eastward side of the building that had been boarded up, but even so, there was a recess that he could shrug himself into in such a way that he could lean back and hug himself into his jacket. There was an elder bush and some brambles that provided a little shelter from the wind, and at first it seemed quite cosy. As time passed, however, it became more and more uncomfortable, and even though he managed to doze off from time to time, he was always aware of the cold ground and the moisture there, and the night-time noises around him. Eventually, he woke fully shortly after five a.m., dawn appearing in the sky and a deep chill permeating his entire body. The cold was so profound that he was beyond shivering. Unfolding his arms was painfully slow. His knees seemed to have locked somehow and, whilst he sat, he had to stamp his feet on the ground to get some movement going, and he winced at the pins and needles for a while before he could even think of standing up.

As he did so he realised that he was ravenous. He stamped a little more, and flapped his arms in an attempt to warm up a little but found that this made his ear ache under its dressing. He wondered how well it was healing and patted the dressing lightly. It felt a little tender, but otherwise fine.

It was still only just before six o'clock, and as he came down the hill he noticed that the town was deserted. He realised with dismay that the day had yet to begin, a day destined to be far longer than the one he'd managed to negotiate. The sea was flat and the light on it almost unbearably beautiful; a palest blue that faded into white so that it wasn't possible to see exactly where the horizon was. A seagull dipped into the water not far from the shore and Mark could see the ripples spreading out from where it had grabbed at something, and he lay back and looked up at the sky, at the white clouds and the blue between them, and he felt. . . nothing. Well, not exactly nothing, but an emotion that he didn't recognise. It was something that seemed almost wholly physical. There was the emptiness of his stomach, and the beginnings of a raging thirst, plus coldness that had seeped right into him. But these things described a feeling too. He was 'cold and empty' and in articulating it in this way, he realised that he had always been like this.

That first full day was, as he'd suspected, interminable. It was dominated by hunger and an awareness of – yet, separateness from – the beauty that was around him. He was able to tolerate this because it didn't seem real, but his feeling of being distanced from his surroundings gradually subsided.

By the next day, after another night up at the lighthouse, he was forced by necessity to find something to eat. Over the course of the day, he found that, so long as he didn't let himself be caught up in the ignominy of it, he could occasionally get hold of some food. He kept an eye out for people who were eating fish and chips, or burgers. Occasionally they would discard some uneaten food which he could reclaim from the bins whilst it was still fresh. He tried to be furtive, but that didn't help as it was a warm day and the town was busy. The bins in secluded places had no food in them, and so he found himself down on the esplanade watching people who were eating. Being in such public places made him feel particularly vulnerable, and he kept an eye out for Sean, but in the end, what else could he do but take the risk? He needed to eat. Finding water was less of a problem as he could drink from the taps in the toilets by the harbour.

This all kept him busy, but he found that it diminished him, in the sense that he was now preoccupied with something that had never been an issue for him before and which left no room for 'ordinary' things such as having a sense of choice about what to do and where to go. In the early evening, however, he had a piece of luck. He noticed a group of three girls eating doughnuts who discarded a supermarket carrier bag that looked suspiciously heavy. Sure enough, when he pulled it out of the bin he found that there was a twelve-pack of jam doughnuts inside, with three left. Three fresh doughnuts! Sweet and sugary, and also loaded with fat, they filled him up and kept him going until the following morning.

He slept for the first part of that night in a bus shelter on the west side of town, but he was moved on by the police at around three o'clock, and he ended up back at the lighthouse again. He tried shouldering the boarding, to see if it would give, but it didn't and so he spent a few hours there, managing to 'sleep' until nearly six this time.

When he got up, apart from the terrible, bone-numbing cold, his first sensation was of being unshaven, unwashed and of badly needing to clean his teeth. Of itself, being unshaven was not an issue as it quite suited him, but his clothes were becoming crumpled and stained. Being unshaven in this context now had a different 'feel' to it. It did not communicate a bohemian lifestyle, but homelessness and undesirability. With this came a feeling of disbelief. He had never considered what kind of people became homeless, but it certainly wasn't people like him.

He managed to wash his hair and clean himself up a bit in the toilets by the harbour, but that was only his upper body so it was less satisfactory than he'd hoped. The bandage that he had over his ear was becoming grimy, but there was nothing he could do about that. He took off his shoes and socks later in the morning and paddled. The water was still icy, but it made his feet feel tingly and fresh which was helpful, and he splashed some on his face.

In the afternoon he noticed the fire-eater again, setting up to perform. Seeing him like this gave Mark a ghastly lurch in the pit of his stomach. He was reminded of what the man had said to him, about ending up sleeping in the gutter, and he couldn't bear the thought that he might be seen looking like this. He kept out of sight of the juggler for the afternoon, but that didn't stop him feeling a crushing sense of humiliation.

The following days were a nightmare as it rained sporadically, and so hardly any people were out, and they certainly weren't discarding food for him to eat. The gnawing hunger he'd already begun to experience became worse than he could have imagined, becoming totally preoccupying – filling his thoughts with desperate need. He sat for a lot of the day in the shelters along the seafront, feeling abject and unsafe and wondering what he would do if Tara didn't offer him a room. He was still clear that he wasn't going to go home, but what he was doing now was unsustainable even with the summer unfolding ahead. He would have to make himself known to the council as a homeless person and see what services they could offer. . .

After a week or so there was a night that was the worst so far, as the temperature dipped and there were squally showers throughout the night as well as one period of heavy rain. He'd managed to find a disused garage behind the station which had a shed-like outhouse that he managed to get into. But it wasn't fully watertight and he ended up getting wet all down one side of his body. Sheltering there was particularly unpleasant as he had no light, and it was pitch dark. He'd found it in the dusk, and had been able to see that the space was empty, but in the dark he could hear occasional scuttling sounds and wondered if it was rats.

As soon as he saw the first crack of dawn's light, he crawled out from his hiding place, feeling worn out, nauseous and sleep deprived. He went down and found a little food on the seafront – a half-eaten sausage sandwich which made him gag a little as he ate it, and which made hardly any difference to his hunger. His empty stomach was causing him pain. The bins along the esplanade had all been emptied in the night, but wedged behind one of them he noticed a discarded, half-eaten portion of fish and chips that had been pecked at by gulls. Quite a lot of its contents still remained, and Mark pulled it out from behind the bin, then ate the congealed, cold food swiftly, before he had time to properly think about what he was doing. It seemed delicious.

After he'd eaten he went and sat on the beach. He still had several days to go and wondered how he was going to get through the time. Gradually, however, he settled into a routine of looking for food, trying to be as inconspicuous as possible, and then crawling back into his shelter at night. And time did pass, in such a way that Mark's waking life came to seem like a dream, from which he simply hoped that he would ultimately wake up. This he finally began to do over the course of the following Friday, which was warm and sunny.

On the Saturday morning, just after seven thirty, he dropped into the Old Oak Hotel and collected his bag, then took it down to the beach. There was still no one there and so he stripped down to his underwear and jumped into the sea. The cold took his breath away, but he forced himself to stay in as he briskly rubbed himself all over. When he got out, he dried himself on his crumpled shirt and changed into a new set of Ingrid and Wim's bright clothes. Then he put his wet shirt and underpants into a side pocket of the bag. After that, he went to the toilets by the harbour to smarten himself up. He washed his hair and beard and, at last, felt a little more presentable. When he looked in the mirror, though, he could see a wild light in his eyes – someone else stared back at him. Someone *in extremis*, and perhaps a little mad. He took several deep breaths, and tried to look more at ease. But it didn't really work and so he gave up and, seeing that it was now a reasonable time of day, left to go and see if Tara was up and about.

He was feeling out of breath when he rang the doorbell to number 11. When Tara answered, he made an attempt at explaining what had happened to his finances, but it sounded rather lame and as if he was making excuses. Tara listened impassively then said, 'All right, I suppose you'd better come in, and we'll talk to Mr Hammond about it.'

She took him up to the second floor. There was a tiny upstairs landing lit by a small window, beneath which was a tall, narrow table with a spider plant perched on it. Nearby, there was a small green armchair with aged velvet upholstery that was worn to a shine on the arms. The chair was positioned so that, if you cared to sit on it, you might look out of the window at the next house up the hill. From here, a flight of narrow stairs led up to the attic room, and they had to negotiate them in single file. Mark smiled as he went because he felt as though he was being called into the headmaster's study for a grilling about some obscure transgression. There was something curiously intimidating, too, about what the barman had told him; that Mr Hammond might be deformed, or mad. He almost laughed aloud at himself for thinking this but then realised that, for the first time since leaving university, he was not absolutely in control of the situation. He was here to ask a favour from strangers, and that made him nervous and uncertain. Tara knocked quietly on the door and they waited for a few seconds before a quavering voice called out, 'Come in.'

They went in. Mr Hammond was sitting on a settee in a long room with a sloping ceiling. He was smartly dressed in a pair of light grey trousers and a blue velvet smoking jacket, with a matching bow tie. He was old – certainly in his eighties, Mark guessed – and frail with it. To Mark, he seemed like an emanation from a bygone age, or like an actor from a period film. Mr Hammond smiled at Mark, and then at Tara.

'Yes, Tara, what is it?'

Once the situation had been explained, Mr Hammond sat in silence, looking out of the window to his side. A high skein of cloud was letting watery sunshine through – bright but hazy. In addition to this window there were a couple of large skylights that enhanced the sense of light in the room. It must be wonderful, Mark thought, to have the lights off in here at night and look up at the stars.

'Maybe Mark could take over Ralph's duties?' Tara said quietly to Mr Hammond. 'What do you think?'

'I think we should discuss it privately for a moment,' he replied, gesturing to Mark with a hint of apology. 'I'm sorry to be so secretive,' he said, 'but I'm sure you understand.'

'Yes, of course,' said Mark. 'I'll wait on the landing downstairs.'

He went down and sat on the ancient green armchair and pondered the fact that under normal circumstances he would never have dared to come back to explain, and to ask for the room to be kept for him. But then, what other option did he have? And there had been something about the way in which Tara had said that he was the kind of person they were after. . .

After a while, Tara opened the door and asked him to come upstairs. Again, a bizarre fear of harsh judgement welled up in him. He felt like a criminal coming back into the courtroom for his sentence. Mr Hammond looked genial but rather distracted, and said, in a slightly over-formal way, 'Tara was mentioning to me that there is another room in the house which has never been let before. It used to be occupied by Ralph, our caretaker. He moved into sheltered accommodation last year and, since then, his room has remained empty. Perhaps, as you have no money at present, you would consider taking on both Ralph's room and his duties. As you have no doubt noticed, the house needs a certain amount of attention. I don't know how good you are at that sort of thing-'

'I've done it to a professional level for several years, although it isn't really my trade,' Mark broke in. 'I used to help my dad do up properties to get pocket money when I was at school. There was a lot of pressure put on me not to go to university, but to go into business with my father. He wanted me to make it my profession.'

'There you are!' said Tara to Mr Hammond, with a hint of triumph.

'Of course,' she said, turning to Mark, 'I'm sure it will only be a temporary arrangement while you look for a better job. And Mr Hammond can't afford to pay much money, but you'll have somewhere to stay. I don't know if you're interested?'

'Yes,' said Mark. 'Yes, absolutely.'

'I expect you'll find much better paid work very quickly with your skills,' she said, 'especially in this part of the world. But this might give you time to settle in and look around before you decide what to do next.'

His small room was positioned at the front of the house on the first floor, immediately above the hall. When Tara had shown him round previously he'd thought it was a cupboard. Yes, it was small, a mere sliver of a room, being only the width of the hallway below, but it was light and the window had a fantastic view out over the town, the harbour and the sea beyond. The fishing and leisure boats looked tiny from this elevation; the sea was mottled with sunshine and occasional showers that were drifting across from the south west. Given the previous ten days, it seemed all he could possibly need. There was a single bed in the room, with an iron bedstead, a plain chest of drawers and a single, simple antique wardrobe in dark wood. It looked like a luxurious prison cell, he thought, and it was, in its own odd way, enchanting.

'Take a day or two to settle in,' Tara told him, 'and then, perhaps, you would like to have a look over the house to see what needs to be done. Ralph was lovely and we were absolutely devoted to him, but he was a *terrible* handyman.'

As soon as he'd unpacked, Mark had a long bath and carefully took off the dressing on his ear. The wound was crusted with dried blood, but most of it came away easily with warm water. Once he'd cleaned it, he carefully snipped the five stitches and removed them. What remained was a livid scar, still a little scabby. The ear itself looked oddly misshapen, but not as bad as he'd expected. It was only face-on that it really showed. From this angle his remaining earlobe seemed particularly long, giving his face an asymmetrical look that was disconcerting.

Later, as he lay on his bed, watching the dusk fall, he thought of the last few days and how relieved he was that he'd been taken in. He also thought of Holly and wondered about her. The Baker's Yard house rule of not asking questions about a person's past meant that she'd remained a stranger in a number of important ways. Everyone at Baker's Yard had. It was unsettling to think how easily he had given them his trust, and how nonchalant they – and especially Don – had been about Sean and their connection with him, and how dismissive they had seemed about his fears.

# 5. Refuge?

Mark spent the next couple of days looking the place over. Externally, the house was shabby but essentially in reasonable repair. The guttering needed to be secured in a couple of places, the woodwork needed to be properly sanded and filled here and there. The windowsills needed the most work, and some of them would have to be replaced. A couple of coats of good, weatherproof exterior paint were in order, too. The roof had some tiles missing.

Inside, the top priority was rewiring. The old wiring was ancient and possibly dangerous. Some of the plaster in the hallway was crumbling. Taking the wallpaper off would probably bring some of it down, and the plaster of the ceiling near the bottom of the stairs would have to be replaced completely. The central heating was woefully inadequate as well as ancient.

How odd, it felt to Mark, that these jobs seemed to be an exciting challenge. Even agreeing to sort out the central heating seemed okay, which surprised him as this was precisely the work that he was refusing to do for his father.

He'd put up with this kind of work during the holidays at university because it gave him spending money, but he certainly didn't enjoy it and would often be incredibly bored, or resentful that he was working when his friends were out having fun or off travelling. The prospect of spending the rest of his life doing this had made him feel breathless to the point of panic. Here, now, he wasn't quite sure what made him feel so keen to get on with it. Was it because this was the house where he was living? But then, he'd be likely to be moving on soon enough. . . It was a mystery.

In the late afternoon he was called up to see Mr Hammond again. This time he was less formally dressed, wearing corduroy trousers and a short-sleeved shirt, and looked – Mark thought – even older. The skin on his forearms was wrinkled, and showed dark patches of discoloration. Mr Hammond asked Mark to bring him a glass of water from the kitchenette.

'I'm sorry,' he told Mark, 'my legs have rather given up on me, I'm afraid. And old age is a condition for which there is no cure.'

When Mark returned with the water, Mr Hammond smiled.

'What do you think,' he asked, 'in terms of getting the house up to scratch? Are we asking the impossible of you?'

'Well,' said Mark slowly, 'there's a lot of work that needs to be done. It depends whether you want a quick tidy up, or the whole works.'

Mr Hammond nodded, and looked at him.

'And you're prepared to do it? The whole works, I mean.'

'Yes,' said Mark.

Mr Hammond smiled and his face instantly became radiant. 'Excellent. I'll make sure that Tara keeps the kitchen stocked with all the food you need,' he said. 'I expect you'll want to work on the interior of the house at first. That way you won't need to go outside for a while.'

'Yes, it will be easier to work outside when the weather improves,' Mark agreed.

'No,' said Mr Hammond, 'that's not what I mean. I mean it will be useful for you to stay inside because you have an urge to hide.'

'Pardon?'

'My boy,' said Mr Hammond, 'it is quite all right for you to seek refuge here. Tara is a very instinctive person and her advertisements are not intended to be seen by everyone.'

Mark felt an eerie sense of *déjà vu* hearing this, and a creeping sense of anxiety.

'You don't seem comforted by this,' Mr Hammond added.

'I'm sorry,' Mark told him. 'It's just that this has happened to me before. I felt that I'd been given a special invitation to come to this town. The invitation seemed specifically "intended" for me, and I assumed that I was being offered refuge. But the people who took me in at Baker's Yard were somehow connected to a man I owe money to, who is looking for me, and who is dangerous.'

He absently touched the scar on his ear and felt the sensitivity there.

'Ah, Baker's Yard,' said Mr Hammond thoughtfully. 'I know of it, and the people who live there. And there's a man that you owe money to. In what way do you owe him money?'

'I took £40,000 that he gave me, mistakenly thinking I was someone else.'

'So, you're a thief?'

'Not in the sense that I intended to take it.'

'But you still took it.'

'Yes.'

'So you are a thief.'

Mark looked down at the carpet.

'Yes, in a way I suppose I am.'

Mr Hammond waited for Mark to look up again, then nodded.

'What have you done with the money?'

'I gave a lot of it away,' he said. 'The rest has been stolen.'

'Who stole it?'

'I would guess either someone at Baker's Yard, or the man who is looking for me. But I don't know.'

'I see,' Mr Hammond said slowly. 'All I can say to you is that, for as long as you stay in this house, you will be safe from anyone who is pursuing you.'

'How do you know?'

'I know.'

Was it something in the man's age and apparent venerability? Mark's instinct told him to believe him. But there was a hard edge of doubt that would not be so easily dismissed.

'I trusted the man who invited me to stay when I arrived here,' Mark said. 'But I lost my trust in him.'

Mr Hammond smiled his radiant smile again. 'But I am not asking you to trust me,' he said. 'It is of no consequence whatsoever whether you trust me or not. If you have decided to live with me, you will be safe for as long as you remain in the house. If you give Tara a list of what you need for your work, we can organise for it to be delivered to the house. I am at the very end of my life, Mark. It may well be that I do not live to see the fruits of your labour. Why would I lie to you?'

'For reasons I am not aware of.'

Mr Hammond laughed, a sad and dry sound that had almost no energy and which ended in a cough. 'Doubt is a vital human emotion,' he said, 'and you are quite right to doubt me. I would advise you always to doubt everything. Even yourself. But – and this is essential – you must never lose the *ability* to trust. This is the paradox at the heart of being human. You cannot base your judgement solely on empirical evidence. If you do that, you will cut out all aspects of this world that are ineffable and intangible; and the great prizes of happiness and fulfilment reside precisely there, in a place that can only be accessed through instinct and trust. And I don't mean belief in God,' he added. 'I mean belief in the truth of what you cannot prove.'

'And yet,' said Mark, 'you are telling me to doubt everything.'

Mr Hammond laughed again, with delight. 'You are right!' he said. 'But perhaps, if you approach doubt with open enquiry, it can turn into something else.'

Mark looked up through the skylight. Ranks of pink and red clouds drifted overhead, as the setting sun slipped towards the horizon. He absorbed Mr Hammond's words for a few moments, then returned to a previous topic. 'What will happen,' he asked, 'when I want to do some work on the exterior of the house?'

'By that time,' Mr Hammond said, 'you will know more.' His skin seemed to glow like red gold in the dusk. 'Perhaps you will know enough to have begun to feel safe.'

There was a pause and Mr Hammond looked at his watch, and Mark realised that their talk was over.

'Please do come and see me every once in a while,' said Mr Hammond, 'and tell me how you're getting on.'

As Mark left, he considered Mr Hammond's frailty. He remembered that when his own grandfather was very old, he'd lost interest in all things pertaining to the future. When Mark used to go round to mow the lawn, as a teenager, his grandfather had never thanked him – seemed hardly to notice that the chore had been done. And yet Mr Hammond, clearly older than his grandfather had been when he died, still seemed interested and engaged with the world. Would he gain pleasure from having a renovated house? After all, he wouldn't be able to experience it in any tangible way if he was too infirm to leave his room. Perhaps it was the *thought* of it that was significant? Mark suddenly felt a great urgency to get the work done while Mr Hammond was still alive. He felt pained by the knowledge that he liked Mr Hammond and that Mr Hammond would, in all likelihood, soon be dead. Thinking this, he realised that he was fascinated by the old man. How was it that he felt so strongly about this person – whom he had only just met – when the death of his own grandfather, whom he had loved, had arrived almost as a surprise to him and had caused him no lasting or intense pain, only a temporary sense of emptiness.

The kitchen, he noticed, had a good stock of food. There was a vegetable rack which always had potatoes and onions, plus a variable selection of other vegetables, most of which needed a good wash and looked as if they'd come from someone's garden. The cupboards also had pulses, rice, pasta and herbs and spices, so that Mark could prepare himself simple meals with ease. There was a conspicuous absence of meat. Each tenant was allocated a cupboard for their own additional stores, but Mark's remained empty at first.

It struck him as odd that, in the first few weeks, when he was working on the communal areas of the house, he didn't meet any of his fellow tenants. Given that he would have to do work in each of their rooms it was inevitable that he would meet them at some point, but it was comforting somehow that so far – with the exception of his brief meeting with Mr Hammond – he only saw Tara. She had keys to each of the rooms and had agreed to take him round them so that he could assess what needed to be done. A notice had been put up above the telephone table in the hall letting residents know what was going on.

In the fourth week, when he was doing some preparatory work in the hall, stripping back the wallpaper and removing the patches of plaster that were crumbling, he met Paul, a man of perhaps fifty or fifty-five, who stopped and said – somewhat belligerently, Mark thought – 'Oh, *you're* the new handyman that Tara's hired.'

His hair was greying and a little unkempt. He had a comfortable suit on and looked to Mark like the sort of person who might want to sell him dodgy car insurance.

'Hello,' said Mark, standing up and extending his hand, 'I'm Mark.'

Paul ignored Mark's hand and said, 'Well, I'm Paul and you can leave my room alone. No one is allowed into my room. *No one*. Ever.'

'I'll give you plenty of warning when I need to have access,' Mark said. 'But there's a few things that I'll be needing to do in there at some point. The wiring, for example.'

'No,' Paul said. 'I mean it. Stay out of my room.'

He marched off up the stairs leaving Mark feeling bemused.

He didn't have any further chance to wonder about him, as at that point the doorbell rang and a delivery of materials arrived.

When he saw Tara, after lunch, he told her of his brief conversation with Paul and she smiled.

'He has no choice,' she said. 'It's not as though rewiring his room is an unreasonable request. Tell me when you want to do it and I'll negotiate it with him. In the meantime, perhaps we can leave his room alone.'

There were eight letting rooms, including Tara's. One of them was empty – the room that had been advertised and which Mark hadn't been able to afford. There was also a kitchen, toilet, bathroom and Mr Hammond's attic suite. This meant that as well as Tara, Mr Hammond, himself and Paul, there were four further residents. Tara took him round all the rooms but Paul's that afternoon. It was an odd experience, they were so different in 'feel'. The first, on the ground floor at the front, was inhabited by a fastidious woman. She had a slightly gothic taste in clothes. A dark red dress with black lace trimmings hung on the back of her door, while a small midnight blue hat – almost a skull cap, but with a voluminous black veil – hung over a vase on the mantelpiece, beside a carriage clock and several small china ornaments of cherubs and angels. The furniture was Victorian in feel, with rather worn velvet upholstery in green and red. The fireplace (clearly not used for its original purpose) had an ornamental fireguard, but the hearth itself contained a fan of peacock's feathers. The patterned carpet had an almost heraldic feel to it, but again was rather worn, especially by the door.

Opposite Mark's room was another smallish room – though larger than Mark's – which was sparse where the first room had been cluttered, and which smelled strongly of stale cigarette smoke. There was an ash tray on the windowsill piled high with cigarette ends. Tara and Paul had their rooms on the first floor. The other two rooms on that floor looked out onto the back garden of the next house up the hill, and were astonishingly tidy and astonishingly untidy, respectively. The first had the most neatly made up bed he had ever seen, the sheet being folded back just so, with a small triangular folded edge that made Mark want to measure it to see if it was precisely equilateral. The last room had coffee mugs, magazines, clothes, shoes and books littered across every surface. There was a smell of incense too, with a hint of something musky underneath it that made Mark want to stay there and browse.

'Well,' said Tara, after they'd finished, 'have you seen all you need to?'

'Yes,' Mark told her. 'The preparation work on the communal areas will probably take me a while longer, and then I can get started on this lot.'

So began one of the happiest periods of Mark's life. It was fascinating to him that each job he did was enjoyable – plastering, rewiring, painting, even the work he did on the central heating and the bathroom, which was so eccentrically plumbed that he had to do more work on the piping than he expected. Some of the work was particularly intricate, and he enjoyed having the time to devote to doing it properly. The sash windows especially needed a great deal of painstaking work. It made him realise that, in the past, the work had propelled him into a bad temper because he resented being asked to do it. It had nothing to do with the tasks themselves. He also realised that, from the age of eleven, when his dad had first roped him into preparing woodwork for redecoration, he'd been learning useful skills. Even though he was unwilling to give up his free time, he'd still been learning a skill. And he'd always had more pocket money than his friends, a fact that he'd enjoyed even though he'd resented having to work for it. Now, he held a conflicted position when he thought of it. On one hand, honestly looking back, if he'd been given the choice, he was clear that he would have chosen to have less pocket money and more time. But he couldn't deny that he was able to make the most of this opportunity here in Mr Hammond's house precisely because of what he'd learned.

He gradually became aware that what had been damaging to him hadn't been what his father had asked him to do, but the resentment with which he'd responded to being asked to do it. He remembered his cousin Rod, and those holiday periods in the summer when Rod had come to stay. Rod had loved all this doing-up of houses and the renovation work that it involved; he'd loved learning the skills, and getting some money for it, which he spent on outdoor things – a bicycle, a surf board, and finally a one-man sailing dinghy. No wonder he'd ended up as a gardener, given his love of the outdoors.

Now, Mark's work became a series of tasks done apparently for their own sake, or perhaps for Mr Hammond's, although that was an odd concept, given that he hardly knew Mr Hammond, who in any case never saw any of Mark's handiwork.

The room that he'd originally been offered became a temporary holding space for the tenants while Mark rewired and decorated their rooms. Oddly, given that Mark was in the house all the time, he never saw any of these tenants, except for the bad tempered Paul. This was partly because Mark was not an early riser and the tenants had usually left the house by the time he got up in the morning. But this only partially accounted for it and only explained the mornings. He would often, especially in the later afternoon, hear footsteps going past the room he was working in, or hear a toilet flushing. Or see washing up on the draining board in the kitchen. But he never saw the people who made these noises, or who left their dishes out to dry. He communicated with them about when he needed access to their rooms by leaving notes on the hall table. Tara had told him their names. Miss Bowley (the gothic one), Mr Pollard (the smoker), Mrs Armstrong (the tidy one) and Ms Wright (the untidy one), plus Mr Bastock – AKA Paul.

Paul saw him on several occasions as the months passed, and was always either irritable or belligerent. Once, when they were in the kitchen together, he said to Mark, 'You do realise you're being taken for a ride here, don't you?'

'In what way?' Mark asked him.

'How much is Mr Hammond paying you to do all this? It's a job worth thousands. I bet he's not giving you anything except your room and your food. You should bill him a proper hourly rate and then he'd realise how he's exploiting you.'

Mark didn't respond to this.

'Anyway, it's all the same to me,' Paul told him. 'I don't give a shit about anyone in this house, least of all Mr Hammond. So long as you leave me alone, and stay out of my room, I'll be happy.'

'Actually,' said Mark, 'I'll need to get into your room next week or the week after that. Tara must have had a word with you about it. You can move into the spare room for a few days while I do the work.'

'I've made it clear to her that you can't. I *hate* change. My room is quite alright as it is.'

'Look,' said Mark, 'I can't rewire the house and upgrade the central heating and just leave your room out of it.'

'Of course you can,' said Paul and left.

A couple of days later, Mr Hammond asked to see Mark. Mark's response to this was one of both pleasure and anxiety. Pleasure because he liked Mr Hammond, and anxiety because he couldn't shake off the feeling that the only reason why he'd ever be summoned upstairs would be to be told off.

When Mark went into the attic room, Mr Hammond looked even more frail – something Mark would hardly have believed possible. He was wrapped in a maroon towelling dressing gown which came up almost to his chin and which was fastened by a golden chord around his waist. He was wearing a pair of grandfatherly chequered slippers. His attitude of cultured poise lent a sense of dignity to a costume that could easily have seemed pathetic.

When asked how he was getting on, Mark explained the difficulty with Paul.

'Ah, Paul,' said Mr Hammond.

'But what should I do?' Mark asked. 'I really do need to get into his room.'

'Yes,' he said. 'I suppose you do.'

'Do you have any advice?' Mark asked.

Mr Hammond smiled kindly. 'No.'

This was rather nonplussing. Mark had somehow imagined that Mr Hammond was a repository of all knowledge, good advice and insight, and it was confusing to find him so unhelpful.

'And how is it going, *apart* from Paul?' Mr Hammond asked.

'It's going well,' Mark told him. 'By the way, thank you for getting decent materials for me. It makes a real difference to the quality of the outcome.'

'And how is it going *for you?*' he asked.

Mark thought for a few moments.

'Actually,' he said, laughing, 'I'm finding all this work incredibly restful.' He paused thoughtfully. 'It feels funny to say that, when I'm keeping myself so busy, but I go for whole days at a time without thinking of my old home, or the people and the job that I've left behind. I haven't felt unsafe, or worried about the £40,000 that I owe. . . I haven't set foot outside the front door, and I haven't wanted to. Every day I can look at what I've done and get a sense of achievement and pleasure.'

Mr Hammond nodded. 'I'm pleased that you have taken this refuge,' he said. 'But I have to tell you that there are two kinds of refuge. It's a semantic trick, in a way, you see. I offered you "refuge", but what does that mean? I said you would be safe here from the man to whom you owe money, and that was true. But you are not entirely safe from yourself. Perhaps I should have made that clear to you when you first arrived here. But you were *in extremis* and needed refuge – as in shelter – which is what I have been able to offer you. But genuine refuge is not something that you can build from bricks and plaster.'

'No,' said Mark, 'I am aware of that.'

Actually, he hadn't the slightest idea what Mr Hammond meant, but he felt too foolish to ask him to explain.

'Good,' said Mr Hammond. 'There is also something else that I must tell you. I shall be going into hospital at some point for a minor operation, but as I am so old I may be away for a week or two. Perhaps you could use that time to do whatever needs to be done to my rooms?'

'Of course,' said Mark, 'that sounds very practical.'

'Good, good, my boy.'

As Mark went back to his work, at the back of his mind he could hear Paul's poisonous assertion that Mr Hammond was simply exploiting him as cheap labour. Although this hadn't previously occurred to Mark, now that it had been pointed out, there was a part of him that felt he was getting a raw deal, financially at least. And yet. . . this time in the house had given him peace of a kind that he had never experienced before. And wasn't peace of mind priceless? Although he wasn't completely sure what Mr Hammond had meant when he'd said there were two kinds of refuge, it certainly made him aware of the fact that what he was doing here was finite. There would come a time when he would have to venture outside, to work on the exterior of the house, and there would come a time when he would have finished the house completely and would have to start looking for work else-where. This thought was so disconcerting that he tried to put it from his mind, not altogether successfully.

The following day, Mark asked Tara if she could negotiate entry to Paul's room for the following week. He also left a note to this effect on the hall table, as he'd done for the other resi-dents. Tara was clear that Mark should simply start work on Paul's room on the appointed day, whether Paul had agreed or not. Over the next couple of days, he completely finished his own small room and the upstairs landing. It was extraordinary to watch a space being transformed from shabbiness to elegance. It only needed a decent carpet to finish it off, but he would lay that last. Despite a sense of impending conflict with

Paul, Mark continued to feel a kind of synergistic connection with the work that he was doing.

On Monday morning of the following week, he let himself into Paul's room and made a start on the rewiring. It was a straightforward job that required Mark to remove a couple of the skirting boards on either side of the door so that he could sort out this part of the first floor ring main. He also needed to chisel a small runnel up the wall to where he was going to install the new plug points. Once he'd done this, he got out the two double plugs that he was going to fit, and his cable. There was something pleasing in the methodical nature of this work. It didn't need a great deal of thought, but it did require a kind of meticulous attention that was totally absorbing. The morning passed in calm concentration. Mark would hum a song to himself from time to time, and whistle a tune that he made up, which reminded him a little of the song that he'd sung in the caves with the Baker's Yard brigade. It made him want to go back to that cave on his own to see what it might sound like, to whistle like this, but with the benefit of those fantastic acoustics. Thinking like this made him miss Holly, Don, Ailsa and the others, and it made him sad to think of how he'd lost his trust in them.

When he'd finished the wiring in Paul's room he collected up the wire trimmings that were scattered about the floor. As he was gathering them into a little heap, he noticed that the cable itself was white lighting flex. He stared at it briefly, confused. He'd been using this very cable for all the other wiring work in the house, and he'd been absolutely sure that it was the correct, standard 2.5mm$^2$ grey cable for a 30 amp fuse. But now, somehow, it was wrong. It was completely wrong, not to say dangerously wrong.

He went back into his own room and unscrewed the plug

socket there. Sure enough, the wiring in this room was incorrect too – white and insubstantial instead of grey and thick. He felt a thump in his chest that was a mixture of embarrassment, disappointment and shame. How could he have put the wrong wiring in without noticing? Surely that was impossible? He would have to ask Tara to order more, and he would have to rewire the whole place a second time. Fortunately, the rest of the house was still on the old circuit, so it wouldn't mean having to switch things off, but when he thought of having to go into each room to take the skirting boards up again, he felt a wave of tiredness and misery.

The embarrassment that went with this reminded him of getting things wrong at school and when he went to see Tara, he couldn't help feeling that she was going to punish him – give him detention, or something worse. He was quite willing to take responsibility for his mistake, but why did it make him feel so ashamed?

Tara's response completely surprised him: she laughed.

'You're blushing so hard I can feel the heat of it from here,' she said. 'Don't worry, I'm not going to tell you off. How much of the wiring had you done?'

'All but Mr Hammond's suite,' he told her.

'Poor Mark,' she said. 'I hope this won't make you give up.'

'No,' he said, 'of course not.'

'You say of course not, but isn't it at precisely this point that people most often *do* give up and wander off into the blue, dragging a sense of failure behind them?'

Mark sighed, but didn't say anything.

'Well, give me the correct specification for the wire that you need and I will have it delivered in due course. I expect there are plenty of other things you can be getting on with.'

'Yes,' Mark agreed.

'Well then,' she said, 'that's what I suggest you do.'

He went to make himself a cup of tea in the kitchen, and sat at the table there, looking out over the town and wondering what he might do next. Despite his upbeat response to Tara, there was something hugely demotivating about getting something so completely wrong, and the thought of having to do it all over again was overwhelming. It seemed inconceivable that he might get pleasure out of redoing a job that he'd already thought he'd done so well.

As he was finishing his tea, Paul came into the room, walked over to Mark, thrust his face so close that their noses were almost touching, and said, 'You've been in my room.'

'Yes,' said Mark.

Paul turned and walked out. Mark watched him go and felt a flash of anger. It wasn't as if there was anything odd or embarrassing about Paul's room, so it seemed particularly unfriendly of him to not have wanted to let Mark in. Privacy was something that Mark respected, but this kind of behaviour had no logic.

Mark made himself a second cup of tea and drank it slowly, considering how to explain himself to Paul in a friendly way. As he was washing up his mug, he heard a sound from the hallway that sounded like an object falling down the stairs. He went out to have a look, and saw immediately that water was pouring through the ceiling of the hall and had brought down the patch of new plastering he'd done above the foot of the stairs.

He ran to the cupboard under the stairs, where the stop-cock was, and turned the water off, then on to the kitchen where he took a couple of the biggest saucepans and the washing up bowl and dashed back to put them where they might catch some of the water that was coming down. The flow was showing no sign of diminishing and Mark stared at it as it cascaded into the hall. He hurried upstairs to check the bathroom but there were no taps running. He went on to his own room and grabbed a towel, then went back down to drop it into the water on the hall carpet, wringing it repeatedly into the saucepans which needed to be emptied several times before the flow of water began to subside. Once it had slowed to a steady dripping, he left his wrung-out towel on the floor, and the pans in place, then ran up the stairs three at a time, and banged on Paul's door.

As he waited, he noticed that he was panting, whether from the exertion of running up the stairs or from anger, he couldn't tell. When Paul opened his door, Mark shouted, 'What have you done! My plastering downstairs has been *ruined*!'

Paul came out and looked down the staircase, and then laughed.

'Good,' he said.

Mark felt rage surging up.

'You!' he said. 'Why did you do this?'

'I won't deny I'm pleased,' he said. 'I'm pleased that your little attempt at home improvement has ground to a halt. If there's one thing I despise it's the smugness of people like you. You're so self-satisfied and sure of what you're doing, I can't help getting pleasure when it turns out wrong. But please don't blame me for what has happened.'

'Come off it,' said Mark, 'you left the kitchen looking purposeful a few minutes ago, and you looked obscenely pleased when you saw what had happened.'

'Like I said, I *am* pleased it has gone wrong, but that's your fault and nothing to do with me. I don't care about you, Mark, or what you think. I want to be left alone.'

Paul closed the door of his room firmly. Mark wondered whether to bang on it again, but decided to find the source of the outpour instead. He could decide how to react to Paul later.

He could find nothing. Although the bathroom had been recently used, there was no water on the floor. Up in the roof, the water tank was full and undamaged and the piping in good shape. So, tentatively, he went back to the under stairs cupboard and turned the stop-cock back on. Nothing happened. He went back into the hall. Still nothing.

There was only one thing it could have been – some problem with the plumbing of the bath. He took his toolbox up to the bathroom and pulled back the lino. He'd done this before, to get the piping done, and it came up easily. Fortunately he was still waiting for some new floor covering to be delivered so it didn't matter if he damaged the old lino in taking it up again. Once the boards were bare, he lifted the two boards that were nearest to the bath: Nothing. By the sink: Nothing. Under the window: Yes, it was soaking under there. On his knees, Mark stared at the plumbing for some time with his mouth open. The pipes under this part of the floor didn't meet at all. It was bizarre. The outflow from the bath simply stopped. There was a gap of nearly a foot between Mark's new plumbing and the old outflow. Either someone had tampered with it, or he'd done an astonishingly bad job. It didn't make sense. Like the mismatching of the electrical wiring, it didn't seem to be the kind of mistake that anyone would ever make. But here was the evidence, writ large. He put his hands to his head. Was there no end to his incompetence?

But there was also something else tugging at a corner of his mind.

He wondered how many people had had baths in the week or so since he'd replumbed the bathroom. He himself had had a quick bath each evening after finishing his work, so the mistake made even less sense, unless. . . unless someone had carefully lifted the lino and the floorboards, removed a length of pipe, then carefully put it all back again. But there were far easier ways to wreak havoc in the house. He might as well wonder whether someone had taken the time to remove all his good wiring and replace it with lighting flex.

It was a mystery.

It wasn't a difficult job to join the two pipes together. He had the blow torch and the materials, but the cause of the mistake was still baffling, and very upsetting. Now, he was going to have to check all his plumbing as well as replacing the wiring, and he would have to replaster the hall and redecorate where the walls had been soaked. Thank goodness he'd been leaving the kitchen until last!

That evening, he went up to see Mr Hammond. He had to wait a long time after knocking before he heard any sound, but eventually he heard Mr Hammond calling, 'Come in.' He went in. The room was catching the evening sunshine, and was glowing with red twilight. It was a warm light, like the inviting glow of a camp fire. As he looked around the room Mark made a mental note of what work needed to be done on it, once he had access to it. The carpet needed to be ripped up and thrown out, for a start. Mr Hammond was sitting in an old, comfortable armchair with a book in his lap, and looked as if he might have been snoozing, wrapped in the same red dressing gown as before.

'Good evening, my boy,' said Mr Hammond. 'How can I be of service?'

Mark explained what had happened, and how surprised and embarrassed he was that all his efforts at doing up the house had gone so terribly wrong.

'I can't understand it at all,' he said. 'I know my competence, and this just shouldn't have happened. It's not that I'm unwilling to accept responsibility for what I've done. I have always taken responsibility for my actions, but it still doesn't make sense.'

'Hmm,' said Mr Hammond, 'that does sound perplexing. What do you propose to do about it?'

'Well, clearly I'm going to have to completely redo a lot of what I'd already done, and I'll have to revise my estimate of how long it will take.'

'Is there any pressing reason why it can't take longer?'

'No.'

'Then there is no problem. Carry on.'

Mark looked at Mr Hammond and realised that he'd again arrived expecting to be told off. He thought of the rages his father flew into whenever things went wrong. The contrast between his father and Mr Hammond was so profound that it almost made him laugh.

'I also want to apologise,' Mark said. 'You must be questioning my competence, and I can't blame you. It's very generous of you to allow me to stay on and continue.'

'It's a question of awareness,' Mr Hammond told him. 'I suppose I should have warned you of this. I'm not quite sure how to put it in words that will capture what I mean, but I would start by saying that your skills as a builder are secondary to the awareness that you bring to your task.'

'But I was under the impression that I *was* paying attention to what I was doing.'

'Ah yes,' said Mr Hammond, 'the material task, you see. You were paying attention to the material task, but where was your intention? *What* was your intention?'

'My intention was to renovate this house.'

Mr Hammond smiled.

'And a very good intention that is. Do you know *why* you are renovating it?'

'I'm renovating it for you,' Mark said, and as the words were spoken, he remembered Don challenging him about the window that he'd intended to replace at Baker's Yard. Was this the same?

'But are you?' said Mr Hammond. 'Really? I will be dead soon. All this rewiring and infrastructure, it's going to last twenty or thirty years, and some of it far longer than that if you do it well.'

'Mr Hammond,' Mark said, 'all I know is that you have offered me refuge. I have felt safe here. I haven't thought of the outside world at all while I've been working on this house, and that is a precious – a priceless – gift. I don't care why you asked me to do this work. If I'm not doing it for you, or if you don't want to explain why you offered me the work, that's fine. I don't need to know.'

'But awareness, Mark, is everything,' he said.

On his way downstairs, Mark bumped into Paul on the landing.

'I'm sorry I accused you of that flooding earlier,' he said. 'It was my fault. I messed up the plumbing in the bathroom.'

Paul frowned slightly. 'I told you,' he said. 'Things were fine as they were. Tara tells me you're going to have to re-do the wiring in my room. She said that it's actually *worse* after your fiddling than it was before. Well, that says it all, Mr Handyman. You're no better than the last one.'

He went into his room, and as he shut the door he laughed loudly and nastily. Humiliation was not something that Mark had often felt in his life, but he certainly felt it now.

# 6. Sloth and Torpor

When Mark woke the following day, his body felt heavy and his mind was dull, as if he was coming down with something. He lay on his back staring at the ceiling, his thoughts wandering here and there but settling on nothing. He watched as three small flies zig-zagged about in the corner of the room. Their sudden sharp turns seemed so purposeful, their trajectories so delineated, and yet they got nowhere. On and on they went, moving rapidly, but essentially standing still. His work on the house had been like that. He'd been so certain of his tasks, he'd been so focused, and yet he'd achieved nothing. He turned his head and looked out of the window at a patch of uninteresting sky. As a moody patch of cloud drifted past, he realised that the enthusiasm he'd had for the renovations had totally evaporated. What could he do now, anyway? He would have to wait for the hallway to dry out before he could begin to rectify the water damage. He also had to wait for the correct wiring to arrive before he could replace that.

Of course, there were plenty of smaller jobs to be done, and quite a lot of painting, which he normally found restful. But somehow he couldn't see the point. There was the exterior of the house to be worked on, too, but Mark wasn't yet ready for the outside world. Instead, he wasted the morning sitting in the kitchen, drinking tea and looking out over the town. It occurred to him then that there wasn't anything he could use to distract himself. He had no access to a television, to music, to a computer or to books or magazines. There were Mr Hammond's books, but to ask to borrow one would be to admit that his motivation had changed. He tried to remember if he'd ever done this before – sitting with no obvious task to do and only his thoughts for company. He couldn't remember clearly, but he didn't think he had. It was maddening.

The sun was shining, and it was warm in his room. The sea looked inviting, and Mark suddenly wondered why he'd been so happy to shut himself away like this. Outside, it was warm. The summer was nearly over – a shocking realisation for Mark, who had hardly noticed it passing as he worked on the house. And now it was waning, and it was no time to be indoors. The danger he'd felt before he moved here seemed almost inconsequential now, as he sat and experienced his boredom. Idly, he ran his fingers over the scarring on his ear, but even then it was hard to remember the terror he'd felt when Sean had sliced the lobe off.

Eventually, in the late morning, he could bear it no more and he changed into some of the clothes that he'd bought from Wim and Ingrid. He'd been living in the previous handyman's old overalls for weeks now, and it felt strange to wear anything else. When he put on his blue trousers he found a £10 note in the pocket. It had been so insignificant when he'd been at Baker's Yard that he hadn't even remembered that it was there. What a difference it would have made, though, when he'd been sleeping rough! He felt a brief prickle of emotion as he thought of it.

He left the house and wandered down through the town to the sea. It was moderately busy down on the seafront. People were wearing tee-shirts and summer clothes. The water, when he got to the shore, was still and lethargic as it lapped slowly in across the sand. The beach was quite crowded, and Mark guessed that it must be a weekend. He'd completely lost track of time, shut away in the house on the hill. It was odd to realise that the world had continued about its business all this time, oblivious to his little life and his problems.

Lots of people were swimming, and he was tempted to join them, but he had no trunks and so he ended up leaving the beach feeling rather intimidated, if he was honest, by the busyness around him. As he thought of the money in his pocket he realised that he hadn't been paid anything in all the time he'd been there. Mr Hammond had mentioned 'pocket money' but none had materialised, and he hadn't thought to ask about it. Besides, pocket money was a relative term. To him the price of a cup of coffee would be decent pocket money today. For some, the £40,000 that he'd been asked to return to the mysterious Jonathan might be virtually insignificant.

There was a smart café above the beach, looking out across the sea and he decided to go in. The coffee, when it arrived, had a curious effect on him. The flavour – strong, and full – and the aroma, were so redolent of the sensations that the outside world could offer him, that he suddenly found himself yearning for some further connection with what he'd always regarded as ordinary life: meeting friends, eating good food, drinking good wine. . . He hadn't expected this experience to be so wistful, or so melancholy.

The cake was delicious, too. He'd been eating basic foods

for a while, and that had seemed right at the time, but this cake was so rich, sweet and satisfying that he immediately wanted to make this café a regular morning stop-off. For some reason, he had no sense of fear or personal vulnerability, and it was difficult to remember that he ever had. A moment of unease flickered across his consciousness but it subsided quickly, as though some kind of protective soothing mechanism was coming into play. For as long as his work on the house had been going well, it was easy to stay indoors and get on with it. Once it had started going wrong, the house had stopped feeling like a sanctuary. What was happening that he now felt able to risk the outside world? At the back of his mind, it seemed like madness, but the part of him that was scared was simply too quiet to make itself heard. It was subtly disturbing to Mark that, at the back of his awareness, he knew that he'd done this often in his life – knowing he 'shouldn't' be doing what he was doing, and yet doing it anyway. Wasn't this how he'd kept at bay the imperative that had kept shouting out to him to change his life? He'd simply ignored that voice, and had taken antidepressants to further subdue it. He had numbed his whole being rather than listen.

In addition, perhaps, there was also a self destructive part of him that felt he no longer deserved refuge in Mr Hammond's house, and so was sabotaging his safety. It was impossible for Mark to bring any clarity to this and so he gave up and subsided into an appreciation of the sensual pleasure of what he was eating and drinking.

He wondered, as he sat, whether he should ask Mr Hammond for some money so that he could come down here regularly for a treat when he'd done good work in the house. But this thought caused an echo of the humiliation he'd felt the previous evening. Good work. Had he done *any* good work?

Did he deserve any reward for the work that he'd done so far?

Before leaving, he went to the cash till to pay. The cashier rang up the bill and as he turned to fish the money from his pocket, he saw her looking at his damaged ear. He distinctly noticed a look of surprise and perhaps shock flit across her face when she saw it.

When he handed the money to her she mumbled something and wouldn't take it.

'Is anything wrong?' he asked.

She looked embarrassed and shook her head.

'No, no, it's nothing,' she told him. 'You don't have to pay. This one's on the house.'

He looked at the note in his hand, and then back to her, but she smiled at him and said, 'Have a nice day.'

He was about to question this, but she'd already started talking to the couple behind him so he didn't have a chance. He left, feeling confused as to why this had happened, and started back towards the house. As he did so, he saw Natalie on the other side of the street. She was with the two friends from Club Covert that she'd been arguing with on the day he'd given her the £4,000. She saw him immediately and blanched. He could see quite clearly that if she had been able to hide, she would have done so. But they'd established eye contact now, and so it was too late.

She crossed over to him, looking anxious.

'Mark,' she said, 'how are you? Oh, God, what's happened to your ear?'

'It's okay,' he said. 'How are you?'

She ignored his question.

'Look,' she said, 'I feel really terrible about all this. You must think so badly of me. But there's one thing you've got to know. I didn't steal your money, I really didn't.'

'What are you talking about?'

'It didn't occur to me that there would be any consequences. I'm so sorry, Mark. You were so sweet and generous, and now look what's happened.'

'Natalie,' Mark said, 'the ear thing has nothing to do with you.'

'I went round to Baker's Yard to talk to you,' she said, 'but a woman there said you'd moved out.'

'I'm living up near the top of the Old Town, now,' he told her.

'Mark,' she said, 'I've got to go. I wanted to come over and say how sorry I am, that's all. Please try to forget that you saw me again.'

She left and went back to her friends and Mark watched as they walked down onto the esplanade, disappearing round the corner and into the sunshine. He was stunned. What had she meant? He turned to walk back up to the house, and as he did so, it hit him. She'd told the person she'd owed money to about his cash! There was no way he could know what she'd actually said, but it was frighteningly easy to imagine the gist of it. She might have taken the money round to pay off her debt, and then she could easily have been asked, 'Where did you get this from?' He could almost hear her response: 'You wouldn't believe it. There's this guy who lives in Baker's Yard and he's got thousands of pounds in cash stashed under his bed!'

The thought that followed this was that Natalie must have owed the money to a criminal, if their reaction to her information was to come to Baker's Yard and steal his money. It fitted, of course. She hated working at Covert, so there must be some reason why she needed to stay on in a place like that.

When he got back to the house, Mark forced himself to do

some work. He chose a single, simple task: he would work on the banisters up to the first floor. Several of them were broken or damaged. It was one of those small, straightforward jobs that he'd been leaving until the major tasks had been done. It was also something that had nothing to do with the other tasks that he'd messed up, so it had no connotations of failure or repetition.

He'd ordered the replacement banisters from a hardware catalogue. They were of a standard size and pattern, so they had been neither difficult to find nor expensive, and he had stored them in the cupboard under the stairs. Going out into the communal area to get the replacement spindles, he heard footsteps upstairs as someone crossed to the bathroom. This had been happening a lot lately, people wandering about the house, heard but unseen. It was a little unnerving, especially as he'd given up on the possibility of ever meeting half the household. These other residents didn't seem like people at all, just increasingly sinister noises in the distance. Taps running, a toilet flushing, an occasional distant click as a bedroom door was shut. Somehow it was easier to face Tara and Mr Hammond, and even Paul, than to constantly worry that he might meet one of these strangers in the capacity of a blundering, havoc-wreaking handyman.

He took the three new banisters to the staircase, and saw immediately that they were of the wrong kind. His stomach lurched. Trying to stay calm, he looked again, helplessly, but the replacement banisters remained stubbornly wrong. Certainly, the newels matched the old ones, but the new spindles were fluted whereas the spindles on the existing banisters were of a classic style that was quite different. He stared at them with a sense of disbelief and an overwhelming feeling of 'Oh no, not again.' He was sure that he'd ordered the correct supplies, so what could have happened? Heavy hearted, he went to get the catalogue that he'd ordered them from, and turned to the relevant page. And there was the evidence, once again staring him in the face: A thick red circle in felt pen, around the type of banister he was currently holding in his clenched left hand. He'd circled the wrong ones. It was his fault. He'd messed up the order.

Mark couldn't believe it. What was happening? He couldn't touch anything without it going wrong. What was the point of doing anything, if this was going to be the result?

He went back to his room and sat for a while, feeling totally blank, and wondered what to do. On one hand, even though Mr Hammond had been kind about it so far, Mark didn't want to admit to him that still more things had gone wrong. It also seemed particularly unfair that he'd been out of the house today and that it had been such an intense and pleasurable experience. He wanted to go out more, and have money to do so. But what could he say now? 'I'm sorry, Mr Hammond, I've messed up every job in the house, and now I want you to give me some money so I can go out whenever I want, to sit in cafés drinking coffee and eating cake.' No, it wouldn't work. Much better to steer clear of Mr Hammond altogether.

He went downstairs, confused and upset, and cooked himself a simple meal from the ingredients in the kitchen. As he ate alone at the big table, he thought about Natalie. If a criminal acquaintance of hers had stolen his money from Baker's Yard, then it couldn't have been Sean, or any of the Baker's Yard lot who'd done it after all. . .

He felt a sudden wash of embarrassment at this realisation, about having worked it out so wrongly. But it figured, in a way. He'd got everything else wrong, so why not this, too? And it didn't change his predicament in any case. The threat still remained. However much he'd disregarded it earlier, he was still £40,000 in debt to Sean, or to the mysterious Jonathan that Sean represented. On thinking this, Mark shuddered. Why hadn't that seemed to matter earlier in the day? Perhaps, he thought, it was a side effect of refuge. You end up taking it for granted. Though perhaps another side effect of refuge was that it could become a prison.

The next few days passed extraordinarily easily. Mark did nothing except sleep late into the morning each day and then potter about, drinking tea and eating his simple food. The cable arrived but it lay untouched in the cupboard under the stairs. September was passing, but the weather was warm and it was remarkable how quickly the hallway dried out after the flooding. Within a week, he could easily have started replastering above the stairs. But he left it. He kept the window open in his bedroom and he could smell freshly mown grass from the meadow at the top of the hill. It was a scent that reminded him of indolence and freedom, but he felt completely separate from it, and there was a vulnerability that went with that. Whereas he'd wandered down to the sea quite happily a few days earlier, now it seemed dangerous to even walk the couple of hundred metres up to the field.

He realised, as his second, and then his third and fourth week of inactivity began, that he was waiting. He wasn't sure what he was waiting for, only that he was waiting. He wasn't even sure which particular quality of the experience made it feel like waiting. It was different to the ten days of waiting that he'd experienced whilst sleeping rough, and it was different to all the other periods of waiting that he could remember in his life – to get the results of his 'A' levels and then his finals; to hear whether he'd got a job; to become a father – in all of these he'd had a goal that either would or would not be achieved. But this waiting had no goal that he could put his finger on, except perhaps to feel safe. But that was too nebulous, and in any case he wasn't quite sure what it meant.

One day, as he stared out of the window at great towers of dark cloud building in the distance, he remembered that during his adolescence he'd spent a lot of time waiting to become grown up. There had been something of the same quality to that experience – it had been both exciting and scary, and the specifics of it were strangely obscure. What had he expected it to feel like, to finally become an adult?

He'd imagined that he would know what he wanted. He'd be sure of himself; he'd feel settled. Know his mind. What a disappointment that had turned out to be, one way and another! All that turbulence. All that longing. All that expectation that it would turn out well if only he could get a good degree and find a woman who wanted to settle down with him and have their children. . .

When the weather broke towards the end of October, it rained heavily and he felt a little happier about being indoors. After another couple of days, he realised something that he'd lost sight of over the years – that waiting is an activity of itself. Hadn't he been doing it always, without knowing it? Having something to wait *for* was the luxury in life because there was focus in that. But what a curious realisation that you can simply be waiting.

Another month of inactivity began, or perhaps even two. Mark didn't know what date it was because he had completely lost track of time. There was so little to differentiate the days it was hard to tell them apart, and when Tara finally came to see him, he had no idea how long he'd been inactive. She knocked on his door and came in.

'Hello Mark,' she said with characteristic directness, 'I expect you know why I'm here.'

'I can guess,' he said.

'Mr Hammond was asking me about your progress, and I said I would come and ask you about it.'

'As you must be aware, I haven't done anything for ages.'

'I don't make any assumptions at all about whether you are doing anything or not,' she told him. 'Just because I don't see you working on anything doesn't mean that you're not.'

'Well, I'm not,' he said.

'Ah.'

She came in and sat down on the edge of his bed and looked at him.

'You see, the thing about refuge,' she told him, 'is that it comes with some strings attached, at least in this case it does. I think we were explicit about that when we offered you this room – that you would work on the house. That you would give us your time in lieu of rent.'

Mark didn't say anything. He could think of nothing to say.

'I'll leave you to think about this,' she said. 'But in the meantime it's important for you to know that this room will not be available to you indefinitely if you don't keep your side of the bargain. Please, don't see this as a threat. It's not meant that way at all. Rather, it is a statement of fact, and may be an incentive to you. Come and see me if there's anything you want to discuss, or if there is any way in which Mr Hammond or I can be of help.'

She left and Mark wondered what he should do. He had no confidence that he could do any job, no matter how small, without it going disastrously wrong. So what was the point of trying at all? Because there was no clear answer to this, he did nothing, and went back to that sense of waiting that had become so familiar recently. It was a state in which time passed surprisingly quickly, without apparent effort.

One of the side effects of this state of mind was that he began to forget why he'd come here. What had he been trying to do, anyway, running away like that when he had a comfortable life and a lovely little son who needed him? To try and find a way to become happy? Or a little less unhappy? But what was that all about? Hadn't he wanted to find a way of living his life without compromise? Hadn't he been looking for integrity? It all seemed a little mad, really. It was as if he'd set out to become more himself, only to find out that he didn't have the faintest idea who he really was. And lying on his bed, looking out at the dark ragged storm clouds, gave him no insight at all as far as that was concerned. His life seemed totally compromised right now. He'd lost any sense of purpose, or confidence. He was trapped in this house, surrounded by jobs that he'd messed up one way or another. He was trapped, too, by a sense of obligation to Tara and Mr Hammond, whom he liked and respected and whom he'd failed, utterly.

Perhaps inevitably, the desire came over Mark to leave the house once more and go down to the sea. He was by this time so bored that the concept of refuge was becoming meaningless to him. It would have been almost a relief to bump into Sean, just so that something might happen. The whole business of coming down here to make a new life for himself now seemed laughable. Part of him wanted to go up to Mr Hammond and say 'I am so useless, I might as well go out and sleep on the street again and accept whatever might be waiting for me out there.'

He'd imagined that, in time, he'd have been able to get some work as a renovator and decorator in town while he orientated himself and his life, but what was the point of marketing a skill that seemed to have deserted him?

'Sod it,' he thought, with wilful abandon, and changed into his colourful clothes and left the house. He still had the money that he'd had last time he'd gone out. The fact that the cashier at the café had refused to charge him for his coffee and cake meant that he'd be able to have coffee and cake again. But even this didn't particularly appeal to him today. There was, in fact, nothing he actually wanted to do. It was as if leaving the house was a deliberate flirtation with danger. Or was it, perhaps, an act of giving up – going out into the world and saying, as it were, 'Here I am. Do your worst.'

The town was quieter this time. He was surprised to find that it was bitterly cold and he had to shrug himself into his fleece as he walked. He realised he did not have a scarf or gloves and was completely unprepared for winter weather. Nevertheless, it was pleasant to walk along to the harbour and see life going on around him. Traders trading, shoppers shopping, even the tourists walking on the front in their thick coats and warm hats seemed to have purpose. A trawler was coming into the harbour and, as he watched the boat being manoeuvred into its berth, the life of a fisherman at sea seemed almost unbearably romantic. He smiled at the thought, knowing full well that a life at sea was a hard one. But it was the thought of activity, really, that he envied. And although wandering in this way was activity of a kind, it had no purpose other than to get him out of the house and pass some time. He noticed a newsagent and stopped, for a moment, to look at a paper to see what the date was. It was February 7th, and he felt a jolt of disbelief at this. He knew that he'd been spending a lot of time 'waiting', but this was ridiculous! Still, there was no denying the evidence. Over three months had passed and he'd done almost nothing whilst time had slipped by.

The sun was shining, and there was a bite to the northerly breeze. As he ambled towards the harbour, he noticed a woman walking towards him. He didn't recognise her, but she stopped in front of him and said, 'Hello there.'

'Hello,' said Mark, not sure why her face now seemed slightly familiar.

'I'm a friend of Natalie's,' she said.

'Oh, yes,' said Mark, placing her now. She was one of the girls Natalie had been with the first time he'd seen her away from Club Covert.

'How are you?' he asked her.

'Oh, you know,' she replied. 'Have you seen Natalie recently?'

'No. Actually, I don't really know her,' he said.

'Forgive me if I'm wrong because this was some time ago, but aren't you the guy who gave her £4,000?'

'Yes,' he said, feeling suddenly embarrassed by it.

'And you don't even know her? Wow. If you'd given *me* £4,000,' she said, 'I'd have used it much better. Natalie didn't do anything except pay off her dealer and take more smack for a while. Great, huh? And what's the end result of that? She's still working at Club Covert, still hating it, and she's blown the only chance she'll ever get of escaping it. That's what I call a lost cause, huh?'

She smiled but looked sad underneath it.

'I'm still there myself, of course,' she added, 'but I started there for a different reason.'

He looked questioningly at her and she paused briefly and looked at her watch, then went on.

'I'm paying off my debts without accruing any new ones,' she told him, 'so I can see a time when I'll be able to stop.'

She laughed at herself, briefly, a more genuinely felt expression, Mark thought, and he suddenly felt friendly and well disposed towards her.

'Do you know who stole the rest of my money?' he asked.

She took a deep breath. 'I can't say anything to you here,' she said in a low voice, glancing sideways nervously. 'Let's go for coffee somewhere where we can talk properly.'

'There's a place just up here?' he said. 'They do great cake.'

She nodded and they walked together to the café and went in. It was moderately busy, and the background babble of conversation gave them privacy. Natalie's friend, whose name was Clare, wanted to take a seat in the window so that they could look out over the sea, but Mark preferred to sit at the back where they could be inconspicuous. She had straight reddish-brown hair and a freckled complexion, and smiled easily and readily as they talked.

'I don't know much about it,' she told him, 'but it will have been one of John Luscombe's men who did it.'

'Do you mean John as in "John", or Jon as in "Jonathan"?' Mark asked.

'John as in John,' she said. 'He runs Club Covert as – well, it's not difficult to guess – a *covert* operation. For petty stuff mostly, I think, but there's some drug dealing too, as you might expect. Natalie was beside herself when she let the cat out of the bag that you had cash hidden away under your bed. I'm afraid I gave her a particularly hard time over that. I mean, what did she expect them to do? Say, "Oh, that's interesting, Natalie," and then leave it alone? That girl's a mixture of surprisingly worldly knowledge and bizarre naïveté. *Not* a good mix.'

'But you're friends,' he said.

'There's something about people in this line of work,' said Clare. 'We stick together, but that doesn't mean that we like each other. Some of the girls, I think I'll know forever, but some I'll be *very* pleased to say goodbye to. We're all very different from each other, with only this one thing in common, which makes us a kind of oddball community. We look out for one another because we know how tough the outside world can be. It's that thing, you know. . . you meet someone in the outside world that you like and then there comes that inevitable point when they ask you what you do for a living. I have a duality about that, actually. Part of me is happy about what I do – or unapologetic about it, anyway – and part of me is quite embarrassed. In a way, I envy those women who have made the decision to really take it on as a profession. They seem so defiant about it. But I'm only here for a while – I hope. . . ' She laughed again, an unselfconscious sound that made Mark smile along with her.

'But never mind that. You wanted me to tell you who took your money and perhaps where it is now. I'm afraid I don't know on either count. I expect it's in a bank, although John keeps quite a lot of cash in his office. . . but the truth is I don't really know.'

'It was all the money I had,' Mark told her. 'Now I have nothing. Well, not exactly nothing – I have a £10 note in my pocket. I've found a little room in a rooming house that I'm getting rent free in return for some renovation I'm doing on the building.'

'Oh, Mark,' she said, 'I'm so sorry. You didn't deserve this.'

He shrugged.

'It's not your fault,' he told her.

'No,' she agreed. 'But I can still feel sad for you. It seems to be quite a talent I have. Being sad for other people.'

They drank their coffee for a while in silence. Mark felt incredibly grateful to be with someone who was so friendly. Like Natalie, she looked too ordinary to be a lap dancer. Not that she wasn't attractive, and she certainly had a good figure. It was all rather confusing. He realised that he had a deeply stereotypical image of "that sort of woman" – someone tragic, someone over-sexualised, someone clearly at the bottom of the heap – and he smiled to himself at his stereotyping. It was another example of the ways in which he misread the world. Without meaning to, he began to tell her about the house, and Tara and Mr Hammond, although he didn't mention how his handiwork had gone so disastrously wrong.

'And what are you hoping to do once you finish at Covert?' he asked her after he'd run out of things to say.

'My girlfriend and I are going to set up a flower stall,' she said. 'Gemma works in the florist's shop between Baker's Yard and the sea, but it's not a very good one, and it's quite badly run. We could do much better. We've even got our eyes on a pitch. Up where the river comes into the harbour. There's that cobbled area between the bridge and the new waterside development. I bet we'd be able to get a licence to put up a stall there. Now that the area's going up-market, I should think a florist would do very well, and once we've built up some capital, who knows, we could even open a shop of our own.'

'It's good to have a plan,' he said.

'Life has no direction without a plan,' she told him. 'What's your plan?'

'Plan A seems to be failing me at the moment,' he said, 'and I find I have no plan B.'

'Has it failed because your money was stolen?' she asked.

'That may have been a part of it,' he said, 'though there are other things too. Actually, coming across the money in the way I did was just a catalyst for a series of events. I put them into motion and everything that followed seemed inevitable.' He laughed in surprise at himself. 'It seems incredible to say this, with all that's happened, but even though things are difficult and confusing, I don't suppose I regret coming here.'

'Still, how much money was stolen?'

'I had £40,000 initially,' he told her, 'but it wasn't mine, that's the thing, and I do have to pay it back.'

He explained briefly how the money had come to him, and about giving half of it to Amy. In fact, now he talked about it, he realised, he'd spent only a tiny proportion of it on himself.

'Poor Mark,' she said. 'And this man, Sean, sounds ruthless. Your ear looks quite sweet, by the way. Not at all disfigured, just *lobeless*, and lots of people have small earlobes.'

'But most people don't have one on one side and none on the other.'

'Yes, you are a little lopsided, that's true,' she said. 'Still, symmetry is overrated in my opinion. I'm a little lopsided myself, on top, which I had never really bothered about until I started. . . displaying myself.'

She sighed suddenly, and Mark felt an intense wash of sadness for her.

'But it's okay,' she added wistfully. 'It won't be long before I pack it all in. And I think being lesbian helps, too, because I get less drawn into it all. The men aren't allowed to touch and I'm happy to keep it that way.'

They talked for a little while longer, but Clare noticed the time and had to leave.

'Look, I'll pay,' said Clare, 'it would be too embarrassing otherwise, considering what you've lost.'

He smiled, a little abashed and shy, and thanked her.

'My pleasure,' she said. 'It's nice talking to someone who knows what I do and doesn't care.'

'My pleasure,' he said.

As they were leaving, she put a hand on his shoulder.

'Could you promise me one thing?' she asked.

'What's that?'

'If you ever see me selling flowers by the harbour, will you come and buy a bunch?'

'Yes, of course,' he told her, 'that's an easy promise to make.'

'But only if you have any money,' she said, 'otherwise, I'll have to give them to you.'

They both laughed, then parted company out on the pavement. It had been a heartening meeting and it made him feel lighter. He crossed to the shore, and as he did so, he noticed that the juggler was down by the sand, in his harlequin suit, juggling and fire eating. Mark walked over to watch, but again the man's act was coming to an end and so he didn't have a chance to do so. The man exhaled a plume of flame and then bowed to his audience, who clapped appreciatively. Some of them came over and dropped money into the hat as they started to disperse. The man looked up at Mark, and recognised him immediately. He didn't say a word, but continued to pack his bag and then picked up the cap with coins in it. He emptied the contents of the cap into the front pocket of his bag, and then put it in alongside his juggling sticks. Picking up the bag, he walked over to Mark without speaking or gesturing in any way, and stopped in front of him. When the man reached out, Mark wasn't sure what was going to happen. He wondered if the juggler wanted, inexplicably, to shake his hand and he started to stretch out his own hand in return. But the man ignored it. Instead, he reached up and touched the scarring on Mark's ear with his forefinger. That was all.

Touched it. Mark wasn't sure if the expression on the man's face was one of pity or respect. No words were spoken. The man simply walked on with his bag and turned up an alleyway leading up into the Old Town.

Back at the house, and perhaps because of his meeting with Clare and the juggler, whose acknowledgement of him had been mystifying, Mark began to feel a new quality of enervation and listlessness. This continued for the next few days. Somehow it was different to the previous months of apathy. Before, everything had seemed pointless and futile, and if it had had a colour it would have been the colour of relentless rain clouds. This new listlessness was different. There was a sense of lightness and a tinge of melancholy about it that seemed almost enjoyable. Well, if not enjoyable, then more comfortable than before. Things were no longer pointless, it simply didn't matter what happened any more. He also knew that a burgeoning need to go to Club Covert and talk to Natalie lay submerged beneath this veneer of painful pleasure. He kept trying to put the thought aside, but there was no getting round it. It was beginning to feel like a primary need – a necessity, a compulsion – as if some irresistible force was going to propel him through the door and down the hill.

He couldn't decide whether he wanted an apology from her for giving away the whereabouts of his money, or whether he wanted to vent some (perplexingly absent) anger at her for causing him to be penniless. He also wanted, from her own mouth, an explanation of what she'd done with the £4,000 that he'd given her. It wasn't that he disbelieved Clare when she mentioned drugs, it was that it didn't really match up with his experience of Natalie. But then, what did he think someone who took heroin might be like? Of course, her paleness was now explained. But lots of people are pale.

A couple of days later, in the evening, he went up to talk to Tara. She looked a little distracted when she opened her door, but she smiled and asked him in.

'Tara,' he said, 'I want to talk to you about money. When you and Mr Hammond offered me a room, there was a mention of "pocket money". I didn't really think about it at the time, because there was nothing I needed to spend money on.'

'But now?'

'Yes, now I need to do something. There's someone I need to talk to and I need some money to do that.'

'How much?'

The sum he requested amounted to a week's rent for the room which he hadn't taken. Tara did not react in any way to his request, but said, 'Please wait here while I pop up and have a word with Mr Hammond.'

When he was on his own, he became a little nervous. Under the circumstances, why should they give him any money? Surely it was an insult to request money right now? He could see that quite clearly. Yet here he was making more demands on these people, having done absolutely nothing to warrant their generosity. He felt a tingle of humiliation as he sat there in Tara's room. This sharp pricking of his pride, however uncomfortable, was better than the maddening, suffocating boredom he'd been suffering from over the previous few weeks. It was not a question of being reasonable. This request was a measure of his desperation.

Tara, when she returned, was as impassive as when he'd left, but she handed him an envelope and said, 'Here you are.'

Mark opened the envelope and the money he'd requested was there. He felt a flush of gratitude.

'Thank you,' he said, genuinely moved. 'Thank you so much.'

'Mark,' she said, 'I have to tell you that there is an obligation that goes with this. It is a question of trust, you see – we are giving you the money in the hope that you will start work on the house again as soon as possible. I am not absolutely sure what that might mean to you – "as soon as possible" – or even what constitutes "possible" for you at the moment, but I guess you get my gist.'

'Yes, I take your point,' he said, 'and I *do* feel an obligation.'

'Good,' she said, 'now go and do what you have to do.'

He walked to Club Covert. The evening was clear and the first twinklings of frost were visible on the roofs of the cars that he passed. He wandered down to the sea enjoying the stillness of the air and the fresh, slightly marine smell from the sea. For some reason, the far side of the harbour looked far more run down this evening, almost sinister and possibly dangerous. As he passed the second hand cars, and the dusty rubble of a couple of demolished buildings, he began to feel the now-familiar creeping feeling of being unsafe. Why had he so completely ignored the possibility of bumping into Sean when he'd gone out before? Sean had happily sliced off his earlobe in a pub's beer garden, where there had been witnesses. Now, here, he was on his own. There was no one around at all, and Sean would be able to do something far worse to Mark with impunity.

Mark continued walking, his unease prickling on his skin. He was particularly struck this time by the location of Club Covert. Why was it out here? As he approached he noticed how anomalous the club's flashy architecture seemed. The nautical look seemed more of a failed joke, here, than an attempt at sophistication. The bouncers did not seem out of place in their padded black jackets, and with their breath visible in the freezing air. They looked as if they would be happy, at the slightest provocation, to take unwanted punters round to one of the poorly lit, derelict spaces in the vicinity for a spot of recreational violence.

He was let in without a murmur, and paid the woman at the cash desk, as previously. Again, he was too late for his complementary table dance, and he was relieved that this was the case. He took the table that he'd sat at before, which was at the back of the club where he would be able to sit relatively discreetly, and again he ordered a whisky with ice from the waitress. Of course, discretion is not what a club of this kind is about, and as soon as he'd sat down, a blonde woman came up to him with a surprisingly authentic smile.

'Hello, I'm Sandra,' she told him. 'How are you this evening? Can I interest you in a dance?'

'Actually,' he told her, 'I'm here to see Natalie. Or Ruby, that is. Do you know if she's here this evening?'

Sandra's expression changed to one approaching pity. It was a subtle change, disguised by her heavy makeup, but Mark spotted it at once. Was it that he'd asked for her as Natalie rather than as Ruby?

'I think she's going to be in a bit later,' Sandra told him, then smiled sympathetically. 'But perhaps you want some company until then?'

'Thanks,' he said, 'but I'm okay for the moment.'

'Okay, wave over to me at any time and I'll come across.'

She wandered off. The music was the same as last time and seemed rather sanitised, he thought. The place was more busy this evening, and at a couple of the tables champagne was being drunk. Several girls were clustered round, smiling and laughing with a group of men who were flirting with casual, drunken abandon. One of the bouncers was hovering nearby to make sure that no boundaries were crossed. Two girls were dancing at poles on the bar area and there really was something hypnotic in the way they moved.

Mark was approached by another couple of girls, but he shooed them away and after a while he was left alone. Then, once he'd got himself a second whisky, he noticed Clare approaching across the room.

'Mark,' she said, surprised, 'what are you doing here?'

'I've come to see Natalie,' he said. 'I want to have one last conversation with her.'

Clare looked dubious, but shrugged and said, 'I suppose I can see why.'

'Can I pay for you to sit with me for a drink?' he asked.

'Okay,' she told him, her voice softening, 'I'll have an orange juice and soda.'

She attracted the barman's attention and made a gesture, and he nodded and started to mix her drink.

'This feels a bit weird,' she said. 'You seeing me "in action" as it were.'

'Sorry.'

Clare shook her head and said, 'Don't be. It's okay. This is what I do and I'm not ashamed of it. As I said to you before, I don't like it, but I'm not ashamed.'

The drink arrived and they clinked glasses, a gesture that is normally a happy one, but there was a touch of melancholy here.

'So, anyway,' she said after a few moments of silence, 'what are you going to do once you've talked to Natalie?'

'I don't know,' he said. 'Let it go, I hope.'

She smiled sadly and leaned forward for a moment. 'Are you the sort of man who *can* let these things go?'

'I let a whole life go,' he told her.

'But did you?'

He looked at her and she held his gaze, intensely, for a moment, before he looked away, down at his empty glass. The barman was looking in his direction, so he raised the glass and the barman nodded. Clare looked across at the club behind him, then smiled again, more brightly this time.

'It's my job to smile,' she said to him out of the corner of her mouth, 'so bear that in mind, because I'm being watched by one of the managers right now. I know it's ridiculously false, given what we're talking about. And, oh. . .' she paused, looking surprised for a moment. 'I have to tell you that behind you, just coming into your view on the left, is the man who owns Club Covert. I didn't know he was going to be here this evening. He's probably the one who ordered the theft of your money.'

Clare smiled across at the man and gave him an astonishingly convincing happy wave. John Luscombe, Mark remembered. A rather handsome man of about fifty, with a head of hair that looked a little too full to be quite real. The man smiled back and Clare gave a little shiver, as if of pleasure, then turned back to Mark.

'Doing that makes me want to vomit,' she said, flashing her teeth, 'but there we go. Grin and bear it, that's what we all say.'

The barman arrived with Mark's drink, and a bill on a stainless steel saucer, which he put on the table in front of Mark. Then he picked up Mark's empty glass.

'Doesn't it kill you,' Clare said as the barman started to clear the next table, 'John's worth millions, and he's such a shit. I never get the best shifts here because I've never agreed to have sex with him. At least I'm not one of the more popular girls here, like Natalie, so he's never pursued it.'

She leaned back and gave a coy look that made Mark laugh. 'But listen,' she said, her eyes sparkling suddenly with genuine emotion, 'this is it. Tonight's the night. I'll have paid my debts off once I get my money at the end of this evening's shift. That'll be it, I'll be in the black!'

'Well done,' he said.

'For the first time, some of the smiles I've smiled this evening have been authentic,' she told him, 'which I thought I'd *never* be able to say about this place. Oh look, here's Natalie!'

Clare stood as Natalie came over. She was wearing a skimpy black sequinned corset. She didn't look at all pleased to see Mark.

'What are you doing here?' she demanded.

'I wanted to talk to you.'

'No,' she said.

'Please,' said Mark.

'*Talk* to him!' Clare told her in a stern voice before walking away.

Natalie sat, quite suddenly, with a sigh and looked as though she was deflating. He could see her eyes welling up.

'Look,' he said, 'I gave you the money. I didn't make any stipulations as to what you should do with it—'

'Clare's told you what I did with it, though, hasn't she?' Natalie asked.

'Yes,' he said.

'So why have you come to talk to me? You know everything you need to know.'

'Let me buy you a drink,' he said.

'I'd better not. Really,' she said, but didn't move. After a while, she smiled what was almost a real smile, and said, 'You look very different from the first time you were here. Do you remember, in that naff jacket and trousers.'

Mark nodded.

'Oh, Mark,' she said, 'I thought I'd be able to pay things off and get out of here, but it's only made things worse. You don't know the half of it, and John, oh God, he's so. . . *persuasive*.'

'Why don't you leave?' he asked her. 'It must be better than staying here if you hate it.'

'If only it was as simple as that,' she told him.

She was about to say something else, when Mark saw John coming towards them. Natalie saw Mark's expression and looked around.

'Ruby?' said John, 'are you okay?'

Natalie smiled, far less convincingly than Clare had.

'Come on,' he said, 'pull yourself together. Is this gentleman bothering you?'

'No, no,' she said.

He looked at Mark, and when he noticed Mark's ear, he stiffened slightly.

'You watch it,' he said to Mark. 'And leave Ruby alone.'

He took Natalie's arm and pulled her slowly, but with brutal force, to her feet. Mark watched as she was marched across the room, John talking to her *sotto voce* as she tried to smile. As he did so, several more bouncers came into the club. When John saw them he let go of Natalie's arm and beckoned to them, then went off through a door beside the bar. As soon as he was gone, Natalie crossed to talk to someone on a table beyond the one that Mark was sitting at. As she passed him, she whispered, 'I could *kill* him!'

Given John Luscombe's attitude towards Natalie this evening, it seemed that Mark's presence had not been helpful. But as he sipped his drink, he thought, 'Why *am* I here?' Did the contact he'd had make him feel any better? No. Clare came over to him. She didn't say anything, just raised her eyebrows.

'This was a mistake,' he said. 'I don't know why I came. I suppose I thought I'd see something or learn something that would help me put it to rest.'

Clare nodded to herself. 'You can't save Natalie from this, Mark. You have no money. She doesn't know you. You're just a stranger who gave her £4,000.'

Natalie was over by the bar, and she beckoned to Clare, who patted Mark's shoulder and walked away. He looked around the bar and felt extraordinarily out of place. His colourful clothes were just as wrong as the dowdy ones he'd worn last time. He didn't look off-duty executive like everyone else. And there was no one else that he could see who'd come on their own. There were two different girls in eyeshot who were stripping and it felt hugely inappropriate that he should be witnessing it. It had felt inappropriate the first time, but this time was worse – the first time he hadn't known what kind of place Club Covert was. He couldn't make a judgement about the other men here, they'd come for such radically different reasons from his that he couldn't put himself in their shoes at all.

He sat for perhaps five more minutes, then downed the rest of his drink in preparation for leaving, and looked around to see where Natalie and Clare were. They were nowhere to be seen, and so he stood to leave. As he did so, he heard the slamming of a door behind the bar. Then one of the bouncers ran out into the bar area and, at almost the same moment, the fire alarm went off. This was followed almost immediately by a billow of smoke from the doorway at the back of the bar.

Instantly, it was mayhem. People shouting, girls running to the double doors at the rear of the club, presumably to the changing rooms, and being blocked by a bouncer. Drunk men were trying to get to their feet quickly, and failing. Mark was mesmerised by it all, rendered immobile for a few seconds, watching. He could see that the lobby was smoke free, so it looked like he'd be able to get out without a problem. Also, he hadn't had much whisky since his arrival and was clearly the only customer who wasn't drunk. A much bigger billow of smoke belched through the door by the bar, causing a wave of panic to run through the room. There was a sudden, undignified race to get out of the burning building, all elbows and knees as people tripped over upturned chairs, and as more people converged on the exit, Mark managed to move swiftly into the lobby ahead of a group of sweating and dishevelled men of around his own age. He was fortunate to have been sitting near the entrance, and was one of the first out onto the paved area in front of the club.

He didn't know what to do. Hang around for some kind of roll call? He tried to work out how many people had been in the club, and thought perhaps something between thirty and forty punters, plus dancing girls, waitresses, bar staff and bouncers, so quite a lot. Perhaps a barman, or a bouncer, would be best able to say who'd got out and who was still inside. Despite the expensive suits, and the sexy glamour-clothes of the girls, they looked a sorry bunch standing out there, bewildered, displaced and shivering. He was the only one who was wearing casual clothes – rust coloured jeans and a yellow shirt under his fleece. Most of the rest were dressed as though they'd come from a high powered business meeting. Worryingly, though, there was no sign of Natalie or Clare – or John Luscombe, for that matter.

After a while, Clare came out. As she walked past Mark towards one of the bouncers, she said 'Meet me at the Harbour Tavern in an hour. Now *go!*'

Bewildered, he had no time to answer or to ask questions,

because Clare was gone. He looked around him but she'd managed to slip away. It was clear that no one was going to make any attempt to organise things, and some of the customers were already beginning to drift away. Mark decided to follow suit, and walked off along the road to the harbour. When he was some distance away he looked back at the club. There was no sign of fire.

It was 10.00pm when he arrived at the Harbour Tavern. The bar was busy but not overcrowded. He bought himself a pint of San Miguel and took it to a small table where he could sit by the window, looking out over the water. From there he could see, through the heavy condensation on the window, the starboard light at the harbour entrance, winking green. He sat, sipping his lager occasionally as he waited. After an hour, three quarters of his pint remained. After two hours, it was warm and unappealing. It was midnight and he wondered what to do. He'd waited for more than two hours and there was no sign of Clare. On one hand, sitting here waiting for her had a purpose to it, as opposed to the other 'waiting' he'd been indulging in lately, which had been characterised by an absence of purpose. On the other hand, he couldn't wait indefinitely. He wasn't sure when the bar closed, but it was still lively so he reckoned it would be open for a while longer. Perhaps he would wait until it closed, then go back to the house if Clare hadn't turned up. He felt curiously detached from the laughter and bonhomie around him, but detached in an almost pleasant way. He didn't envy these people their pleasure, he was simply aware that he wasn't a part of it. Time was rung at the bar at about ten to one. Mark sighed and felt almost nothing. Not anger, not disappointment. Nothing. He might as well have waited here as go back to his room. Staying up late was of no consequence, as he had nothing to get up for in the morning. Dimly, he was aware of the feeling of obligation to Tara and Mr Hammond, which he'd felt so strongly earlier on, to get on with the work on the house. But now it seemed to have no substance and so he ignored it.

As he was getting up to leave, Clare came in. She was wearing scuffed jeans and a black cowgirl jacket with a mud stain on the sleeve. She had a small rucksack slung over her shoulder, and she came over to him at once. Her face was pinched with cold, and her cheeks glowed red.

'Thank God you're still here, Mark,' she said. 'I'm sorry I'm so late.'

'That's alright,' said Mark. 'You're here now.'

'Are you still up for a drink?' she asked. 'There's a bar by the station that stays open late.'

'Okay,' said Mark, 'so long as you tell me what's been going on.'

'Let's go then, but not together,' she said. 'You go straight there and I'll go round by Terminus Street and meet you inside.'

She left immediately, and Mark – somewhat bemused – followed her out a few moments later. She'd already disappeared when he came out onto the quayside, and so he walked along and up the main street towards the station. The bar that they'd agreed to meet in was at the back, beside the large hotel there. There were only a few late-night people inside, and Mark ordered himself a coffee to try and fight off his sleepiness while he waited for Clare, who turned up about ten minutes later. She looked distracted but very alert and she smiled quickly at him, then went to the bar to buy a large glass of red wine before coming over to his table.

'So,' he asked as she sat down, 'What happened?'

'The fire,' she said, 'that was all Natalie's doing – she lit a pile of paper towels in the ladies toilet and threw some along the back corridor and then chucked the rest into John's office. While he was in there with his thugs.'

'Woah!' he said. 'But why?'

Clare dumped the rucksack on the table between them and said, 'Have a look in there.'

Mark loosened the drawstring at the top of the rucksack, and saw the neat pile of bundled banknotes immediately. He fastened it quickly as Clare leaned in towards him.

'There's £40,000 in there,' she whispered. 'I've counted it.'

'Wow!' said Mark, handing the rucksack back to her.

Clare laughed and pushed the rucksack towards him across the table.

'No, Mark, it's for you,' she told him.

As she spoke, he noticed that her forearms were scratched.

'I don't understand,' he said. 'And what happened to you? You're scratched and muddy.'

'There was a lot of activity at Covert tonight because there was some cash coming in,' she told him. 'John's not usually in the club, and there aren't usually that many bouncers around, so we all knew something was happening. The whole fire thing was a spontaneous idea on Natalie's part. I guess she snapped, or something, after he'd been so harsh with her and because of all the stuff that's being going on for her, and I guess because you turning up like that gave it all some kind of perspective for her. It was stupidly dangerous. She created a lot of smoke in the corridor and then cleared the office by throwing some of her burning towels in there. There are two doors to John's office, so I guess everyone would have been forced out of the far door and into the back of the bar. She grabbed as much money as she could whilst the room was empty, then put it in a rucksack and threw it out of the window of the ladies toilet.'

'Where you picked it up? Is that what all those scratches are?'

'Yes. It's waste ground out there, with brambles all over the place.' She sipped her wine and closed her eyes for a moment, as if suddenly tired. 'I didn't know anything about any of this until she came running up to me and asked me to go and get the money and give it to you. Then she ran off while the place was in uproar. The bouncers at the door didn't know to stop her.'

Mark was amazed that Natalie had risked so much to get his money back to him.

'What about the two of you,' he asked, 'I hope you've both got something out of this?'

'No. Nothing,' said Clare. 'That's all there was. Natalie fluked the exact amount.'

'I can't take it,' he said. 'Or not all of it. Although I owe £40,000, there was a lot less than that stolen from Baker's Yard.'

'If you don't take it, Mark, it will all be pointless,' she told him. 'Don't you see? You gave money to Natalie and expected her to take it, didn't you? Well, now it's your turn to be on the receiving end.' She smiled again, and patted his hand. 'Go on, take it. It's for you. This whole thing would amount to nothing if you didn't take it all.'

Mark grinned for a moment. 'It's hard!' he said. 'And now I know why Natalie seemed so unbelieving.'

Clare shrugged and looked at him with a subdued grin.

Mark was speechless for a few moments, then laughed. 'This solves everything,' he said, smiling. 'It's. . . well, it's amazing!'

'And there's a poetic justice in it, too,' Clare added with a smile of her own. 'Natalie wanted to piss John off, which, of course, she's managed to do very well.'

'But the stakes are so high,' Mark said, suddenly becoming serious. 'I was accidentally handed some money, but this. . . they must know that Natalie did it. Someone must have seen her, and that means she'll be in real trouble.'

'You mean you weren't?' said Clare. 'What about your ear?'

'Where is she?' he asked.

Clare looked worried. 'I don't know,' she said, 'I slipped away as soon as I left the building, to go round and pick up the rucksack. That's why I was so late, by the way: there was a Fort Knox fence I had to get over. Natalie chucked the rucksack into the brambles and it wasn't easy to get it out. Once I'd got it, there was no way I was going to come back round to the front carrying a bag full of money. It was quite surreal really. I sat there and counted it while I waited for the club to go quiet. But it never did go quiet. There were guys running all over the place. So, eventually, I made my way along to the harbour. There's a lot of concrete debris around there, and a couple of old jetties, and some more fences, so it took a lot longer than I thought it would, especially in the dark.'

She looked at her scratches, and at the dirt on her jacket. 'I hope Natalie is okay,' she said, suddenly sombre.

'Maybe we should go looking for her.'

'No,' said Clare. 'I'm sure she managed to get away from the club because I saw her leaving ahead of me and no one tried to stop her. She'll know not to go home. That's the first place John would go looking for her.'

They sat in silence for a while and Mark felt a beat of dread in his heart.

'So,' Clare asked, 'what are you going to do with the money?'

'That's easy,' he told her, 'I know where Sean lives, so I'll go over there tomorrow and give it to him. It's months late, but maybe that won't matter.'

They sat on and chatted a little, but both of them were tired, and it was becoming more and more difficult to think of anything to say. Mark could feel a tingling sensation deep in his stomach that was a mixture of euphoria and fear. He wondered what price Natalie might pay for her actions. He remembered his own fear when he'd realised that Sean was in town looking for him. He wouldn't wish that sort of precariousness on anyone, let alone Natalie.

He could see Clare wilting with fatigue opposite him. 'Look,' he told her, 'you'd better get home, you look washed out.'

'Yes,' she said, then looked at her watch. It was nearly 2.00am.

'It's odd,' she told him, 'I'm usually still in the club at this time on a Friday night. It seems impossible. . .'

He looked at the bag for a moment, then up at Clare. 'Let me give you some money to cover your wages for the evening,' he said. 'I presume you weren't paid?'

Clare smiled. 'Mark,' she said emphatically, 'give the money to the people you *owe* it to. It's not going to work if you give them less than £40,000, is it? Be sensible. I'll be okay. I'll borrow what I've lost tonight from Gemma. We'll be fine.'

She stood.

'Now, I'll leave on my own,' she told him. 'Wait five minutes, will you?'

'Of course, if that'll make you feel safer.'

She kissed him and smiled sadly. 'You deserve some good things to happen to you, Mark. You're a kind man, and that's all too rare these days.'

*

Mark waited five minutes and then walked along to the Old Town and up towards the house. The night was dead still and, in the silence, his footsteps sounded unnaturally loud. As he climbed the hill he could see a half moon rising in the east. He found himself shivering in spite of his exertion. The adrenaline that had fuelled him was now beginning to wear off and the coffee seemed to have had no effect at all.

He realised that he wasn't far from the cave that he'd been to in those early days in the town, with the residents of Baker's Yard. Although he'd never been far from it since he'd moved to his current address, he'd never thought of going there again. But now he remembered that Holly kept a candle and lighter in the recess by the cave's entrance, and he felt a sudden yearning to revisit it. He walked the couple of blocks to where he could see the railing protecting the entrance to the cave.

It was easy to clamber round and into the tunnel. Once inside it was pitch dark and he had to feel his way along carefully, trying to remember how far the tunnel went before it descended into the cavern. When he came to the steep decline it was easier than he expected because he could take it slowly and feel his way forward step by step. Being in profound darkness was an extraordinary experience of itself – it wasn't something that was familiar to him at all, and he could imagine it being terrifying under other circumstances.

When the path levelled out, he searched the wall for the recess where Holly kept her candle. It took him longer to find it than he'd expected, because it was a little higher than he remembered, but he managed eventually, and when he flicked the lighter on the flash of light made him blink. Once he'd lit the candle, he looked around. The single flame made a small pool of light that didn't extend far into the engulfing darkness, so he had the eerie sensation of being in an underground space that went on forever. It was cold in there, too, which gave him an odd feeling of being refrigerated. This was what a morgue must feel like, he thought, and he smiled slightly at the thought which, although a little morbid, was not at all scary.

He tried humming, and the resonance of a single voice was curiously full in the echoing space. But he couldn't find a tune that seemed appropriate, and so he didn't bother trying to find one, and hummed a single note instead, 'Mmmmm. . .', over and over until he felt dreamy and connected to the darkness, which seemed to hold the sound that he was making, like a bottle might hold a liquid. And although he was alone here, he didn't feel lonely. It did occur to him, though, to wonder where Holly, Don and the rest of the Baker's Yard lot were and what they were doing. He wondered if they'd visited the cave since the night he'd come along with them. Perhaps they'd been here earlier this evening. . .

He thought of Natalie, too, and where she might be, and what a great hiding place this would be, and how perfect it must have been in the old days of smuggling. The weight of history was almost palpable, and he felt connected, suddenly, to all the people who had sought refuge here over the centuries. It made him realise that he wasn't the first person to have sought refuge. Perhaps it was a universal need, and he had missed that – that Amy and others back home might benefit from it, too.

With that thought, sleepiness arrived as if seeping into him from the darkness. He blew out the candle and replaced it in its recess with the lighter, then carefully edged his way back along the tunnel and out into the fresh air and moonlight.

*

He walked back to the house, let himself in and went upstairs. He felt almost peaceful as he crossed the landing, and certainly ready for bed. When he opened the door to his room, he found that Natalie was sitting on his bed.

'Hello Mark,' she said.

'Natalie! What are you doing here?'

'I couldn't go home, could I?' she said. 'So I came here.'

She looked extremely pale, tired and dishevelled. Her hands had black smudges on them. She was wearing jeans and a soft beige jacket, under which Mark could see that she was still wearing her black sequinned corset from Club Covert.

'How did you know where I live?' he asked her.

'Clare told me she'd bumped into you the other day and she said a little about what you were up to. I know this place because one of the girls at the club used to have a room here. I came over sometimes on Sunday or Monday afternoons to chat and drink weird herbal tea.'

She smiled sadly and looked around Mark's room with a neutral expression. Mark found it impossible to guess what she thought of it.

'I've met Tara several times, too,' she went on, 'so she knows who I am. She was very supportive of my profession and I was grateful to her for that. When I rang the bell this evening, she was kind enough to let me in.'

Mark sat on the bed beside her, and she noticed his rucksack.

'Oh, good,' she said, 'Clare got the money and passed it on to you. I'm glad. Is there enough?'

'Spot on,' he told her. 'But what about you? You must be in real danger, now.'

She shrugged and he asked, gently, 'Why did you do it?'

'Seeing you at the club like that made me realise how I'd

ruined everything for you. I'd ruined everything for myself anyway, so there was nothing left to lose on that score. It was odd, I knew even before I started the fire that John's body-guards would have killed me without a qualm if he'd told them to, or if they could get their hands on me, but that didn't really seem much of a deterrent. I got quite a blaze going almost immediately, you know, which was a blessing, and that took their attention off me even better than I'd hoped.' She laughed grimly. 'I'll leave town tomorrow. There are a couple of people I know who will be happy to put me up in a pinch.'

'Let me give you some of this money, then,' said Mark.

'No,' she said firmly. 'That money's for you to pay off your debts. Don't start giving it away again, Mark!'

Mark thought for a few moments. 'Perhaps you could stay here,' he said. 'I know that the room I was originally going to take is still free. Maybe you could lodge here. You'd be completely safe, I'm sure. When I came here, Mr Hammond was clear that if I stayed indoors I would be safe from the people who were looking for me. Maybe the same would be true for you.'

'You met Mr Hammond?' Natalie seemed impressed. 'The girl who lived here never did. She thought it was all a bit odd, even a bit creepy, that there was an old man up there in the attic that no one ever got to see.'

'He's an amazing person,' said Mark, 'but too immobile to get out and about, that's all.' Briefly, Mark stopped to wonder why he'd described Mr Hammond in this way. What, exactly, was so amazing about him? He was an old man whom he hardly knew. What had he done or said for Mark to be so profoundly affected by him?

There came a knock at the door. Mark looked at his watch. It was nearly 4.30am.

'Come in,' he called.

Tara put her head round the door before coming in. She was wearing an oriental dressing gown and looked neat and awake, as though she might have been up quite naturally at this time.

'Hello Mark,' she said, 'I just needed to check that it was okay for me to have let Natalie in.'

'Yes, it's fine,' he told her. 'I'm glad you did.'

She turned to Natalie and said, 'Are you all right, my dear? You look as if you've just escaped from a fire!'

'That's it exactly,' Natalie said, and laughed. 'I guess I'm lucky to be alive.'

'And you look cold, too,' said Tara. 'Do you want a dressing gown?'

'No, I'm fine,' said Natalie. 'I'm sorry if I'm shivering a bit, it's the shock of it. I just can't go home this evening, that's all. I'll be fine in the morning.'

'By the way,' Mark said, 'would it be okay to put Natalie up in the spare room?'

'Only for tonight,' said Natalie quickly.

'Of course,' Tara told her. 'And you must have a good hot bath before bed. Come up to my room and I'll sort out something for you to wear tomorrow under that jacket. A corset is hardly casual day time wear.'

'Thank you,' said Natalie, looking both grateful and embarrassed at the same time. 'I'll be up in a minute, I'll say goodnight to Mark first.'

Tara nodded and then left.

'She's a sweetheart,' Natalie whispered.

Mark nodded, feeling suddenly self-conscious. The fact that Tara had seen them together, in his room, made the atmosphere seem sexual, somehow, where before it had been uncomplicatedly friendly, as though they were brother and sister. Natalie noticed the change in Mark and stood up.

'Mark,' she said, 'I'm so sorry I accepted your offer of a coffee that day. I was using you for my own reasons, and that's unforgivable. I dragged you into all this, and although I've managed to get the money back for you, it doesn't really make amends, does it? I could stay here and sleep with you–' she glanced down at the single bed '–but it wouldn't help, would it? I'd still have to leave in the morning, and I'd only be doing it as a favour. I'm sorry if that sounds cruel or callous, because you're handsome and I like you, but that makes it all worse, really. In fact, you're exactly the sort of person I used to dream about when I was a teenager, before I got sucked into a world of. . . extremes. But now, well, let's just say I need to get away from here and face up to some of the major mistakes that I've made over the last two or three years.'

'You don't need to go,' said Mark, 'Tara was so welcoming and friendly, I'm sure she'd be happy to let you stay on until this all blows over.'

Natalie scrutinised Mark intensely. She stared into his eyes. He tried to look back, but there was too much pain there and so he looked away.

'If I asked you to,' she said, 'would you help me run away?'

'Yes of course,' he said.

'Would you come with me?'

'Yes,' he said, without hesitation. As he uttered the words he felt a painful stab of emotional pain. Was it any better if two people were running away together?

Natalie looked into his troubled eyes and put her finger to his lips. She nodded to herself and said, 'We'll talk about this in the morning. I'm far too shattered to think straight now, so we might as well wait until we can be sensible.'

She leaned towards Mark and kissed him on the cheek. 'Poor Mark,' she said quietly, and left.

Considering how late it was, Mark took a long time to get to sleep and even when he did so, it was fitful. He seemed to dream a lot, but it was the sort of dreaming that he didn't remember; the sort that left him exhausted and melancholy. The following morning he woke at around nine, after less than four hours sleep, and immediately got up and went to the kitchen to put the kettle on. Then he went up to knock on the door to Natalie's room. There was no answer. He knocked again, and waited for a while, and when there was still no answer, he opened the door and looked inside. The room looked untouched. The curtains were open and sunlight streamed in. The bed was perfectly made. He saw the note straight away, on a sheet of lined A4 paper, and picked it up.

*Tara even lent me pen and paper*, it read. *Can you give the pen back to her? I have slipped away to get the first train to London. I have some decent friends there who will take me in. Your offer to help me run away meant a lot to me, Mark, and I will never forget that you offered so readily of your own free will. But I couldn't take you up on it. Meaning well is not enough, I'm afraid, and I need to be around people who understand addiction. I'm not the sort of person who could have asked for refuge here in this house. What would I have done? You're doing up the house in payment for your refuge, but what skills have I got that would be of any use at all? Please try to take responsibility for your own life, as I am trying to take responsibility for mine. You're too kind to be able to offer me the kind of tough love that I need right now. xxx Natalie.*

\*

Mark read the note twice then crumpled it in his hand. He was struck by her request that he should take responsibility for his life. It seemed to him that he'd been trying – and failing – to do exactly that ever since he got here. The melancholy sadness of his dreams welled up again and he got up and left the room. He could think of nothing except that Natalie had gone; that she represented something for him psychologically that seemed to bring out both the best and the worst in him. He was also aware that he wanted, desperately, to see her again. Back in his room, there seemed nothing to stay awake for and so he pulled the blankets over him, fully dressed, and drifted off to sleep.

When he woke up again, it was late lunch time and he felt rested but empty. He remembered the money and lay there wondering what to do about it. From where he was lying he could see a sliver of blue sky and it seemed to him that even the winter was slipping by. He got up and went through to the kitchen. As he was boiling the kettle, Tara came in.

'She's gone,' he told her.

She didn't respond immediately.

'Tea?' he asked.

'Please,' she replied, then smiled sadly and added, 'Yes, I guessed she would go when she asked me for pen and paper last night.'

She sat down as Mark made the tea and handed her a cup. She took a tiny sip, noticed it was too hot, and then put it on the table.

'She would never have fitted in here, you know,' she told him. 'Mr Hammond would certainly have offered her the room upstairs if she'd asked for it, but refuge means such different things to different people and I fear that our sort of refuge would have been unbearable to her at this point in her life.'

Mark sat down at the table and they remained in silence for a while.

'She told me I should take responsibility for myself,' he said. 'But I find that I don't really understand what responsibility is. When I left home and came down here, I seemed to be taking responsibility for the fact that my life was suffocating me and that I needed to get away from it or else it would kill me. But here. . . Well, I tried to fit in at Baker's Yard but it didn't work. I've tried to do useful jobs around the house and that's been a disaster. I have accepted your refuge, but ultimately it seems to me that taking responsibility for my life will have to be done by facing the world outside these walls first, and not by hiding from it.'

He sighed. 'When I talked to Mr Hammond about how all my handiwork has gone wrong, he spoke of awareness, of bringing awareness to what I do. In a way I think I get a hint of what he means, but I seem to be helpless in spite of my willingness to make an effort. Things seem to go wrong around me. I try to act consciously but afterwards I realise that I have acted from motives that I'm not clear about and which have nothing to do with what's best for me.'

'Awareness,' said Tara. 'Awareness and responsibility. You're setting yourself lofty goals here, Mark, if you want to achieve these things.'

Mark smiled.

'You've been here before, with other tenants, I expect.'

'That's irrelevant,' she said.

'I suppose it's a bit naïve to take on such aspirations,' he said.

'They're the only things worth living for,' said Tara. 'I

can't understand why anyone ever strives for anything else.'

He mulled that over for a short while, then looked at her. 'So, do you think I've got it in me to manage it?'

She looked at him carefully, as if trying to sum him up. 'I don't know,' she told him. 'It's funny, you have come here with an intention, and intention is vital, but it seems to me that your intention is to run away *from* something rather than running *to* something.'

Mark remembered the alacrity with which he'd agreed to run away with Natalie, and blushed.

'Maybe you won't really get anywhere until you know where you're heading,' Tara told him.

It was cool and sunny and Mark felt light on his feet as he walked past the station, then down to the river and on up towards the big house by the lake. How different this was from the day he'd fled in fear on his bicycle. The gate to the garden was open, and he noticed that there was a thick dew on the grass. The chestnut tree, which had been verdant with new leaves last time he came this way, was bare and sharply defined against the sky. Crocuses were out in profusion at the edge of the lawn, with the last of the season's snowdrops amongst them. The lake looked placid and dark.

As he walked up the gravel path by the lawn, the ornate red-sandstone mansion came into view. Not huge by stately home standards, but far too large to be a family house. He could see into a large drawing room with bay windows to one side and French windows to the other. It seemed deserted and so he followed the drive round to the front where larches shaded a mossy drive. Here, he ascended the two shallow steps up to the ornate front porch, and rang the bell.

He waited for some time before he heard footsteps

approaching, and when the door opened he was relieved to see that it was Sean: tall, rather pale, with his hair still swept back into a pony tail.

'I have the money,' Mark told him. 'I'm sorry it's late, but it's all here. All £40,000 of it.'

# 7. Doubt & Indecison

Sean looked at him for a few moments without any discernable expression, and then said, 'Come in.'

Mark stepped inside the house. There was a huge marble fireplace, ornately carved with dragons and grape vines. The floor was of marble too, in a black and white chequered pattern. Above him, the cornicing was almost obscenely intricate.

'Wait here,' Sean told him and walked off through some large double doors.

Mark watched him go and then looked around. A white marble staircase swept up in front of him. Portraits hung everywhere in heavy gilt frames. The place was so cool and hushed and silent it was almost unnerving. The wealth that was represented by a place such as this. . . it was incredible. It reminded him of a city, rather than a provincial, museum.

After a short while, Sean came back.

'Jonathan will see you now,' he said. 'Follow me.'

Mark walked behind Sean as they went through to the drawing room that Mark had glimpsed earlier from outside.

This room was quite different in tone to the hallway. It was warm and made Mark think of summer. It was bright and airy, the walls pale gold and hung extensively with contemporary art. The carpet was of a muted yellow, with such deep pile that Mark could feel his shoes sinking into it. The watery sunlight which came through the large windows seemed to intensify the vibrancy of the room. Even the air seemed to shine. It was strange – as if there was more light in here than there was outdoors. Sean gestured towards a sofa. Mark sat down, and was left on his own for a minute or two before the door on the far side of the room opened and a man of about fifty came in. He was tall and a little formal, with short, well cut grey hair and an expensively cut suit of Italian design. It was of the palest pastel yellow, and made of very fine cloth. He was perfectly of a piece with the room, as if he was a part of the fixtures and fittings. Mark found it hard to look at him.

'Hello,' he said as he crossed the room and shook Mark's hand. 'So you're Mark? I'm pleased to meet you.'

Mark didn't know what to say, so he said nothing. He noticed that one of Jonathan's well manicured fingers sported a large gold ring.

'I hope you like tea,' Jonathan said, 'or perhaps you would prefer something stronger?'

'Tea is fine,' said Mark.

'Good, it will be with us in a moment. Sean tells me that you wanted to see me?'

Mark took a deep breath. 'Yes. I have the money I took from him,' said Mark. He surprised himself by wanting to call this man 'sir', and wondered at himself. It wasn't something that would normally occur to him.

'I've brought it with me,' he added, gesturing towards the rucksack.

'I see,' said Jonathan. He turned and looked out of the window for a moment, as though he'd forgotten that Mark was there, or as if he was thinking of something completely different. 'Tell me,' he said, turning back to Mark, 'did you think that you might simply hand the money over to me and that I would say "Thank you very much, that's very kind of you"?'

Mark made no reply.

'Did you think I would leave it at that and simply let you go, with no further consequences?'

'I hoped that you would be pleased to get your money back,' said Mark carefully.

The door to the room opened and a well-dressed woman came in, carrying a tray of tea and pastries, which she placed on the glass coffee table in front of them.

'Thank you, Anna,' he said.

Anna nodded silently and smiled at Mark briefly before leaving. Jonathan poured the tea, added milk and handed a cup to Mark.

'A fine Darjeeling,' he said, taking a sip. 'It's quite difficult to get a tea of this quality these days.'

He looked at Mark, then out of the window, as if savouring the tea, and then back to Mark again. 'But have you thought to wonder,' he asked, 'about the inconvenience you might have put me to by absconding with my money? And what about interest? If you ran off with money from a bank, say, don't you suppose that, as well as prosecuting you, they would demand some interest.'

'If you tell me how much interest I owe on the money, I'd be happy to get it to you as soon as I've got it.'

Jonathan laughed. 'No, no, no, Mark,' he said, gesturing elegantly with his left hand. 'Don't you see, it's the *principle* of it. I don't care about the £40,000. Do I look like the sort of person for whom £40,000 would make any difference whatsoever? It wouldn't buy the least of the pictures in this room.'

He paused to look around appreciatively then got up and walked over to the window and looked out. He stood with his back to Mark for a few moments and then turned round. 'Tell me,' he said, looking carefully at him, 'what does wealth mean to you?'

'I'm not sure I know what you mean.'

'I am most usually judged by my material wealth,' he said, inviting Mark to look around him. 'But this is wrong. Every man in this world should be judged, not by the quantity of wealth that he has, but by what he does with the resources available to him. This house, these pictures, this furniture, it is all *meaningless*, unless it represents another kind of wealth, too. You see, Mark, I can *afford* to give sanctuary to people, and that is what I do.'

Mark felt strange. Jonathan was standing in the window so that Mark couldn't see him properly. With the sunlight behind him, streaming in through the window, Jonathan had become a dark silhouette limned by dazzling gold. For an instant, Jonathan reminded him of Mr Hammond although he couldn't be sure in what way, and then Jonathan moved away from the window again.

Mark shook his head, confused. 'In what way did you give me sanctuary?' he asked. 'I mean, you had Sean cut part of my ear off.'

'Is that what you think?' Jonathan said thoughtfully. 'Yes, I suppose you would. But actually, *you* are the one who set in train the series of events that would lead to you having your earlobe cut off. I didn't order anything. From the moment you received my £40,000, it was your own actions that led you on your own journey – and they have led you here, too, of course, to drinking tea with me.'

'I had a bag thrust into my arms,' said Mark. 'I didn't know it had money in it.'

'What did Sean say to you when he gave you the bag? I believe he said "Make sure Jonathan gets this," or something of that sort. And here you are. How obedient of you. Where did you get this particular set of banknotes, may I ask?'

'I was given it.'

'You mean given it in the same way that Sean "gave" it to you?'

'No, not exactly,' he said. 'I didn't steal it. But it *is* stolen money, if that's what you mean.'

Mark sipped his tea and tried one of the pastries, which was light and seemed to be filled with some kind of sweet almond paste. It was delicious.

'It is not necessary for me to know how you got the money,' Jonathan told him. 'It is not me who will be facing the consequences of its acquisition.'

'But I guess, by your logic,' said Mark, 'that there will be consequences for you in taking this money from me.'

'Ah, no,' said Jonathan. 'You see, I am not going to accept your money. Of course I use the term "your money" in the loosest possible way.'

This came as a shock to Mark, and was completely unexpected. 'What are you going to do then?' he asked, suddenly fearful. 'How can I pay you back?'

Jonathan laughed, a sudden burst of bright merriment. 'Mark,' he chuckled and came back to sit beside him on the settee, 'you're still stuck in thinking of these things in terms of you and me. Take the scenario that we have here. I wonder how you would describe it if you were to be reductive about it? Let's see. Perhaps you might say that you took some money, then you gave it back, and now, hopefully, all is well. But this leaves out the most important aspect of the whole business. You take some money, *and that has consequences.* You spend some of the money, and maybe you give some of it away, *and that has consequences-'*

'I had a lot of it stolen.'

'Well, that would certainly have consequences, wouldn't it? And now you're giving it back to me, but even if I were to accept it, there is still a whole web of consequences that are in the process of working themselves out. My accepting money from you wouldn't be the end of those consequences, would it?'

'I hoped it might be.'

'Of course you did, but that – in effect – is giving up *responsibility* for the consequences that you have set in motion. You hope that you will give the money to me now, and then, miraculously, and in spite of everything that has happened since the day you took the bag from Sean, I will call everything off so that you can go back to your home and be left in peace.' Jonathan spread his arms wide and shrugged. 'I'm sorry, Mark, but it's not something that I can do for you.'

Mark didn't respond straight away. 'It's funny,' he said eventually, 'but there's something about responsibility that I don't understand. I've been doing some renovation work on a house recently-'

'Yes, Mr Hammond's house in the Old Town. I made it my business to find out where you were staying and what you were doing.'

'Oh,' said Mark, shaken by Jonathan's knowledge. He paused for a moment before continuing. 'Well, anyway, the point is that even though I'm competent at what I do, I've still managed to mess up every job I've done there. And, this is the thing, I *have* taken responsibility for that. I didn't for a moment try to hide it or pretend I hadn't got it wrong, and yet I still seem to be stuck.'

'I suppose this is the hardest thing of all,' said Jonathan, 'to know *what* it is you have to take responsibility for. For example, how do you intend to rectify the situation? Not by running away, I hope.'

Mark felt a stab of accusation, and sighed. He might so easily have run away with Natalie, if she'd let him. 'I suppose you mean I should take responsibility for the consequences that you referred to earlier,' he said.

Jonathan smiled. 'Now you're getting the idea,' he said.

'I suppose there's no point in asking your advice on how to do that? You would just say I wasn't taking responsibility for myself.'

'Advice can be both good and bad, you know,' Jonathan told him. 'My advice to you is to make good on your original intention, whatever that was.'

'My original intention was to leave my old life behind and go out into the world to find something better.'

'Then try to do that. That is my advice,' he laughed. 'But of course, I haven't answered your question about *how* to do that, have I?'

He picked up a small golden bell from the table, and shook it gently. It gave a sweet, penetrating ring.

'Mr Hammond is a friend of mine,' Jonathan said into the fresh silence. 'As soon as I understood that you were taking refuge in his home, I cancelled your debt. As you now know, this money means nothing to me, so don't thank me for that. It was you who made that happen by taking up residence where you did. You see, consequences can be positive as well as negative.'

Anna came in to take the tray away and, as she did so, Jonathan stood. Mark followed suit.

'Please,' he said, 'say hello to Tara for me when you see her. I have a great respect for her, as well as for Mr Hammond. And please, also, feel free to use my garden whenever you want. I'm often away and then the lower gate is locked, but the garden is available throughout the year to everyone that I have met and for whom I have high regard. And I am happy to say that that includes you, Mark. We have a couple of boats, too, if you should ever want to get out onto the lake. Sean has the keys to both the garden and the boathouse and will happily let you have them if you ask.'

Mark felt strange about having yet another bag with money in it under his bed. He felt no desire to spend any of it, and so it seemed academic and rather pointless that he had it at all. He wasn't quite sure what he felt about having the debt cancelled by Jonathan (or Mr Jonathan as now he referred to him in his head), but chagrin was definitely part of it. It was almost irritating to know that, all this time, he had in fact been free to roam the town without threat. From the moment he'd accepted Mr Hammond's refuge – or at least, from the moment Jonathan knew he'd done so – he'd been safe from pursuit or reprisal.

The first thing he did was to go down to Baker's Yard to look for Don and the others. As he walked there, he remembered seeing Don accepting the boathouse keys from Sean in the spring. How suspicious Mark had been! How angry and betrayed he'd felt when he'd seen Holly holding them! And yet, Don and Ingrid must have been given permission to use

Jonathan's garden and boathouse, just as he had been. In fact, it was clear now that Don had asked Sean to borrow the keys specifically for the purpose of making Mark's birthday into a special celebration. That was why he'd been so secretive about it when Mark had challenged him at the harbourside café. God, what a fool he'd made of himself! How stupidly narrow. He'd completely ruined a burgeoning friendship through his lack of trust.

But when he got to Baker's Yard, he found that the house was boarded up and there was no one there. Mark felt desolate as he looked at the rough boards that were nailed over the windows. Where was everyone? Where had they gone? It was disconcerting and rather worrying, but there was no point in standing there looking at the place. There was nothing to learn from staring at the impersonal boarding. He left the yard and went across the road to the off licence, where a bearded young man was serving.

'Hello,' said Mark, 'I'm trying to find someone who used to work here last year. A woman called Holly?'

'Holly?' said the man. 'Oh yes, with a piercing in her lower lip? She left as I was starting. I'm sorry, I don't know where she went. I think she got a job which had something to do with mental health, but I don't know any more than that.'

Mark went back to the house. He felt unsure what to do with himself. He still didn't want to start on any of the jobs he had to do because, if nothing was going right, what was the point in even making an attempt? And, of course, he now had £40,000. He could move out if he liked. But where to? That was the question.

The following day, Mark felt somewhat unnerved by the fact that there was no imperative for him to stay on in the house.

Wasn't that the one thing that had defined him recently: the fact that he had no choice but stay there, to keep danger at bay? Wasn't that what refuge was all about, anyway: being allowed to have a safe space in a hostile world? But what if the world was no longer hostile? Did he still need refuge? It was all too much to take in right now. He accepted the fact that Sean was no longer looking for him to get the money back. But he wasn't sure what sense he might make of that, for himself, in terms of what he could do with himself and where he might go.

The weather was clear again over the next few days, with a touch of spring in the air, and so he went out walking. Beyond the town, on the far side of the harbour, there was a series of cliffs and inlets that he'd never felt inclined to explore at first, and then latterly it had not been safe to do so. He wasn't sure of the rock, but it looked like gritty sandstone to him. It was certainly crumbly and unstable, and the cliffs themselves had skirts of fallen rock at their feet, where the high tide lapped quietly. He could imagine the winter storms being spectacular here – and dangerous. The inlets were narrow and uninhab-ited, with tiny beaches of unwelcoming cracked stone that was full of fossils.

The place was wonderfully peaceful down by the sea, with only the sound of waves and gulls to break into his thoughts. When he glanced up, he could see birds circling above the cliff, apparently effortlessly, lifted by the updraft. One day, he saw a couple of cormorants on a rock a short way out, looking stately and serene. A trawler was chugging back to harbour with a swirl of seagulls behind it and Mark suddenly felt a kind of wild openness within himself that seemed to match the landscape in front of him. Being stuck in the house had prevented him from getting out here, and that was a shame. Climbing the cliff path was particularly invigorating, with its fresh sea breeze and stunning views. From up there the horizon looked pale and sharp.

Back in the house, he began to feel more relaxed than he'd been since he arrived in the town, and although there was a tinge of loneliness to his experience, it was bearable. This state managed to last for some time, and Mark fell into a routine of eating simple food in the house and going out for daily walks. One afternoon, a few weeks after he'd met Jonathan, Mark came in and saw a note for him on the hall table, in Tara's handwriting.

*A woman called Gemma dropped by to talk to you. She said she would call again this evening.*

It was 3.30pm. Mark wondered about the name. It was familiar, but he couldn't place it, until he remembered that Clare had a girlfriend called Gemma – a florist who worked at the rather second rate shop down from the station. He left the house and went straight out to see if he could find her there. When he got to the shop he found a woman outside, arranging some irises in a galvanised bucket and so he went up to her and said, 'Are you Gemma?'

She looked worried, Mark thought.

'Why do you ask?' she said cautiously.

'Because someone called Gemma left a note for me earlier,' he said. 'My name is Mark.'

'God!' she exclaimed. 'Of course, I should have recognised you straight away because of the ear. Come inside, please.'

She took him to the back of the shop, where they couldn't be seen through the shop window.

'I've got a message from Clare. It's about John at Club Covert. He knows that you have something to do with the money that Natalie stole.'

Mark felt confused.

'What do you mean?'

'John's been away for several weeks, but now that he's back he wants to clear this up. He sent a couple of the bouncers round to talk to Clare,' she told him. 'She was seen talking to you on the night that the money was stolen, and they were suspicious of that, because you were also seen talking to Natalie, just before she did her fire trick. It's all got something to do with your ear, apparently. Apart from anything else it makes you very distinctive, but also, John seemed to think it meant something very particular, and he seemed sure that it proved you were the one who masterminded the theft.'

'But–'

'Yes, I know you didn't. But suspicion has fallen on you. They were asking where you lived. Of course, Clare didn't tell them.'

Mark felt a familiar sense of panic welling up.

'Also,' Gemma said, 'Clare has reported Natalie missing to the police.'

'She left town the morning after the fire at the club,' Mark told her. 'She stayed the night at my place and left in the morning.'

Gemma considered that for a moment.

'I hope you're right,' she said eventually, 'but still, it's almost impossible to imagine that she would have left and not contacted Clare to say that she was okay.'

'Natalie implied to me that they weren't that close,' said Mark.

'That's not true. They argued quite a lot towards the end, but that was only because Clare was trying to support Natalie in getting herself together, so that she could move on from Club Covert and get her life back. Natalie appreciated that Clare cared enough to keep on trying. But she could really lose her temper, too. You know how it is with heroin.'

'No, I don't, actually,' said Mark. 'But I guess I can take your word for it.'

'Anyway,' said Gemma, 'you need to be careful. I'm sorry you came down here to see me because it may not be safe.'

'What about Clare?'

'I don't really think they're suspicious of her. They were a bit rough, but they didn't beat her up. She's never been into drugs, and has never been unreliable, so there wasn't any reason why she would ever want to try to do something dangerous. She'd made the money she needed, too, and they knew it. Why would she want to steal more? They just wanted to frighten her a bit. They succeeded, too. I don't suppose that will be the end of it, though, which is worrying.'

Mark looked down at the floor and noticed the trimmings of greenery scattered there. Debris. 'Okay,' he said, 'thanks for letting me know. I hope that Clare really is all right.'

'I hope that Natalie is.'

'Yes, of course,' he said. 'Let's hope she did go off as she said she was going to.'

Gemma nodded.

'Listen,' he said, 'tell Clare that I'm sorry she's got involved in this. It has nothing to do with her and it's a shame.'

'We're all inescapably caught up in each other's lives,' said Gemma. 'There's nothing you can do about it, Mark. Sometimes that works in your favour, and sometimes it doesn't. If you tried to live in a vacuum, well, for a start, you'd fail, but you would also die. Of loneliness, as well as lack of oxygen.'

Mark nodded. 'You're right,' he told her. 'You are so right.'

He took a deep breath. 'Could you tell Clare that I wish her well?'

'I'd be happy to,' said Gemma. 'And I wish you well, too. I would also warn you to be as careful as possible. The men who have been asking about you are dangerous. I mean, as in "they might kill you" dangerous. Chopping a bit of your ear off seems positively tame in comparison to what I've heard of this lot.'

'Yes,' said Mark, 'I got that impression.'

He left the shop and went straight back to the house. Along with a sense of fear and lack of safety, there was an almost amusing – albeit blackly amusing – feeling of *déjà vu*. He'd had a few days off, and now it was all starting again! There were dangerous men out there looking for him, to try and recover a stolen £40,000. The difference was that he actually had the money this time, so if he wanted to he could just go down to Club Covert and hand it over. But this seemed far less straightforward than it had done when he'd gone looking for Sean. This time, for instance, there would be all the fire damage to the club to consider, and although John Luscombe may well have been insured for both the damage and for any loss of income incurred, there was still the ill will of it all, and – potentially – the desire for revenge to be taken into account.

The best thing, he decided, was to go upstairs and talk it through with Mr Hammond. Mr Hammond might be cryptic, but he was obviously sensible and Mark trusted him, so when he got back he went straight up and knocked on the door of the attic suite. He waited for a while, wondering what he might say and realised that he didn't know what advice he was actually hoping for.

No one answered, and so he knocked more loudly and waited again. After a while a door opened on the floor below, and he heard Tara's voice.

'Hello there, are you after Mr Hammond? Oh, it's you Mark,' she said as he came down. 'I'm afraid he went into hospital this morning.'

'Oh,' said Mark, 'I didn't know.'

'It was going to be next Wednesday,' she told him, 'but there was a cancellation on a bed and they've let him in a week early. I'm glad I bumped into you because I want to give you the keys to his suite, so that you can get to work on it while he's away.'

'He's going to be away for a while, isn't he?' Mark asked.

'Well,' said Tara, 'it's a bit worrying, really. It's likely to be at least two weeks before he's home, but it's not at all straightforward to have an operation at Mr Hammond's age.'

'Oh,' said Mark.

'Yes. But that doesn't affect the work that needs to be done here. I hope you don't mind the short notice?'

'I don't know whether I've got the competence for it,' he said. 'You know what a mess I've made of things.'

'Mark,' she said, 'I won't deny that I've got some real concerns about this, but I'm still willing to give you another chance. Even so, you do need to know how things stand.'

'How do things stand?'

'I'm afraid I can't offer to let you stay in the house unless you start working on it again. If you can't commit yourself to working on Mr Hammond's apartment while he's away, then I will have to get a professional builder in. I am placing an advertisement in the paper next week for the room that is currently vacant, and if I have to get a builder in, then it would seem pragmatic to let out your room to raise money towards the costs of that.'

'Let me have a look at what needs to be done,' Mark told her, 'and I'll have a word with you later. And anyway,' he added, 'I can start paying rent, that's no problem. I have some money now.'

Tara ignored him and went back into her room to get the keys.

'Here you are,' she said coming out and handing them to him. 'Let me know if there are any further supplies that you need. I'll come and have a chat with you this evening after you've looked over the suite.' She looked him directly in the eyes. 'This is it,' she said. 'Now, it's up to you.'

Mark lay on his bed, trying to pull his thoughts together. There seemed to be no end to his troubles. How deep did the rabbit hole go, he wondered? Everything was happening as Jonathan had said it would. Consequences. When he thought about it logically, it was obvious. If you pushed a boulder off the top of a hill, it wasn't going to stop half way down just because you wanted it to. No, it would roll on down, relentlessly gathering speed and momentum, bringing all sorts of other debris with it, until it came to rest somewhere below. And what sort of mess would that make? Mark didn't want to wait around to find out. His first impulse was to leave, cut his losses and make a fresh start elsewhere. What was the point in staying here? Why not go to the station and get the first train out of town? He could even go home. He could probably set himself up in business using the money he had. . . and even if he didn't want to see Amy again, perhaps he would be able to see Ty. There was that pain again, of love and loss as he thought of him.

But what was it that Jonathan had said? *How do you intend to rectify the situation? Not by running away, I hope...*

He was sobered by a sudden realisation, which washed over him like ice cold water. Coming down here hadn't allowed him to escape from Sean, so why did he think that going home would be an effective strategy for freeing himself from John Luscombe and his thugs? He saw very clearly for the first time that he was stuck in a loop of his own making. Events seemed to be repeating themselves, but only because he insisted on making the same choices. And this time the stakes were even higher. It was vital that he did the right thing, whatever that was.

Mr Hammond's absence was palpable, and upsetting. Mark had felt safe and protected in the knowledge that Mr Hammond was up there in the attic, if not actually looking out for him, then imbuing the house with benevolent energy. And there had been the reassuring knowledge that he could pop up and have a word with him at any time. Even as he was thinking this, Mark recognised that his thoughts were shot through with an unhealthy self-pity, but there was also a genuine sadness that Mr Hammond was ill. And a genuine sense of potential loss – loss of that simple wisdom which could communicate so much in so few words. There was no sense of purpose that Mark could hold onto any more. He didn't know what to do, and now there was nobody to ask about it. He wondered if he should go up to look over Mr Hammond's room now that he had the chance, but didn't quite have the energy for it.

He remembered Tara mentioning that it was Wednesday, and he knew that once a month, on a Wednesday, the residents of Baker's Yard went to the Harbour Tavern for the live music night there. He wondered if tonight might be the night.

The thought of going down to see if he could find them seemed risky, but on reflection – and just as he had done before in a similar situation – he felt that he might as well do something. Lying here, with his thoughts endlessly going round in circles, would achieve nothing.

He walked down to the Harbour Tavern feeling furtive, almost criminal. He felt particularly exposed once he got down to the quayside, as if the eyes of the whole town were upon him. He tried to resist the temptation to look around him, but failed. On reflex, he glanced about as he went, half-expecting a gang of thugs to leap out at him from the shadows. But everyone looked perfectly ordinary.

It was shortly after seven-thirty when he got to the bar, but there was no sign of a band setting up their equipment.

'Isn't there live music tonight?' he asked the barman as he bought a pint.

'That'll be in a fortnight, mate,' he replied, 'the last Wednesday of the month.'

'Oh,' Mark murmured.

He took his drink over to the back of the bar, where he could sit as inconspicuously as possible to drink it. The bar wasn't particularly busy, so he had a choice of table. He noticed a discreet position behind a pillar at the edge of a large alcove, so he went there and sat down, feeling extremely unsafe. Now that he knew there was no chance of meeting the Baker's Yard gang it seemed like madness to be out in public.

He decided that he would finish his drink and then order a taxi at the bar so that he wouldn't have to walk through the streets. He could feel a tremor in his arm as he lifted his glass and it was this, more than anything else, that made him realise that he was genuinely afraid. Fear. It was familiar to him, but it wasn't something he'd ever expected to feel so often as an adult.

He took a gulp of beer and as he did so, he heard a strange noise behind him, a choking sound of distress. He turned and saw that, at the table in the alcove, there were three women. They hadn't attracted his attention before because he was on the lookout for menacing-looking men, but now that he looked at them properly, he noticed that one of the women had a black eye and a contusion on one of her cheeks. It was she who had made the noise, and as Mark looked at her she raised her head and they made eye contact. They both recognised each other in the same moment. She was the other friend of Natalie's, who had been with her that first time he'd seen her, along with Clare.

'Oh!' she cried, 'it's you!'

He got up and crossed to her table.

'Are you okay?' he asked.

'They've got Natalie,' she said in a sort of strangulated whisper. 'They let me go, but not before they did this. I think they're taking her to the east pontoon – that derelict wooden pier on the far side of the harbour.'

'Oh my God!' he exclaimed, feeling a sudden panic welling up, followed swiftly by pounding urgency. 'Okay,' he asked her, 'where's the east pontoon? That one out on its own, on the far side of Club Covert?'

'Yes.'

He nodded to himself. He remembered looking down at it from the cliffs.

'Have you been to the police?' he asked.

'No,' she said, and made the same choking noise that had first attracted Mark's attention. 'They said that if I did, they would. . . kill me.'

This was clearly not an empty threat.

'How long ago was this?' he asked.

'About an hour.'

He looked at her briefly then turned and ran from the bar, leaving his drink virtually untouched.

He sprinted along the harbour side, but it was impossible to keep up that pace for very long. He had to slow down before he'd got very far and then continued at a more modest loping run, a stitch starting to catch him just below his diaphragm, his breath coming in ragged gasps. He ran down towards Club Covert and as he passed it he noticed a large padlock on the front doors. The place looked well and truly closed. He could dimly see that the waste ground beyond had a lot of broken concrete rubble on it and random mounds of hardcore waste, and so it was slow going to pick his way through it in the dark. More than once he nearly turned his ankle on the uneven terrain in his hurry. The evening was getting cold now, which was just as well because he was working up a good sweat as he scrambled over some particularly awkward concrete slabs with metal rods sticking from them at odd angles.

The east pontoon was near the eastern edge of the harbour and there was some more light here, from the harbour, lighting the huge timbers, many of which were missing. The tide was low, and the exposed lower parts of the stanchions were thickly encrusted with mussels, and the dark mud they stood in looked sticky and unappealing. The shadowy under-side of the pontoon was darker still and he couldn't see much at all down there.

Then, with a shocking jolt, he saw something pale in the dark; a hand perhaps, immobile, drooping over a barnacled rock, in a deep recess. He jumped onto the pontoon and nego-tiated a couple of missing planks. Then, at a point where some of the structure was missing, he found that he could crouch down and peer amongst the struts. He could just see something – or someone. With a sickening thump in his chest, he realised that it was probably Natalie, but he couldn't see her well enough to be sure. Carefully, he lowered himself down onto the level of the criss-crossing wooden supports below the walkway. Here the wood was green with fine tendrils of slippery weed, and as Mark tried to put his weight on the angled surface he slipped and lost his footing, sliding a couple of feet before going over backwards. He landed agonisingly on his coccyx and then tumbled another six feet or so down into the deep sticky mud below. He was unable to move for a few moments. The pain in his spine was overwhelming, and the breath had been knocked out of him, so he lay there in agony, looking up at the underside of the pontoon. After a while, though, when the intensity of pain began to subside, he tried to move, but the freezing mud seemed to suck at his arms as he pulled his hands from the sludge, and he felt a wild, panicky revulsion. The cold was taking his breath away, too, and the smell of decay rose up nauseatingly around him. He twisted over, trying to right himself, and as he did so, he found himself looking up into the gloom, at the silhouette of a bare foot a couple of feet above him.

He painfully pulled himself up from the mud, which made dreadful sucking sounds as he wrenched one of his feet free, and saw that the naked leg was at an impossible angle. The body beyond – also naked – was face down. Even so, against the harbour lights, he could make out Natalie's hair. He didn't really need to see her face. As he looked across at her, resting on a wide beam three or four feet above the mud, he felt a sudden chill of paralysing horror that made him shake. This lasted for a few breaths, until he could gain some control and allow the trembling to subside. Then, he pulled himself up and onto the mussels so that he could sit beside her. Gingerly, he pulled back some hair. Yes, it was her. Eyes closed. He could just make out a red welt on her neck.

As he looked at her, the feelings of creeping horror, panic and revulsion gave way to intense waves of sadness and a welling up of sickening, impotent rage. It seemed especially wrong that she should be naked. The tears that sprang up seemed so inadequate a response to what had happened that he dashed them from his eyes with a violent swipe of his forearm.

He found that he was gritting his teeth so hard that his jaw was cramping. Turning away from her, he was startled by a sliding, clattering sound that made him jump. He looked up to see if anyone was coming, but as he did so he realised that the sound had been caused by Natalie's body slithering slowly over the mussels, finally giving in to gravity. His fall must have dislodged her from her temporary resting place. She slipped down, her head bumping once against another beam so that she seemed for a moment to be trying to look up, and then she was off over the far side, with a splash, into a weedy pool.

It was considerably darker down there, and as Mark looked at her and saw the faintest silhouette of her body, face down in the water in the darkness, he realised that, really, all he could do was to leave her there. There was no point trying to cover her up or even to get down to where she had now come to rest – however temporarily.

He sat and looked at her shadowy form and the sorrow came back, the rage switching itself off so suddenly that it was like a physical jolt. He sat for a while and allowed himself to feel the sorrow. *If I hadn't given her that £4,000 this would never have happened*, he thought. Guilt welled up, this time, along with self-hatred and a blistering gust of self-blame. Everything had gone wrong since he'd got here. His failure to get things right in the house seemed totally insignificant under the circumstances, but even this fed the wave of self-pity that shook him as he looked down into the gathering gloom. It was one thing to have ruined things for himself, but to have dragged Natalie into it in this way. . .

Even as he was thinking this he knew it was faulty logic, but it was all a part of the welter of feeling that was banging in his chest. It didn't seem to have any way out, least of all a logical one. It wasn't until he felt the cramp in his legs that he thought about his own safety, and that perhaps he ought to try to get away. Perhaps John Luscombe's men were on the lookout for him, even now.

He stood as well as he could and, reaching up to the planks above him, hauled himself up into the night. As he stood and looked down at himself, he could see how covered in mud he was. Conspicuous wasn't the word for it. He needed to get it off before returning to town.

Now that he was in the open he felt far more vulnerable than he had before. He remembered, from looking down on this part of town from the hills, that if he carried on eastwards along the shoreline he would reach the foot of the cliffs. If he could only get there, he could double back across the hillside to the top of the harbour without having to retrace his steps or go anywhere near Club Covert. Padlocked up or not, the club seemed worth giving as wide a berth as possible.

He picked his way along the tide line, feeling shivery and wet. It was only another couple of hundred yards to the place where the cliff path led up and away from the shore. As he scrambled onwards he came upon a short, disused concrete jetty, beyond which were the beginnings of the cliffs. Once on the jetty, Mark looked down at the cold, stinking mud that was clinging to his clothes. He was a mess. Then he looked down at the sea from the jetty, and with hardly a thought he walked to the end of it and jumped. It was about eight feet down to the water, which was quite deep at that point. There was an almost pleasing moment of apparent weightlessness as he fell, then the explosion of water against his skin. The sea was breathtakingly cold and, as he went under for a moment, he found that he was gasping involuntarily, which made him choke as he resurfaced. He swam awkwardly in his shoes, but managed to reach a rusted ladder on the jetty wall and, grasping it with one hand, his breath coming in shocking gasps of cold, he ruffled his shirt, and then his trousers, in the water. He could dimly see the mud coming away from his clothes and making the water cloudy around him. He kicked his legs vigorously in the water then, just as the cold was becoming overwhelming, pulled himself up the ladder and out of the sea. Water spattered from his clothes and onto the cracked concrete of the jetty as he stood up. Dripping freely, he walked to the fence at the foot of the burgeoning cliff, clambered over it and found himself on the footpath he had walked several times in the previous weeks, when he'd felt so free of threat and danger.

There was a breeze up here which made him shudder, and so he ran up the hill, breathless again. At the top, he paused. He was dripping less now and so he figured that he wouldn't be too conspicuous in town. He shook his head and ran his fingers through his hair to stop it feeling so matted. As he did so, he wondered what to do next. On one hand, he wanted to call the police, but on the other, John Luscombe's men had told Natalie's friend that she would be killed if the police were called. One person was already dead. Would it be fair – and would anyone be brought to justice – if he alerted anyone? He tried to discount any thought of his own personal safety when deciding what to do. He wanted to do what was right. Mr Hammond, as well as Jonathan, had banged on about consequences, and here he seemed to be right in the thick of them.

By the time he got to the bridge at the top end of the harbour, he had stopped dripping completely, and this was a relief as he made his way up to the house, trying to be inconspicuous and avoiding the main streets as far as possible. When he got back, he let himself in and went straight to his bedroom. Once he'd closed the door, he looked down at his clothes. Their apparent cleanliness in the dark had only been relative, and here, in the revealing light of his room, they still looked a state. He took them off and towelled himself down, then pulled on a pair of jeans. He seemed to be doubly shivering, with shock as well as cold. As he was putting on a tee-shirt, there was a knock on the door. He didn't have a chance to say anything because the door opened immediately and Tara came in.

'Hello Mark,' she said casually, as if continuing a conversation that had been momentarily interrupted, 'have you had a chance to look at the attic yet?'

She stopped and looked down at the wet clothes that were lying at his feet. Her expression changed.

'My goodness, are you all right?' she said. 'And what's that smell? It's like stagnant water.'

'No, I'm not all right,' he said, 'Natalie is dead. I found her body by the east pontoon about an hour ago.'

'Oh, Mark,' she said, 'how terrible! What happened? You've gone white. And you're shaking. You poor boy. Was it an accident?'

'No, she was murdered,' he told her.

'But this is terrible! Have the police been called?'

Mark hesitated. 'It's not as simple as that,' he said.

He wanted to have a bath, and to think. He knew that it might be important to talk this over with someone, but was Tara the right person? And where would he start? He was acutely aware that Mr Hammond was in hospital, and that he would have chosen to talk to him if he'd had the option.

'Come on,' she said. 'You shouldn't be on your own. Come and tell me all about it.'

'I need a bath,' he told her. 'I need to get warm and I've got the smell of this mud right up my nose.'

'Of course, you'll make yourself ill if you don't warm yourself up,' she said, turning and coming back into the room to pick up his clothes. 'I'll see to these for you. Come to my room as soon as you're warm enough.'

Half an hour later he was drinking tea with Tara and telling her his story, right from the day he went to see Don – in his guise as Ewan Rees – doing his comedy routine. He recounted everything that had happened to him in an almost impersonal way, as if it had happened to somebody else; as if it was a story he had heard rather than one that he had lived.

'I feel so guilty about what's happened,' he told her. 'I feel responsible for Natalie's death.'

Tara looked at him carefully. 'You have this all back to front,' she said. 'When Mr Hammond and Jonathan talked about the consequences of your actions, they were referring to your taking the money from Sean and coming down here. These are actions that will have certain consequences for you, because you *chose* to do them. Do you see? Giving Natalie £4,000 will have consequences for you too, but only up to a point. What she did with the money, that was her volition and the results of that are her consequences, not yours. You didn't ask her to steal money back for you. She knew the people she was dealing with and she took the risk. I know it's an appalling tragedy, Mark, and you are caught up in it because you are connected with Natalie, but her death is not your fault. Many things have led to that outcome and only a small proportion of them are to do with you. Surely you can see that?'

'In a way, now that you've cast an outsider's eye on it,' he said. 'But there's this voice that keeps saying, *If I hadn't given Natalie that money, she'd still be alive.*'

'Well, for one thing, that is something that we can't possibly say with any confidence,' Tara told him. 'Who knows what would have happened if you hadn't given her the money when you did? She might have killed herself in despair. Look at it this way: the car salesman who sells a car to a person who subsequently dies in an accident is not responsible for that person's death, is he? Even though he might say, quite rightly in one sense, *If I hadn't sold them that car, they'd still be alive.*'

'Oh, I don't know,' said Mark with a heavy sigh. 'None of it seems clear. In the end it doesn't matter. Natalie is dead, and I'm still wondering whether I should go to the police.'

'Under the circumstances, I don't think you should,' said Tara. 'For what it's worth, I think that doing so really would be jeopardising Natalie's friend. Those men are obviously dangerous, and their death threats are not idle, as we now know. Natalie's body will be found soon enough and then the police will know anyway. You did say that this girl Clare has reported Natalie missing? Well, leave it at that, Mark. There's nothing more you can do. The trick is to know when to take responsibility for your own actions and when to leave others' alone.'

Mark looked at Tara. Her face had less colour than usual, he thought, but she seemed calm and serene. 'You don't seem particularly shocked by my story,' he told her.

'Should I be? All human beings have a story.'

'What do you mean?'

'Anyway,' she added, 'I knew that something was afoot with you, otherwise you wouldn't have seen our advertisement, would you? I've heard much worse than your story, believe me. It's quite heartbreaking about Natalie, though, poor girl. I always thought there was something tragic about her, when she came over from time to time to see Rachel. Some people try, but I'm afraid they haven't quite got what it takes to escape from themselves.'

Mark slept fitfully that night. His mind endlessly replayed that first glimpse of Natalie's hand, and then that awful, creepy sound as her body slithered off the musselled stanchion and slipped into the dark water. And the gentle quality of her expression, as he pulled her hair back and saw her eyes, with the dark smudge of their long lashes, closed gently and forever. And then there was the sense of threat. If they could kill Natalie without compunction, so nonchalantly, what would they do if they found him? Was there any reason to imagine that the house offered refuge from this new threat?

The cyclic nature of what was happening was becoming more and more abundantly clear. He had £40,000 in a bag in his room, and there were people after him to get it back. The situation had an unnerving symmetry.

He pondered this, but felt on reflection that there was an important difference. *He* was different, surely? He understood that the only real thing to do was to stay where he was and somehow break the cycle. He thought of Mr Hammond, and knew in his heart that he was safe in the house, and so he decided that he would go up to the attic rooms in the morning and have a good look at what needed to be done.

The attic suite was in the same condition as the rest of the house. It needed to be rewired and redecorated. The little kitchenette, which occupied a recess by the chimney breast, was a bit old but still functional. Perhaps the taps in the sink should be replaced, but that was about the extent of the work. It obviously hadn't seen a huge amount of use, and all the units were made of good, solid wood. In fact, the whole long room was a beautiful space, light and airy. It reminded Mark of the room in Jonathan's house, although he couldn't say why. That room had been huge, and filled with beautiful objects. This one was small, Spartan and functional. Perhaps it was something to do with the light? The air seemed to be alive in some way.

# 8. Going Forth. . .

The next week was a strange experience for Mark. Before he did any of the re-wiring in Mr Hammond's attic rooms, he checked and double-checked that he was using 2.5mm heavy-duty cable on a 30 amp fuse. He even asked Tara to come up and witness that he was using the correct, heavy grey cable before he removed the relevant skirting boards to lay the circuits. But once he'd started, it was so absorbing that he could lose himself in his task for hours at a time. And, when it came to decorating, there was something transformative about painting the walls in pleasing pale colours.

Personal safety was not something that occurred to him whilst he was at work. He *knew* that he was safe here, and he felt a sense of purpose in getting the place ready for Mr Hammond's return from hospital. Tara told him on the second day that Mr Hammond's operation had been a success and that he would be recuperating in hospital for another week or two before coming home. Because it was something abdominal, he had to be under observation for the first part of his recovery.

As he worked, Mark's internal landscape bloomed with moments of deep sadness. Curious surges of grief would arise apparently from nowhere. He was aware that he'd never had a chance to get to know Natalie, and there was a sense of missed opportunity in that, but he also acknowledged that most of the grief was an ancient grief, from deep in his past. An upwelling that he couldn't quite grasp, but which felt cathartic and healing.

Tara was helpful. She seemed to be around quite a lot and he would bump into her in the kitchen, and her simple acceptance of him had a healing effect, too. In the second week – almost shockingly – as he continued with his work, he found himself having odd moments of extraordinary happiness. He remembered how happy he'd felt last time he'd given himself up to the task of sorting out the house. This time, though, there was something different. He was here of his own accord. And what a fundamental difference that was. He was doing this because he wanted to do it, and not in order to pay for his refuge. He was doing this to try and get a job well done. And for Mr Hammond, a man he respected more than he thought possible, considering how little time they'd actually spent together.

When he finished the work at last, his sense of satisfaction was intense. But before declaring it officially completed, he took the precaution of removing one of the skirting boards to make a last check that the rewiring was in order. All was well. He went down to Tara's room and knocked on the door.

'It's all finished,' he told her. 'Do you want to come and have a look?'

She came up and they stood in the long room, sunshine streaming through, radiantly.

'It should look great when we get some new carpet down,' he said.

'It looks great now,' said Tara.

'I think I'm almost ready to put the rest of the house right,' he told her as he surveyed his handiwork. 'It seemed insurmountable before, but, really, what else do I have to do? There's no point in waiting, is there?'

He stopped and looked up at the sky through the skylight.

'Well done,' said Tara into the silence. She squeezed his arm lightly.

'You know, it seems to me,' he said slowly, 'that I have spent my entire life *waiting*, and I don't know why. Even when I was doing things, I was waiting for what was going to happen after I'd finished doing them – and never enjoying *that*, because I simply started waiting again, for the next thing. I suppose I was waiting to become happy, although what I was doing was actually *preventing* that from happening.'

Tara was smiling at him. 'You're right,' she said. 'And so many people never quite discover this.'

'Although, I guess I'm still waiting, in some senses,' he said. 'I'm waiting for Mr Hammond to return so that I can talk to him. I'm waiting to do the exterior of the house.' He paused and thought for a moment while Tara watched him carefully.

'Such terrible things can happen in the outside world,' he told her. 'And I really do feel safe here.'

'And yet,' said Tara, 'this *is* part of the outside world, you know. It's not separate from it at all. And what you describe is a process. You are in the process of doing up this house. That's not really waiting, is it? It's a kind of *doing*.'

He thought about that for a few moments. 'Maybe that's true,' he said, a little doubtfully.

'It's the key thing,' Tara told him. 'Otherwise, what use

would refuge be? You can't spend your life in hiding, can you? You'd end up waiting again; waiting for the outside world, whatever that means, to become safe, whatever *that* means!'

'But Natalie's killers *are* still out there. They know who I am and what I look like.'

'Yes,' said Tara, 'you're quite right. Don't be lulled into a false sense of security, please, Mark. There are always dangers.'

'At least I don't seem to be waiting for my life to "happen" any more. This is it. Right now.'

Tara smiled broadly. 'Some people seem to think that happiness resides only in being able to look ahead to a certain future,' she said. 'But what does that mean? Happiness often comes at precisely the point that life seems most uncertain.'

The following day he began working on the rest of the house. He decided that he would do the rewiring first, and began by removing the plug sockets from the wall in the mezzanine. He knelt by the socket with the plastic covering in his hands and peered at the wiring. The thick, grey cable of the ring main was immediately visible. *It was the correct wiring.* He looked hard again, nonplussed. But it was true. The wiring was perfect.

In a way it was more shocking to discover that he had unaccountably got it right, than it was to have discovered that he'd unaccountably got it wrong.

He went downstairs and looked up at the ceiling in the hallway. Yes, there were some dried-out water stains, but the plaster itself was intact. Now that he looked at it closely, he realised that all it needed was a couple of coats of paint to put it right. As he stood there, the front door opened and Tara came in. She looked composed, but calm and thoughtful.

'Oh, hello Mark, I'm glad you're here. I've just come back

from the hospital. I'm afraid Mr Hammond has had a stroke. They're not clear how bad it is. He's still unable to speak at the moment.'

Mark took a deep breath but was unable to say anything himself for a moment.

'Of course, he was in exactly the right place,' she said, 'so he got immediate help, which I'm told is vital for an almost complete recovery.'

'It seems unfair,' said Mark, 'given that his operation went so well.'

'Risk of stroke was always the big thing,' Tara told him. 'He may well make a good recovery, but he won't be coming home as early as expected.'

She looked in the carrier bag that she was holding and pulled out the day's paper. 'Here,' she said, 'you should look at this when you've got a moment.'

Mark took the paper from her and Tara went upstairs. After a few moments he followed her and went on up to the attic. The brightness of the sunshine seemed to accentuate the emptiness in there.

He sat on the settee and looked up through the skylights above him. Small clouds were moving slowly across the sky with a gentle grace. Their beauty was uplifting even as Mark's heart filled with sadness. He picked up the paper and unfolded it. The headline read: 'Local Businessman Questioned Over Lap Dancer Death'. Under that, it read: 'John Luscombe, local businessman and owner of table dancing venue Club Covert, was being questioned last night regarding the death of one of the dancers from his club. He was arrested yesterday morning on charges of fraud and was already in custody when the dancer's body was found.' Mark quickly read the rest of the article which wasn't particularly informative and which ended up vaguely speculating about the (possibly large) extent of Mr Luscombe's wealth. There was a reference to a seafront residence and a countryside 'retreat'.

Mark was aware of two immediate reactions: firstly, he felt relief at the arrest, and secondly, a curiosity as to how this would affect him. On one hand, the mere fact of John's arrest would not necessarily stop him from having Mark pursued. There were his lackeys to be considered and they might still be acting on orders. But on the other hand, it might just as easily put paid to all activity of that kind. Maybe a lot of people, in the town and elsewhere, were a lot safer as of today.

Mark couldn't help smiling. He sighed and felt a tension coming out of his body as an extension of his sigh. Along with the sigh came a pulse of sorrow. Why was it, he thought, that everything seems to be so caught up with everything else? He couldn't simply be happy because John Luscombe had been arrested, because the shock of Natalie's death was still too fresh in his mind. He couldn't feel simple pleasure that his work on the house was going so well, because of the worry he felt about whether Mr Hammond would ever get to see it.

As he was considering this, Tara called to him. 'Mark, there are some people downstairs to see you.'

'Okay,' he called back, 'I'm coming.'

He left the paper where it was and came downstairs. In the hall were Clare and Gemma.

'Hello,' he said, 'come on into the kitchen. I'll make us some tea. How are you both?'

'Have you seen the paper?' Clare asked as she followed him in.

'Yes,' he said, 'isn't it good news?'

'Fantastic,' she laughed. 'Who'd have thought it?'

'They're not offering bail, either,' said Gemma, 'so they obviously think they've nailed him properly.'

'This means that you'll be safe,' Clare told him.

'Does it?' he asked.

'One of John's bouncers came round a few days ago, asking for further information from me and Wendy. He said he was going to come back the next night, but he didn't arrive, and we haven't seen anyone from the club since. We wondered about that, but when we saw the paper, we realised that explained it. There's no one to give orders. I bet all John's thugs have left town already. I shouldn't think they'd want to be questioned by the police.'

Mark made tea before broaching the subject of Natalie. 'Was reading it in the paper today the first you knew of her death?' he asked.

Clare welled up with tears. 'No, that was in the paper the day before yesterday,' she said, 'although it was obvious by then that something like that must have happened, considering what they did to Wendy. But there's a huge difference between suspecting something and having it confirmed. Wendy said she bumped into you in the Harbour Tavern on the night that she was beaten up, and that you sprinted off. What happened?'

'I found her,' he said quietly. 'But it was already too late.'

He briefly told them what had happened, without going into full details. He also said why he hadn't told the police. 'And I didn't feel safe enough to come down and talk to you,' he said. 'I mean, it might have been unsafe for you to be seen talking to me.'

'I'm so sorry, Mark,' said Clare, 'I don't know what to say. It must have been terrible for you to witness that.'

Mark shrugged. He found that he was unable to speak

and so they sat in silence for a while before Gemma spoke.

'The whole thing has been such a worry,' she said. 'Clare has been stoical about it, but it's taken it's toll on all of us. Still, now that John's been arrested, I can breathe a little more easily.'

Mark nodded and they lapsed into silence again.

'It's odd,' Gemma continued eventually, 'we take our freedom so much for granted. When it's threatened, it's only then that it begins to seem precious.'

Clare sighed and turned to Mark. 'What are you going to do?' she asked him.

Her practical question broke the tension and the lump in his throat subsided.

'There's still a lot to do here,' he said, 'there's a lot of exterior work on the house that I didn't feel able to get on with for as long as I needed to keep out of sight. What about you?'

'We've made some preliminary enquiries at the council, but they're very resistant to the idea of a flower stall at the harbour side, which seems a bit mad to me, but there we are. I'm sure we'll come up with something.'

They talked on for a little while, but there was not much more that could be said and they soon left. As he saw them off, Clare said, 'We'll have to have some sort of memorial for Natalie. What do you think?'

'Yes, that's a great idea,' Mark told her.

He kissed them goodbye and felt for the first time that he could stand there and watch them wander down the street without wondering who might be spying on him. He went back inside and, for the first time, the house felt like home.

*

The next day, while he was painting the hall ceiling, Tara stopped at the foot of the step ladder that he was standing on.

'So, Mark,' she said, 'what are you going to do now?'

'What do you mean?'

'I hear your enemies have left town,' she said. 'You don't need to stay here any more.'

'I don't know about that,' he said, 'I have a job to do. I'll certainly stay here to finish it. As you know, there's quite a lot of work still to do on the exterior of the house. Another month at least, I'd say. There's the summer to enjoy and it'll be lovely to be working outside.'

'You could be out there earning a lot more money with your skills.'

'What you and Mr Hammond have offered me is beyond price,' he told her. 'I wouldn't walk away from that just because I can.'

Tara nodded.

'Thank you Mark. Some people accept refuge and never even notice.'

'Well, I've noticed and I am grateful.'

It was May 20th. It was over a year since he'd come to the town, and Mark realised that the Baker's Yard night out at the Harbour Tavern was the following week. He wondered if they would still be going there, even though they'd moved away from Baker's Yard.

'I'd like to see them all again,' he told Tara that afternoon, as he took a tea break in the kitchen.

'And why is that?' she asked.

'Because I misjudged them. They're good people.' He laughed. 'And I thought they had it in for me!'

\*

He had plenty to be getting on with for the time being. It was going to take longer than he'd thought, too, because he wasn't working so hard on it.

He bought himself some swimming trunks and went for a quick, bracing dip in the sea each day before lunch. He could only manage a couple of minutes at first, but as the days passed, he could stay in for longer. This was partly because the sea was warming up, and partly because he was becoming acclimatised to it. He noticed that the entrance to Baker's Yard was boarded up, and a sign had gone up which read, 'A new development of seven luxury one and two bedroom flats.' He wondered where the Baker's Yard lot were, and what they would think of this development. Unless this was the secret deal that Don had been planning all those weeks ago?

At the end of the week, he put his £40,000 into a small box which he then put in a carrier bag and took down to the florist's shop where Gemma worked. He left a note in with it:

*Clare: I hope this helps you find somewhere to open a flower stall, and don't you DARE try to give it back to me. You made me take it when it was important for me to do so, and now it's my turn to pass it on to you.*

Mark was surprised at how much pleasure it gave him to pass the money on. It had just seemed like something he 'should' do, but he realised that it was also a gift of love and that this kind of gift was also an act of healing. He returned to his work on the house with an extraordinary feeling of contentment and purpose.

Mr Hammond's death, after nearly six weeks in hospital, was a real blow when Tara told him of it, even though it was hardly a surprise. Mark realised, on hearing of it, that he'd been saving up a few things to say to – or ask of – Mr Hammond, and the loss seemed almost palpable. He mentioned this to Tara, before going for his swim that day, and she smiled sadly, and said, 'Mr Hammond is irreplaceable, but his wisdom was the wisdom of the world, and you are in the world, Mark. It is all around you.'

He absorbed that for a moment, and nodded. 'Now I come to think of it, you're surprisingly wise yourself,' he told her.

She smiled again. 'Thank you Mark, I have managed to pick one or two things up along the way.'

She paused, as if not sure whether to continue, but then said, 'There's one other thing I must tell you, though, Mark. I don't know if he ever mentioned it, but I am Mr Hammond's executor.'

'Oh?' said Mark. 'I'm sure you were very close, so I guess that's appropriate.'

'Yes,' she said, 'I think it is. And the thing is that I've known for a while what was in his will, and I want you to know that he's left the house to you.'

Mark was stunned. He stared at Tara dumbly. 'To *me?*' Mark said. 'Why did he do that?'

'He just has,' she said. 'He gave no reason. Actually, he's left you everything, but that's mostly the house and its contents. He had a pension which stops with his death, of course. He also had a modest amount of savings, which I am able to put at your disposal immediately.'

Mark was speechless.

'So,' she said, 'in theory, you are now my landlord, though only for a short while. It's time for me to be off, you see. My mother is eighty-four and I've been saying for the last year that I will go and look after her. Now that Mr Hammond no longer needs me, I'm free to go, which I will do as soon as I can pack my things together and say goodbye to a few people.'

He looked at her with an almost expressionless face. 'This is too much to take in,' he said.

'Don't worry,' she told him, 'go and have your swim. Probate takes months to sort out, so it's not going to happen tomorrow. Now go. Go! And don't forget,' she called after him as he left the room, 'consequences can be *good*, too!'

He walked down to the sea in a daze. His body was carrying an incredible amount of tension and so his swim was especially welcome. He was the only one swimming today, and the water felt clean against his skin. There was something about being in bracing water that made his muscles feel alive and invigorated. By the time he returned to the beach, he was only just beginning to get a sense of physical calm. The air was still and warm, and so he dried himself quickly and lay back for a few minutes to enjoy the early season sunshine. As he looked up at the sky, he realised that this evening it was the Baker's Yard gathering at the Harbour Tavern. He was ready to go along and see if he could meet up with them.

Back at the house – the house that would soon be his – he cooked a meal, an activity that always helped him to feel settled in himself, and then, in the early evening, he set off down to the harbour. He felt tingly, somehow, and alive and filled with a mixture of expectation and trepidation. As he arrived at the harbour itself, he saw the juggler some distance ahead packing up his juggling sticks. To his surprise, Mark saw that Don was with him, and they were conversing in a friendly way. Don said something and laughed, and the juggler replied, and Don turned and walked towards Mark along the water's edge. After a few moments, he saw Mark, and raised his hand in a welcoming salute.

'Mark!' he called. 'How are you?'

'Hello, Don,' Mark said, 'I was hoping I'd bump into you this evening. Are you off to the Harbour Tavern?'

'Yes, of course,' said Don, 'as ever.'

'Is it okay if I come along?' Mark asked.

Don just laughed and put his arm round Mark's shoulder and patted him and they fell, quite naturally, into step. When they crossed the road, Don noticed that the juggler was walking behind them on the far side of the road, and waved over to him. The juggler waved back and smiled. For a moment Mark thought the juggler was waving at him rather than Don, although it was impossible to tell from this distance.

'You know him?' he asked Don.

Don laughed again and said, 'He's my brother. My twin brother. Non-identical, of course, in more ways than one. . . He's definitely got a different way of using his gifts, but we undoubtedly come from the same place.'

'He certainly made me unwelcome here when I arrived in the town,' said Mark. 'The opposite of you, I suppose, although you've both got an apocalyptic air about you.'

Don laughed. 'So,' he asked, 'where have you been?'

'I've been doing up Mr Hammond's house. I guess you know who he is? He'd certainly heard of Baker's Yard.'

'Yes,' he said, 'I was told that he died recently. I was sorry to hear of it.'

Mark felt a sudden prickling of emotion and stopped, just before the door of the Tavern.

'Don,' he said, 'I'm so sorry I misjudged you. I realise now how badly I misread you at my birthday party last spring. You were all being so generous, and I was so paranoid.'

Don shrugged slightly and said, 'I think perhaps I pushed

you a little too far, too fast. It was a gamble on my part, but I felt a kind of urgency with you that I've rarely felt before with anyone else. What more can I say? We were sad that you ran off like that, but we all understood why what was happening might have been too much for you. And, of course, you haven't got off unscarred.'

He gestured towards Mark's ear and then opened the door to the pub and they went in.

It was bizarre, as though time hadn't passed at all. There was Ingrid and Wim, and Ailsa and Gareth, and various other people, including Leon, whose house was up by the entrance to the cave that they'd all sung in. Mark was welcomed in such a friendly manner that apologies seemed unnecessary, although he did apologise to everyone in turn and his apologies were accepted. Gareth, when he spoke to him, gestured with his potter's hands and said, 'I'm so pleased you made it, Mark. It always makes me happy when someone pulls through. But I'm especially pleased that you managed it.'

'Thank you,' said Mark, genuinely moved.

He couldn't see Holly, and wondered whether to ask about her, but then he saw that she was up on the small stage helping with the set-up there, and holding a violin, which she was clearly going to play. How little he knew of them, and their talents!

The evening turned out to be relaxed and enjoyable. He bought himself a pint of ale, but he'd drunk so little alcohol over the last year that it went straight to his head and he abandoned it half way through and drank juice instead. The band that Holly was in played a kind of modern folk fusion and she played clean, simple music on her violin. She greeted him afterwards with friendly enthusiasm, and introduced him to her boyfriend, a young man called Doug, and although

Mark felt a beat of disappointment at this, he was also pleased for her. They certainly looked happy together.

Later on, Mark ended up chatting to Don once more.

'I'm here to stay,' he told Don, 'although I guess I've still got a lot to learn about what it means to be a resident here.'

'Well done,' said Don, 'not everyone wants to stay on here, you know. In fact, not everyone *survives* the attempt to come and live here.'

'Yes, I know,' said Mark, thinking of Natalie. 'Who would have thought the stakes would be so high? I certainly didn't.'

'Yes you did,' said Don, simply.

Mark was surprised by this statement, but as he thought of it and remembered the jittery feeling that he'd had, over a year ago now, as he'd thrown his phone into the river and jumped on a train away from his old life, he realised Don was right.

'I don't know what I would have done if I'd stayed where I was,' he said.

'You would have died,' Don told him. 'Not physically, but in a way that's even worse.'

Mark nodded. 'It's true,' he said, and they lapsed into a thoughtful silence for a while.

'I see that Baker's Yard is being developed,' Mark said eventually.

'Sadly,' said Don. 'And there was nothing we could do to stop it.'

'Where are you living now?'

'Here and there,' said Don. 'No fixed abode, really. I'm staying with friends and not really looking at the moment. I've been away quite a lot over the winter doing my thing. I'll be back for the summer soon, and then I'll scout around for somewhere to stay. There are two or three of us who have lived at Baker's Yard and who will be on the lookout for somewhere to share.'

Mark had a sudden exhilarating thought. 'Look,' he said, 'for some reason known only to himself, Mr Hammond has left me the house he lived in. Of course, there's probate and so on to go through before it becomes mine, but as you know it's a house with letting rooms. There's already a decent room on the first floor that's empty, as well as the attic suite. And Tara Keane will be leaving soon. . . You could all come and live with me.'

'Well,' said Don, breaking into a delighted grin, 'that does sound like a possibility. Maybe I could come and have a look at some point?'

'Of course you can,' said Mark.

That was all that was said about it that evening, but Mark made a mental note to make sure he didn't lose touch with Don and the others this time. At the end of the night, as people were getting ready to go, Mark had another thought.

'It's my birthday next week,' he told them, 'and I'd like to invite you all to a party. I'll check that it's okay, but if it's free, perhaps we could have it at Jonathan's house, where we were last year. I've become one of the approved users of the garden. Maybe I can get hold of the boathouse keys and we could actually get out on the lake this time.'

There was general enthusiasm for this, and when Mark left some time later to go back to the house, he felt that he'd instigated something important. He decided to take the long way back, and walked down to the harbour mouth, then along the esplanade, before turning up into the town. How different it was to walk along the seafront now! There was a curious feeling that went with this, and it took him some time to recognise it as happiness; a thoughtful happiness, that was tinged with sadness, but which was happiness all the same.

He thought, as he walked, that maybe he was ready to try to get back in touch with Amy again, in a friendly sort of way. Perhaps he would be allowed to see Ty. What had seemed to be an irrevocable and permanent separation, no longer seemed so, and he wondered why he'd felt that way about it. Perhaps Amy would have found someone else by now, too, and that would help. How much more of *himself* there seemed to be, that he could give to Ty – not just the desperate efforts of a lonely and desperate man.

As he walked, there were pools of light on the esplanade beneath the lamp posts, and he noticed that the juggler was standing in one of these, his jacket on the ground beside him, idly juggling with his unlit firesticks. It seemed very late to be out doing this. There was hardly anyone around, and none of them looked as if they'd want to stop to watch a street performer. As Mark neared him, the juggler looked across at him.

'Practising?' Mark asked.

'No,' he said, 'I was waiting for someone.'

He picked his jacket from the ground and held it out to Mark. Mark laughed, but the juggler gestured again.

'Go on,' he said, throwing it to him.

'No,' Mark laughed, catching it, 'really.'

'Put it on, have a go,' the juggler smiled.

After a moment of embarrassed hesitation, Mark shrugged and pulled on the jacket, then the trousers that were handed to him.

'I wish I had a camera,' he said. 'How do I look?'

'You look like a juggler,' the man said, picking up the juggling sticks and dipping them in a container of kerosene. He took out a lighter and lit them. 'The trick is, don't think about it – just do it.' He held the flaming sticks out to Mark.

'No,' said Mark, 'no. It's such a skilled thing to do. I've never practised. It must be dangerous.'

The man looked at him with such intensity that Mark found he couldn't resist. He smiled a little and took the flaming batons. He hefted them in his hands, where they felt comfortable, almost light. He tried throwing one up, and it twisted over in the air in such a precise arc that he found he could grab it quite easily as it fell back towards his waiting palm. After that it was a question of trusting his body. It was easy, really. All he had to do was be *aware* of what he was doing.

Smiling with pleasure, he looked around. But the juggler had gone.

# Acknowledgements:

To Simon Lovat, Keith Elliot, Seb and Jess Jäger, Charlie Porter, Ray Bisson and Rhian Bowley for their help with my manuscript. To Ed Handyside at Myrmidon and particular thanks to Anne Westgarth, my editor.

Sebastian Beaumont was born and raised in Scotland. He graduated from Manchester Metropolitan University with a degree in Creative Arts, in which he majored in Creative Writing. He now lives in Brighton where he works in private practice as a psychotherapeutic counsellor.

Also from Myrmidon, a gripping psychological thriller. . .

# **Thirteen** by Sebastian Beaumont

Stephen Bardot, is a taxi driver working the night shift in Brighton. He works such long shifts that he is often driving while exhausted, and it is then that he starts to experience major alterations to his perception of reality. People start to take lifts in his cab who know things they shouldn't, and who ultimately may not even be real, although the question of what constitutes reality forms one of the basic themes of the novel.

He regularly gives lifts to Valerie – beautiful, haunting, but terminal – from 13 Wish Road to her 'positive thinking classes' at the Cornerstone Community Centre on Palmeira Square. When he is no longer asked to collect her, he fears that she is dead, and queries this with Sal, one of the night operators. Her response turns Stephen's world upside down.

'But Stephen,' she tells him, 'there is no such address. Wish Road doesn't have a number thirteen.'

As time passes, the world gets weirder. People appear (and disappear) who know far too much about Stephen and his past, and who lure him further and further into the twilight world of Thirteen. But if he asks any questions, he gets hurt. Ultimately, he decides, for the sake of both his safety and his sanity, he must walk away. . . but Thirteen has no intention of letting him go.

"COMBINES A VAST EXPERIENCE OF HUMAN NATURE WITH INTELLIGENCE AND IMAGINATION."
**Kate Saunders, *The Times***

"READERS MAY FIND THEMSELVES SHARING STEPHEN'S COMPULSION TO TAKE THIS SCARY JOURNEY AND UNABLE TO PUT BEAUMONT'S NOVEL DOWN."
**Nicholas Clee, *The Guardian***

"THE BEST BOOK OF THE YEAR. . . A MODERN MASTERPIECE."
**Scott Pack**

Available in:   Paperback ISBN 978-1905802128 (£7.99)
Hardback ISBN 978-1905802029 (£13.99)
Trade Softback ISBN 978-1905802036 (£9.99)